WHERE DO WE GO FROM HERE?

WHERE DO WE GO FROM HERE?

Doris Dörrie

Translated from the German by
John Brownjohn

BLOOMSBURY

Copyright © 2000 by Doris Dörrie
Translation copyright © by John Brownjohn 2001

All rights reserved. No part of this book may be used or
reproduced in any manner whatsoever without written
permission from the Publisher except in the case of brief quotations
embodied in critical articles or reviews. For information address
Bloomsbury, 175 Fifth Avenue, New York, N.Y. 10010.

Published by Bloomsbury, New York and London.
Distributed to the trade by Holtzbrinck Publishers

A CIP catalog record for this book
is available from the Library of Congress

ISBN 1-58234-319-5

First published in English by Bloomsbury Publishing Plc 2001
First published in German by Diogenes Verlag A.G. 2000
under the title *Was machen wir jetzt?*

First U.S. Edition 2001
This paperback edition published in 2002
10 9 8 7 6 5 4 3 2 1

The publication of this work is supported by
Inter Nationes, Bonn.

Typeset by Hewer Text Ltd, Scotland
Printed in England by Clays Ltd, St Ives plc

The principal character, Fred Kaufmann, expresses opinions on Buddhist retreats and Buddhism that do not represent those of the Author, who owes a special debt of gratitude to Rigpa, Sogyal Rinpoche, Plum Village, and Thich Nhat Hanh.

D.D.

Row, row, row your boat
gently down the stream.
Merrily, merrily, merrily, merrily,
life is but a dream.

American children's song

I

I'M IN THE PROCESS of losing my family. My marriage is on the rocks and my daughter Franka has fallen for some guy who wants to whisk her off to India.

Call me sometime, my wife says quietly. She's standing in the middle of the street with her arms crossed. I can see the goose-flesh on her bare skin.

A cold, rainy July evening. At least the weather will be better in France. That's something, at least.

Call me, the pair of you, Claudia says a trifle louder. She smiles first at me, then at Franka. Franka props her chin on the roof of the car and gives her mother a blank, silent stare. Her jaws move twice as she shifts her chewing gum from one cheek to the other. Her hair, dyed jet-black, flops over her face and hides the pierced eyebrow. Her skin is as white and smooth as paper. Franka never goes out in the sun.

She opens and shuts her blue eyes a couple of times. She gets them from me. When she was little I used to sing her a mawkish song addressed to a blue-eyed girl: *Deine blaue Augen machen mich so sentimental* . . . She always shook with giggles like a little jelly.

These days Franka's laughter is as rare as a hot summer in Germany. She eyes us as expressionlessly as a polar bear whose body language conveys no hint of its intentions. Is it about to pounce and tear you to pieces, or will it give you a confiding nudge in the ribs with its snout? A parting gesture: she slaps the roof of the car and slumps on to the back seat. I'd assumed she would sit up front with me, but even that's too close for her. I sigh.

Of course I'll call you, I tell Claudia.

Got the battery charger for your mobile? Claudia's voice falters. Promptly, because she could well start crying again, I put my arms around her.

She feels small. Smaller than usual. I try to sense something, a faint pang at parting from her or a trace of affection – anything at all – but no, there's absolutely nothing. I might be holding a laundry bag in my arms, not my wife. I've mislaid my love for her like a key and simply can't remember where I saw it last. Not that I've genuinely been looking for it. That's the real problem. I don't know what I want any more.

I give Claudia a clumsy pat on the shoulder and she detaches herself. Her lipstick is smudged. Now I've got it on my shirt collar. Only three shirts with me, and one of them's ruined even before we get started. Why bother with lipstick when she's only come downstairs for a moment to see us off? I could debate that point for a long time if I wasn't already aware that there aren't any rational answers to such questions. Claudia gives a spurious smile and backs away toward the front door. Her feet are bare. Lipstick, yes, but no shoes. No tears, either. We've almost made it. I'm relieved.

I raise a hand in farewell and get in myself, start up, pull away, and watch Claudia receding in the rear-view mirror. She gets smaller and smaller, a tiny, motionless doll in a red dress, alone in the deserted street. She waves. I don't know if I'll ever come back.

I take the Schwerer Reiter Strasse route out of town. Franka has already turned on her Discman. The music assaults my ears from the back seat like the hum of a swarm of insects. I turn on the radio. They're playing a Dylan number: 'Don't Think Twice, It's Alright'. Nothing's *alright*, Mr Dylan, even though it's ages since I stopped thinking about it.

My daughter has fallen in love with a lama. A lama, not a llama. Something like the Dalai Lama, that's how I picture my daughter's beloved: red-robed and shaven-headed. He's twenty-four, apparently. Eight years older than Franka. I'm taking her to join him at a Buddhist meditation centre in the South of France and keep an eye on her in case she runs off with him, and some day we get a postcard from the Himalayas.

Dadfred, says Franka, can't you turn off that shitty radio? She doesn't remove her earphones. I turn the radio down a bit and try to catch her eye in the rear-view mirror, but she's keeping her head down. We hardly ever look each other in the eye these days.

Seeing that big, peculiar, black-haired creature on the back seat, I try to reconcile it with the baby it used to be, but I can't. There isn't the smallest connection between the two. Except, perhaps, the fact that I found the infant as alien as I now find the sixteen-year-old.

How often we used to drive her around Munich's inner ring-road at nights, when nothing would stop her crying except a car ride. I sometimes imagined, during those phantasmal drives through the deserted city, that the only other road users were equally desperate parents and their infants. But when she finally went to sleep – ah, when she finally nodded off – what joy! What sheer, unbounded joy! I had everything: a wife, a child, a car, and a clear run into a wonderful future.

We listened to the Talking Heads and Tom Waits and Van Morrison, and sometimes Claudia would roll a joint and rest her head on my lap, and I would drive on and on without stopping – I couldn't afford to, not at any price, or our peace would be shattered within seconds. Every red light triggered a fear that Franka might wake up. She's stirring, she's opening her eyes . . . Help! Oh God, dear God, please, please let her sleep a bit longer! On and on we drove, round and round the city. I don't think we talked much. We didn't need to in those days.

In the blue light of dawn we'd pull up in the parking lot of the Euro Industrial Estate while Claudia breast-fed Franka and the first weary, disgruntled housewives wheeled their trolleys into the supermarkets. I'd get us some breakfast from McDonald's, and there we'd sit with a well-fed, well-rested, good-humoured baby on our laps, drinking beakers of coffee and eating McMuffins, warm rolls with an egg and a slice of ham inside. They lay on the stomach like soft little cushions.

In some mysterious way, our nocturnal excursions invested the whole of the rest of the day's work at the *Seventh Heaven*, our vegetarian snack bar, with a special quality. Although dog-tired and tremulous with exhaustion, I had a sense of space and freedom in our little kitchen. As I slid spring rolls and spinach soufflés into the microwave, I could see the dark, deserted road ahead of me and felt sure I would never become imprisoned, like everyone else, in the daily round.

I turn left on to the Lindau autobahn. The motorway stretches ahead of us, grey and interminable. I step on the gas like all the other drivers, under the illusion that speed can release me from the gravity that weighs me down a little more each day.

Dadfred, Franka groans from the back seat, turn off that lousy music, can't you? I turn it off. Franka has evidently turned off her Discman as well, because the car is silent. I look at her closed eyes in the rear-view mirror, the baby-smooth skin of the forehead behind which I envision a murky labyrinth of tempestuous thoughts, of pain and hatred. Who knows, though? Perhaps it's a little, well-tended garden – tulips, narcissi, neat gravel paths – that would put Claudia

4

and me to shame for our persistent inability to conceive of what goes on inside our daughter's head.

What the hell is she thinking about? *If* she thinks at all. I sometimes look at her and get the feeling that there's nothing inside her head but milk shakes sloshing to and fro. Does she realize that we're bound for the meditation centre because she stubbornly refused, some six months ago, to entertain even the glimmer of a thought?

2

I WAS SITTING IN the darkened living room one evening last March, TV screen flickering, when Franka came in and flopped down on the sofa without a word. I only glimpsed her out of the corner of my eye. She didn't say hello, which annoyed me. Couldn't the girl say a normal good evening? Was it impossible to have even the most rudimentary human contact with a teenager?

Good evening, I said. I kept my eyes glued to the screen and doggedly resolved not to let her spoil my mood. *The X-Files* was on, I remember. A gruesome tale about a serial killer who sucked the adipose tissue out of his victims because he needed it for his own monstrous body. Special Agent Scully was as cool and composed as usual, and I was just thinking how much she would interest me in real life – and wondering if she was the kind of woman who shouts 'God, oh God!' or whispers 'Yes, yes, yes!' – when Franka said quietly, I'm pregnant.

Abruptly, I killed the sound. Sitting there in the gloom, we both stared at the little figures scurrying around inside the rectangular, illuminated box. Then I said, Oh God.

I couldn't think of anything else to say. We sat there, mute and motionless, and we'd probably be sitting there still if Claudia hadn't come back from her meditation hour. We both leaned forward a little and listened to the key in the lock. We both heard the miniature bell on Claudia's bunch of keys. She needs it to discover if her keys really are at the bottom of the huge shoulder bag she totes around wherever she goes.

She came into the room, her fair hair shining like a halo. She would save us both the way she always did.

What are you doing here in the dark? she asked, laughing. On the screen, a body was decomposing under our and Special Agent Scully's eyes.

Franka, Claudia said sternly, as if Franka hadn't drunk up her cocoa, packed her school satchel or tidied her room. When, exactly?

December, Franka mumbled.

Three months ago? Claudia exclaimed in horror. When, exactly? Try to remember, Franka. When, exactly?

I watched Agent Scully silently grilling a suspect. She was probably asking him just the same question: When? When, exactly? Try to remember!

Franka remembered. It must have happened on the school trip to Prague, three days before they came back. Claudia and I were in London at the time, trying to save our marriage. I'd just bought myself a hideously expensive pair of brogues. I stared at them intently, trying to discern an answer in their pattern of punch-holes.

Who? Claudia asked sternly. I was convinced Franka wouldn't name names, but she did. Tobi, she said in a low voice.

Oh God! It was Claudia's turn to say that now. That big baby! And I bought you some condoms myself.

I continued to stare rigidly at my new shoes. Three days before Franka's return from Prague I'd gone to Church's in London's Bond Street and spent eight hundred marks on a pair of shoes for the first time in my life. Forty-five years old, and they'd made me feel grown-up at last. My daughter had probably been impregnated at that very moment. At that precise moment, naturally. Your children always catch you napping. Always.

3

O UR TRIP TO LONDON started badly. You sometimes
know, in the very first minute, that a situation is past
saving. You can't just take it lying down, though; you still feel
you'll be able to alter course. It all began in the taxi to the
airport, when Claudia discovered she'd forgotten her high-
heeled shoes, the ones that went with her blue dress, and I
could tell from the way she said it that she'd had a mental
picture of herself in London in the blue dress and the blue
shoes – and now the shoes were missing.

We'll simply go and buy you some shoes, I hazarded. Her
thin-lipped smile told me it was a naive suggestion. Besides,
women don't want to be offered solutions to their problems,
they want to *talk* about them.

She turned away and stared morosely out of the window. I
took her hand in an experimental way, but released it when
she didn't respond. I was glad she didn't, to be honest, because
I'm no great lover of hand-holding. Either my hand is sweaty
and I'm unpleasantly aware of the fact, or the other person's is,
or I nervously wait for one of our hands to grow moist. Mine,
as a rule.

But Claudia loves clinging to my hand. If it was up to her,
she'd do so for hours or days on end. It makes me impatient
and edgy. I sometimes feel like wrenching my hand away and

running off. When I finally get it back, the skin on the inside is as soft and wrinkled as if I'd spent hours in the bath.

If she declines to hold my hand, I know we've got a problem. Exactly what problem, I can't tell. I'm supposed to guess, and after almost seventeen years I'm out of ideas.

She smiled in my direction, trying hard to register good humour, and I smiled back. That was the moment when we should really have turned around. We should have had the guts to acknowledge that our weekend trip to London wouldn't save us – that only a painful awareness of our impasse had set us in panic-stricken motion.

Instead, I deplored my failure to book us business class seats. It would have given Claudia a nice surprise, and besides, we could genuinely afford it now we'd exchanged our politically correct little chain of vegetarian snack bars for a franchise from *coffee & bagel*, the fastfood giant. But would Claudia really have welcomed a somewhat more capacious seat and slightly better food? She could be terribly pigheaded, and her political convictions might well have ruined us.

After a shortlived boom, when every businessman suddenly enrolled in yoga classes and drank soya milk, nobody could stand the sight of tofuburgers and root vegetables any more, and all our efforts to win back customers with esoteric dishes from all over the world, from recipes according to the five Tibetan Exercises to Chinese 'six elements' cuisine, were to no avail. We were eventually left with the pale and anorexic but health-conscious secretaries who had been with us from the outset and would never have gone without their tofuburgers – but we couldn't subsist on them alone. We were compelled to close our branches one by one, until even Claudia realized that we'd have had to look around for a new livelihood if the bagel hadn't descended on us like a big UFO with a hole in the middle: a bread roll of Jewish provenance, come to Munich to save our bacon.

Ours was the first bagel restaurant in the whole of Germany. The dough was initially delivered from the States in the shape of prefabricated bagels that had only to be placed in the oven. The coffee, too, came in huge sacks complete with detailed instructions on how much to use per cup and size of cup. The menus we deliberately printed in English only, with the result that we were promptly besieged by swarms of American girl-students eager to introduce the German nation to the bagel.

The bagels sold like hot cakes, and we were very soon able to reopen some branches: two after six months, four after a year, six after eighteen months.

Business class would have been a possibility, therefore, but I still wasn't used to thinking in those terms. In contrast to the old days, I was ashamed of this and felt hopelessly bourgeois and old-fashioned. In the old days, I reflected, money used to be considered bourgeois. The moment you use that phrase, 'in the old days', you're old. So here, on board a Lufthansa plane bound for London, I'd become old.

We squeezed into our narrow seats. Feeling hot, I waited impatiently for the plane to start taxiing. I opened the *Süddeutsche Zeitung* and was trying to concentrate on the world's various wars when the captain made an announcement. He hurrumphed a couple of times, then apologetically informed us that we would all have to get out again: the steps had jammed and wouldn't retract. Claudia heaved a sigh. My heart sank. This trip had been my idea.

We shuffled slowly out of the plane and down the jammed steps to the bus. Claudia gave me a noncommittal smile of the kind she usually reserves for customers when taking their orders. Another advantage of our bagel paradise: neither of us had to stand behind a counter any more. Claudia seemed to miss this, though, because she made daily tours of inspection and often lingered in one of our six establishments. She would serve behind the counter until it got her down, then hand over to one of those healthy-looking, ever-smiling American girls and go home.

But not working made her as restless and unhappy as a dog bereft of its master. She didn't know what to do with herself, even though she at last had plenty of time to do whatever she'd always wanted. She took Spanish lessons and even dragged me along too – an injudicious move, because I fell in love with Marisol, our twenty-five-year-old teacher. She went into town for rendezvous with women friends, but nothing really seemed to fulfil her until, one day, she came home with a slim red volume entitled *How to Transform Happiness and Suffering into the Path of Enlightenment: How to be Happy When You Aren't.* Thereafter she perused this book with dogged enthusiasm. It was all she ever read, and when she reached the end she started at the beginning again.

The author was a lama named Tubten Rinpoche, whose photograph adorned the back cover. Shaven-headed and attired in a monk's red habit, he was seated on a rock holding a yellow can that might have been a beer can, though one couldn't tell for sure, even with a magnifying glass. I actually studied this individual through a magnifying glass because he was threatening to rob me of my wife. Her whole life now revolved around him and his happiness doctrines. While Claudia was gently snoring to herself in her sleep, I would sit on the edge of the bed and run a magnifying glass over a Tibetan lama to discover what brand of beer he favoured. A beer can would have rendered him far more congenial to me.

All living creatures crave happiness and wish to avoid suffering, said the book. Nothing wrong with that. But, the book went on, people fail to find happiness because they're forever yielding to their desires. That I found more questionable. Claudia very seldom yielded to her desires these days, hence the evanescence of my own desire. I needed a cue from her, just a little, tiny cue, otherwise – silly as it sounds – my nerve failed me. It usually sufficed if she didn't open a book as soon as she came to bed. Or gave me a fleeting smile. Or brushed my cheek with hers instead of pecking me on the forehead. That was enough. Without such cues I found her inaccessible. But the cues became steadily rarer, and at some stage she stopped signalling altogether. That was the end of our sex life. And all because of a bread roll with a hole in the middle, because it was our success with bagels that had ultimately transformed Claudia into a woman who chanted to herself in Tibetan, wore a red thread round her neck, hurried off to a meditation centre nearly every evening, and prostrated herself a hundred and eight times before getting into bed.

I tried to ignore this just as I ignored my daughter's pierced eyebrow, periodically masturbating in the bathroom. I can't pretend I was genuinely distressed, but I did experience the kind of faint, lingering sense of loss that ensues on the death of a beloved family pet.

Like a flock of sheep, we shuffled slowly out of the bus and into the airport building. Ahead of me, a short, plump man with a bald patch detached himself from the herd and resolutely made for another door. I seized Claudia's hand, and we followed the little man, whose bald patch was encircled by a halo of sparse fair hair.

No one who peeled off and opened forbidden doors on his own initiative could possibly be German, I thought. I myself would never have tried to open the other door. It must surely be prohibited, even if there wasn't a notice to that effect, and was bound to be locked in any case. But no, the little man opened it without more ado, and a few minutes later we were back in the departures hall, where the airline issued us with meal vouchers. The little man smiled at us and said, in a faint Dutch accent, Now we begin again, huh?

We queued up together for our free drink and sandwich. Holding an ice-cold minibottle of sparkling wine to his cheek, the little Dutchman informed us in fluent German that he'd had a wisdom tooth extracted only that afternoon. While we were cracking hackneyed jokes about dentists my eye lighted on his fleshy neck. Knotted around it was a strand of red wool like the one my wife wore.

I'd never really inquired its significance. A lucky charm conferred by a Tibetan lama, that was all I knew. Claudia spotted it almost at the same moment. Smiling, she removed her scarf. The Dutchman saw her woollen thread, and within seconds they were swapping the names of Tibetan lamas the way other people swap holiday resorts.

I had to restrain myself from crying out loud. I turned away, feigning boredom, but was able to follow the conversation closely.

There's one of Tubten Rinpoche's meditation centres in the South of France, said the little Dutchman, who introduced himself to Claudia as Theo. I've always wanted to go there. Going on retreat, that's my dream . . .

It was just a word, but I sensed that Claudia sucked it in as a bee sucks nectar. *Retreat* . . . I didn't know what it meant, not then. Seclusion, summer camps, school excursions. Courses for unhappy people in beautiful scenery. *How to be Happy When You Aren't* . . . Oh yes, Claudia replied fervently, I'd like to do that too, some day. Go on retreat . . . I can give you the address, said Theo. I'll send it to you as soon as I get home.

He pulled out his Filofax, and Claudia's blond locks almost brushed his hands as she dictated our fax number.

My wife wanted to go into a nunnery. I'd failed her – I couldn't make her happy any more. I was tempted to throw a tantrum and hurl myself, childlike, to the airport's marble floor. Perhaps I should simply have grabbed her and made a scene. Maybe, just maybe, she might even have liked that.

But I'm a well-trained, modern man. I don't do things like that. Instead, I took up with a twenty-five-year-old Spanish teacher.

From a distance I watched Claudia talking to Theo, whose bald patch had now turned pale pink. His wispy fair hair was standing on end with excitement. Claudia gesticulated wildly, her hair swaying to and fro, and smiled until I could see her teeth flash. Her whole body was in motion. She looked young and vital. She was never like that with me, not any more.

When we finally landed at Heathrow hours later, warm night air came flooding into the taxi. Claudia rested her head on my shoulder, and for a moment all seemed well.

The motorway's quince-yellow lights showed us the way ahead. There was a smell of sea and damp sheets, and my heart immediately became a few pounds lighter. We did this too rarely – we went away far too seldom. Franka was old enough now, we had no need to wait for some school excursion before treating ourselves to a little trip abroad. I gave Claudia a hug. She went soft in my arms, and I caught the scent of her hair. She laughed happily, perhaps because of the little Dutchman. Jealousy gnawed me like a mouse nibbling cheese.

Turmoil reigned in the London streets. Crowds of young people were loitering outside the pubs, which had already shut; tipsy men in suits, their ties loosened, guffawed as they staggered across the road; giggling girls in clumpy boots and short skirts were leaning against the walls. Police cars roared past. The night air was as warm as it usually is in Spain or Italy.

One chilly July night more than twenty-five years earlier, I and a French girl and hundreds of other youngster had sat, shivering with cold, on the steps of Eros in Piccadilly. I could clearly recall the green of the girl's sweater and her small breasts, which were as hard as tennis balls. I also recalled the cloying hangover induced by too much Guinness.

I longed to get out of the taxi with Claudia and mingle with those sweating, pleasure-seeking, pulsating people – to stand around just like them, doing nothing, and be just a little bit like we used to be. Instead of that, because I was afraid my peculiar notion would bounce off Claudia like a squash ball, I said, I suppose we'd better turn in, huh? I was really hoping that Claudia herself would suggest getting out, but she merely nodded and said nothing.

In addition to peanuts and chocolate, the minibar contained a throwaway camera and a floppy disk. Claudia sat down on the high bed and drew her legs up under her backside. She grinned. I feel like the princess on the pea, she said.

There it was: my cue. A cue at last! Although I wasn't really in the mood I promptly stripped off my sweaty jeans and plonked myself down beside her. The mattress wobbled like a blancmange. Her smile faded.

It's like a trampoline, she sighed.

I'm sorry.

You know I can't sleep when the whole bed wobbles every time you turn over.

Yes.

You should have specified twin beds.

We could ask at the desk if –

I don't feel like getting dressed again.

I promise I'll keep still.

I put out my hand and stroked her back. She didn't move, and that was that. One false move, one false word, one wrong bed, and it was all over. I tried nonetheless. She suffered me to tickle the nape of her neck awhile, then got up and went into the bathroom.

16

I reached for the zapper. On MTV some young black men and women were saying things I couldn't understand. They launched into a sexy dance, but not for my benefit.

Claudia had removed her make-up by the time she returned from the bathroom with a towel draped over her shoulder. She looked perceptibly younger without make-up. It staggers me every time. Don't women realize that? She took a pair of old, cut-down tennis socks from her grip, pulled them over her wrists, and spread the towel on the floor beside the bed. Stationing herself in front of it, she raised her folded hands to her forehead, throat and chest in turn, knelt down, slid across the towel on her belly, put her hands behind her head, got to her feet, and began again. The hundred and eight prostrations . . . I wasn't sure whether she performed them to strengthen her thigh muscles or further her spiritual advancement. I'm taking refuge, she had told me. Refuge? Refuge from what? That she didn't disclose.

Buddhist gymnastics, Franka called it. She used to turn up her nose and avert her eyes when her mother engaged in these activities, but she conscientiously joined in after falling for her lama. Side by side, my wife and daughter prostrated themselves on the old kilim I'd brought back from Turkey during my student days, when I was still ferrying Mercs to Iran.

On the TV screen, a girl was singing in time to Claudia's prostrations. Around twelve years old in appearance, she was wearing baggy trousers and a lilac T-shirt and singing of a love that had gone stale while a fair-haired youth nibbled her earlobe with an air of boredom.

The French girl hadn't been as young as that. She was twenty-one, two years older than me. Her name was Dominique, I now recalled. Dominique was something of a trial because she never knew whether or not she was hungry but talked about food incessantly. She would be hungry whenever I wanted to go to bed with her, so we'd get dressed again. Once

17

outside the fish-and-chip shop, however, she couldn't make up her mind and ended up eating nothing. She was out of sympathy with her stomach, she explained, and she had a very dominating mother. I never met her mother, but I soon became more interested in her than in her daughter with the eating disorder. Women have always interested me more when absent than in the flesh.

Dominique's green sweater tended to feel a bit damp because, true to London's reputation, the rain never stopped. We used to cling to each other, shivering, in the icy bed in our gloomy London boarding-house, and didn't discover the electric blanket beneath the sheet until we were leaving. Dominique was a moody, complicated creature. Sticking my prick in her without scaring her – that was really my one, constant preoccupation. That way I felt warm and alive and didn't need to ponder on my existence.

Then a student at the Munich Film School, I quaked at the prospect of never becoming a great director, never making a decent picture. Being as scared and diffident and afflicted with complexes as I was, I behaved in a cold and arrogant manner. To my bewilderment, this stood me in good stead with women. But one couldn't be artistically creative in women's company, I felt; for that one had to live alone in splendid isolation. I was quite clear on that point, but I had no great desire for solitude because I never knew what to do on my own.

Sometimes, though, I was conscientious enough to leave the green sweater and its French contents behind in our chilly London boarding-house. Armed with my Super8 movie camera, I would take a train ride out into the countryside and shoot blurred pictures of cows in the mist and lonely road signs, deserted, rain-sodden streets and raindrops on window panes. While peering through the viewfinder I sensed that my camera's-eyes view of the world was nothing out of the ordinary, and that I possessed no attribute that marked me out from the rest. I had no vision, as they used to say at the film school, and I've never quite recovered from that realization.

Nearly eighteen years ago, when I walked into *The Seventh Heaven*, a little vegetarian snack bar, because I had an inexplicable craving for a spring roll, I was twenty-six years old and had long since given up shooting cows in the mist. I was floor-managing TV talk shows to earn some money while vainly trying to place my screenplays. For this I despised myself and, consequently, half the human race. Orson Welles, Louis Malle, Steven Spielberg, Truffaut, Godard – at my age, they all had masterpieces to their credit. Seething with hatred, I saw former fellow students acclaimed for their first, second or third feature film and invited to expound their personal philosophy on television. I went to see their films, and the better I found them the more they depressed me. I inwardly bled from a thousand cuts because I was no longer one of the their number and never would be. Although I still styled myself 'Fred Kaufmann, Film Director', I knew it was a lie. I had lost at a game I should never have been allowed to play. I found this so unfair, my mood was permanently black.

Claudia, by contrast, was young, cheerful, and efficient. She smelled of good food, even if it was only vegetarian, and I first saw her on 26 May, just as Travis Bickle saw his white fairy in *Taxi Driver*. Like Travis, I was seeking deliverance. Claudia was wearing a long, white apron. Her mermaid-green eyes smiled at me with untrammelled optimism as she asked if she could help me. Yes, I wanted to shout. Help, I'm drowning! She put out her hand. I took it and let her haul me ashore, but when she hung on to it I felt uneasy again.

To begin with, however, I was delighted. Claudia wanted to be herself, no one else. That impressed me.

What do you do? She didn't ask me that for quite a while. I

told her about my big, expensive film projects, all of which would materialize very, very soon – in the immediate future, in fact. She smiled faintly and never raised the subject again. A few months later, feeling relieved, I gave up my floor manager's job and started work at her snack bar.

A year later I took over the management, and five years later the *Seventh Heaven* had five branches in Munich and one in Augsburg. Fred Kaufmann had become what his surname portended, a businessman, and he abominated himself on that account because his dreams had been so different.

A hundred and eight, Claudia grunted, peeling the tennis socks off her wrists. Her T-shirt was sweat-sodden and her hair clung damply to her forehead. She looked sexy. I ought to have fetched the throwaway camera from the minibar and snapped her, but I didn't, of course. We'd grown out of young love's spontaneous exuberance a long time ago.

Well, I asked, still holding the zapper, any closer to enlightenment? I'd channel-hopped my way through a queasy-making multitude of news broadcasts, commercials, whodunits and pop videos during her prostrations.

No, she said, but I've done something for world peace. Panting, she flopped down on to the bed beside me. The mattress rebounded with such violence, I was literally catapulted into the air. When I landed she reached for my hand. I switched the zapper from one hand to the other. You think I'm crazy, don't you? she went on.

I didn't answer.

I know you do.

If the weather's fine tomorrow, I suggested, we could go to Hyde Park and hire a couple of deckchairs for 50p.

All I know is, the prostrations do me good. I can't explain why, not exactly. I don't do them just for myself. It's—

—for world peace, I broke in.

But it's quite logical, she said. I mean, the theory that you've got to make peace with yourself before you can achieve peace worldwide.

With me too?

What?

Peace.

She pulled her T-shirt over her head and gave me a searching stare. I didn't dare look down at her breasts. We were having a serious discussion, after all, so boobs were off-limits. I'm pathetically well brought up.

It wouldn't hurt you to be a bit more peaceful in general, she said soberly.

And tomorrow we've got to buy you some blue shoes, I said.

She kissed me on the tip of the nose. Her lips were cool.

Our marriage is going to the dogs, she whispered.

I promised you some blue shoes.

If I didn't prostrate myself a hundred and eight times a day, I'd have to leave you.

I hadn't the courage to ask why.

She went on kissing me, and I inferred from her unexpected use of the tongue that she wanted to have sex. Instead of gratifying me, it startled me, and nothing worked. Twenty minutes earlier everything would have worked, but now she'd sabotaged it. Unfailingly bad timing: a knack we both possessed, and suffered from, in the highest degree. Her comparatively rare manifestations of desire had a coercive effect on me *because of their very rarity*. I was like a child that stubbornly hides a hand behind its back when told to hold it out. There was nothing to be done. I'd tried to explain the problem and implored her not to take it personally, but more personal than that you couldn't get. I fantasized about having sex with unknown women who had no faces and didn't take things personally.

She confiscated the zapper and slid my hand between her

thighs. It was warm and wet down there, which was only to be expected, but she might just as well have deposited my hand on a pizza for all the effect it had. I actually found myself wondering if I would be able to tell a pizza and my wife apart by touch alone, and my uncertainty saddened me immeasurably.

She arched her body against mine, and I felt her desire surge over me like a tidal wave.

In a moment it would break on the reef of my incapacity, dissolve into chagrin, and then subside. I shut my eyes and, as quickly as I could, pictured white-skinned Japanese girls thrusting pickled gherkins into their shaven pussies and big black women being violated by Alsatian dogs. But my underdeveloped pornographic imagination filled me with disgust, and anyway, it didn't do a bit of good. Eyes still shut, I felt Claudia desist. She turned over – my hand slid out from between her thighs – and sighed.

We were both at our wits' end.

The next morning we put a good face on things, which made us feel even sadder. Outwardly, however, we were an affectionate, cheerful, relatively good-looking couple. Claudia possessed natural elegance. As for me, I looked passable only because she had resolutely taken charge of my sartorial education seventeen years earlier. She knew how many shirt buttons a man should leave undone if he wanted to look cool as opposed to pimplike. She bade me buy expensive black underpants from Calvin Klein and told me to give up wearing my Erdmann leather jacket except in an emergency. I kept abreast of the times, thanks to Claudia, and was eternally grateful when I saw men of my age still sporting leather jackets, al-Fatah neckerchiefs, and drainpipe jeans.

It was Claudia too, of course, who resolutely steered me into Church's, the exclusive little shoe shop in Bond Street. There she watched and waited while I carefully tried on and eventually bought a pair of handmade brogues – the kind of shoes I'd always considered to be the hallmark of the reactionary.

Skinny Indian shoe salesmen in white shirts and black trousers sat perched on little stools. Angelically patient, they explained the merits and disadvantages of various models in mellifluous English and removed their customers' shoes with almost tender, loving care. I was scared my socks might smell but consoled myself by reflecting that we hadn't walked far because Claudia had decided, halfway to Harvey Nichols, that she didn't want any new blue shoes at all. But you, she said, you really *do* need some new shoes.

Beside me sat a couple of our own age – though I'd gladly have believed them to be much older – and their son, who must have been about eighteen. The father was wearing a grey flannel suit, a pale blue shirt and a pair of classic Church's Oxfords. The mother, in a sleeveless white dress and white shoes with gold buckles, had tinted fair hair and a well-preserved face – or well-tweaked, which seemed more likely in the modern world. Ignoring her husband and son, she addressed herself exclusively to the salesman, who hurriedly fetched shoebox after shoebox, but she shook her head disapprovingly at every pair her son tried on. The latter, a pale, pasty-looking youth, wore a blue shirt and grey flannel trousers like his father's, and his movements were slow and sluggish. The whole family might have been embedded in aspic. There was no love lost between any of them, but they all kept still.

I wanted to shake the boy by the shoulders and whisper in his ear, For God's sake be a man! Buy yourself a cool pair of Nikes out of your pocket money and then split! Take off, quick, and don't look back! But the son stared sadly at his expensive shoes and didn't budge.

'My' Indian firmly tightened the laces, and I took a few steps in my surprisingly comfortable 800-mark shoes.

My whole life unfolded before my eyes like shoes on parade. My very first pair: the tiny, pale blue button-ups which my mother still keeps on top of the voluminous flesh-coloured knickers in her lingerie drawer; my first Salamanders, which came complete with Lurchi, a black-and-yellow rubber lizard, and some little storybooks describing his adventures. Then came an exciting period during which my feet, when encased in new shoes, had to be inserted in a machine whose little window reproduced them in the form of pale green skeletons. These contraptions were later banned because they were X-ray machines, and a whole generation of feet, mine among them, will probably exhibit radiation damage in due course.

Like every other child, however, I loved X-raying my feet. I sometimes prevailed on my mother to take me into a shoe shop, purely for that reason, and ask the salesman to see if her boy's shoes still fitted. The salesman would take me by the hand and lead me over to the machine. Expertly, I inserted my feet in it. Then came a dull hum, and there they were again, those mysterious green bones. It was weird, the thought that they were actually inside my body, almost like another person within me. I usually forgot about that green skeleton but sometimes remembered it, quite without warning, in the middle of playing or just before going to sleep, and it sent a shiver down my spine.

As a teenager I wore Hush Puppies, which created a rather inhibited impression. I came to sex late. Girls thought I was 'cute', and that was the opposite of sexy.

At film school I affected some black leather half-boots that lent me a dandyish appearance, or so I thought. I was desperately keen to seem interesting. As time went by I acquired a black Citroën DS (*déesse*, goddess) to go with my boots, and treated it better than any woman. Later came boxing boots with wafer-thin soles designed to give me a look of unsurpassable speed. On my first trip to the States I discovered genuine cowboy boots, which for nearly ten years made me walk as if I'd just dismounted from a horse. Then, on the grounds that only provincial Country fans still wore them, Claudia prescribed sneakers. Thereafter I wore Nikes, replacing them annually with the latest model. They were comfortable, but not image-enhancing except among teenagers. Somewhere or other I'd picked up a saying attributed to the inventor of the Nike: 'A decent sneaker is like a vagina – slip into it and feel good.'

So now my Nikes stood discarded at Church's in Bond Street, down at heel, smelly and spurned, and my conscience pricked me as if I were being unfaithful to them. My heart wasn't as heavy when I ratted on my wife a mere eight weeks later. That's bullshit, of course. Well, to be honest, not altogether. It was light *while* I was ratting on her; it only became heavy after the event.

For me, every new pair of shoes had heralded the start of a new life. I should have given the fact a little more thought that Saturday morning in London. I paid, the Indian held the door open and handed me the paper bag containing my old Nikes, and we emerged into the street as if nothing had happened.

Not that I knew it yet, my new life had already begun – far away in a youth hostel in Prague.

4

I WAS SENT OFF to get a pregnancy test, although there was really no point. When the nice chemist on Elisabethplatz smilingly handed me the kit through the night hatch, I half expected him to congratulate me.

Hearts pounding, Claudia and I stared at the little test strip while Franka sat in the corner, motionless as a lizard on a warm boulder. I nearly fainted when the first pink streak appeared, but Claudia reminded me that it was only the first one, and that we still had a full minute to wait.

We reached for each other's hands and held them tight, really tight. It was a long time since we'd felt as close. Sixteen years earlier we'd sat in the *Seventh Heaven*'s tiny kitchen, staring at the test strip like rabbits mesmerized by a snake. But when the second pink streak appeared, materializing like the first, faint flush of dawn on the skyline, we suddenly burst out laughing and fell into each other's arms, somewhat mystified by our spontaneous delight. From one moment to the next it seemed logical and right for us to have a child.

And now it was all wrong, utterly wrong. I almost felt sick when the second streak showed up.

We sat down beside Franka. Claudia twisted a strand of hair, and I could think of nothing better to do than stare at the new shoes I polished twice a week, as instructed. I even massaged their soles with the tincture supplied and made regular use of their pale cherrywood shoe trees. They were the first shoes I'd ever had that benefited from shoe trees.

We'll help you, said Claudia. Of course we will. We're your friends, after all.

Franka glanced at her. You aren't my friends, she said, you're my parents.

And your friends, Claudia insisted stubbornly.

No, said Franka.

Fred, Claudia said sternly, what are we going to do now? We'll help her, won't we?

I nodded, but serious reflection was beyond me. My brain had lapsed into stand-by mode and preferred to think about shoe trees.

Claudia vigorously knotted her long fair hair into a chignon, picked up the phone, and asked Franka for Tobi's number.

No, Franka wailed, please don't!

Does he know?

Franka shook her head.

Then it's time you told him.

Please don't, Franka whispered. She looked at me imploringly.

You don't have to face the consequences on your own, said Claudia. It takes two to tango.

I never want to see him again, Franka wailed. Never!

But you see him in school every day, Claudia said coldly.

Big tears welled from Franka's eyes and rolled slowly down her cheeks. I could imagine what a trial those daily encounters in school must be. I had only a very vague recollection of Tobi, a gigantic youth with a shaven head, yellow tinted glasses, and baggy trousers that made him look rather infantile despite his size. Not for nothing were such trousers nicknamed 'Pampers', but it was clear that this big baby's nappies concealed a pretty grown-up pecker.

I didn't want to picture my daughter copulating with him or any youngster – not my little Franka, my little mouse. It seemed only yesterday that I'd taken her to the playground.

Here! Claudia held the receiver under Franka's nose. I want you to call him and get him here or I'll do it myself – *and* I'll speak to his parents.

I groaned. Franka was weeping bitterly, the way she used to when she'd grazed her knee.

He's not going to get off that easy, Claudia said firmly, and before I could object Franka astonished me by complying. Three-quarters of an hour later the four of us were sitting at a table in the Pizzeria San Mulino.

5

T OBI ORDERED A *pizza quattro staggione*. He looked a trifle uneasy, not knowing what he was in for, but his teenager's arrogant self-assurance was such that it was all I could do not to hit him there and then. Franka and I dispensed with food, Claudia ordered – as usual – a salad. (Women and salads . . . In my next life I'd like a wife who never touches them.) We took care not to look at each other.

Franka and Tobi were sitting side by side. Franka had tried to avoid this, but Claudia and I were so averse to sitting next to him that we slid on to the banquette in quick succession and left the chairs to them.

Tobi grinned at us uncertainly, then buried his huge head in his huge cola and orangeade. His wrists were as thick as my biceps, his biceps as bulky as my thighs. How, I wondered, could any woman have given birth to such a monstrosity? He was only sixteen, the same as Franka, but he looked like a mutant.

Franka had propped her chin on her hands and was staring at the red-and-white check tablecloth, screwing up her eyes like someone viewing a three-dimensional picture.

Claudia was nervously plucking at the red thread round her neck and giving me sidelong glances. Did she expect me to have a man-to-man talk with the boy?

I felt infinitely weary, incapable of explaining to myself how it had come about that I was sitting in this pizza parlour with my wife and daughter and a youth I barely knew. Try as I might, I couldn't put my finger on a point in my life at which I'd embarked on the course that had brought me here. Was it my sudden yen for a spring roll that had prompted me, nearly eighteen years ago, to walk into the *Seventh Heaven*? Had that spring roll conduced to a pregnant teenage daughter? Were things as banal as that? Perhaps that's all it was: banal, normal, utterly normal. I breathed a little easier at the thought. Maybe a spring roll was to blame for everything.

A professionally genial Italian waiter brought the salad and the pizza, garnishing them with a few words of Italian like Italian waiters the world over, as if it were part of the service. Although they speak the local language fluently, it seems that their job requires them to say *una pizza quattro staggione* and *una insalata mista, prego* . . .

Franka opened her mouth and said, in the waiter's direction, You knocked me up that time in Prague. The waiter ignored us with smiling indifference.

Tobi put the fork to his lips and hesitated for a moment before opening his mouth and engulfing the piece of pizza. We all watched him as he chewed it slowly. Then, with his mouth full, he said, I can't have.

But you did, Claudia said sharply. She had her head down and was weeding the black olives out of her salad.

I can't have, Tobi repeated, slowly shaking his head. And suddenly he looked like a man in his mid-forties. I could see his puppy fat turn into middle-aged flab and render him a prime candidate for a heart attack. He would smoke and wear pale blue shirts and overly wide neckties, have a wife and three children and an administrative job on the senior executives' floor. Perhaps he would be a Christian Democrat politician. No other party would suit his bull neck and the bald head he would involuntarily reacquire in thirty years' time. I was immutably prejudiced in that respect.

Only a whisker separated that man from the big baby that had only just learned to dress itself and wield a knife and fork with reasonable dexterity. It not only had its teenage worries, big and small, like all the rest, but might even be embarrassed by its ludicrous size. For a moment I almost sympathized with the big baby, but then it occurred to me that my daughter, my pretty child, my little girl, must have chosen this monster herself, and I could have thrashed him for it. Not her, strangely enough.

But you did! I repeated Claudia's words with sheeplike stupidity, feeling weak and thoroughly unmanly. Tobi raised his head. His watery, pale blue eyes regarded me defiantly. But I took care, he said to me, to me alone – man to man, so to speak.

What do you mean? Claudia hissed like a viper. What do you mean, you took care?

Well, I yanked it out, said Tobi. He picked the chillies out of his pizza and carefully manoeuvred them to the edge of his plate.

I felt myself turn puce with shame, and the breath issued from my nostrils like red-hot dragon's breath. Franka was scratching a pattern on the tablecloth with her fork. I couldn't see her face, but beads of sweat were gathering on her forehead.

You imbecile, Claudia snarled. That's just for Catholics and cretins, didn't you know?

No, Tobi said truthfully.

Never heard of condoms?

Tobi cut the crust off his pizza and steadfastly continued to eat. We watched him, dumbfounded by his total impassivity.

Well, what happens now? demanded Claudia. Can you tell me? What happens now, pray?

Tobi gave an almost imperceptible shrug, not looking at anyone. Franka pushed her chair back with a fierce movement and hurried off to the loo.

You imbecile, Claudia said in a low voice, and I almost feared for the big baby's safety, because I could tell from her tone that she was within an ace of hurling herself at him, scratching his eyes out, beating him senseless, sinking her teeth in him. You, you . . . You simply stick it in and yank it out and don't give it another thought, do you? Why isn't anyone on this planet too dumb to fuck? Your kind should be banned. You ought to wear a sign round your neck: Too dumb to fuck – don't touch! Better still, you ought to be castrated!

Claudia, I said quietly.

She rounded on me. Don't tell me you're defending this idiot?

She really wanted it, Tobi mumbled, continuing to circumcise his pizza. That was when my hand misbehaved itself. I saw it shoot across the table and land on the boy's fat cheek, jolting his head back and knocking his absurd yellow glasses awry. In one movement I leaned over, grabbed him by the T-shirt, and hit him again on his big, red, shaven head. But then up came our waiter, no longer speaking Italian, and Claudia tugged at my sleeve, and the waiter hung on to my arm, and Tobi was holding his cheek, and a second waiter came hurrying up, and I was hauled out of the restaurant like a vicious dog. I stood there in the cold night air, panting and seething with fury. It almost made me laugh, but then Claudia and Franka and Tobi emerged, and as soon as I saw him I hurled myself at him once more, colliding with his barn door of a chest and lashing out blindly with my fists. And when he started to defend himself and caught me a haymaker in the chest that nearly knocked the breath out of me, I was almost happy because it finally felt as if a decent punch-up could dispose of the whole problem. A decent punch-up, and all would be well.

I vaguely heard Claudia call something, but it didn't matter because what mattered was that something was being *done* after all that futile blather. Just then I saw the big baby's massive fist heading straight for my face. It grew bigger and bigger, comic strip fashion, until a black pain wrapped me in cotton wool and robbed me of my senses.

When I came to I was lying on a park bench, dazzled by the street light overhead. My wife was sitting at my feet and my daughter pillowing my head on her lap. It was quiet and peaceful, the only sound a faint hum of traffic in the distance. I smiled, because apart from a dull ache in the jaw all was suddenly well again.

You're awful, Claudia said from down by my feet. What did you hope to achieve?

Oh, Dadfred, said Franka, it was almost like a movie.

Stupid, said Claudia. Utterly stupid.

I felt like a hero and couldn't stop smiling. As far as I could recall, I'd last experienced such a moment with my wife and daughter in Italy, when Franka was three years old and we were lying together on a beach lounger counting shooting stars on San Lorenzo's Night. It was a moment filled with happiness and acceptance of all that had happened between now and that spring roll of eighteen years before. I took Franka's hand in one hand and Claudia's in the other and gave them both a squeeze.

Everything'll be fine, I said. Neither of them answered, and I sensed how ridiculous I was.

6

WE'RE DRIVING THROUGH SWITZERLAND on a pitch-black night. The white central strip has been gliding past for hours and is starting to hypnotize me. There's very little traffic. I'm tired and in danger of losing myself in time and space. I don't know where I am any more. I still think I'm somewhere in the middle of my life, but it hasn't really been the middle for a long time now.

My daughter's asleep on the back seat. I'm taking her to her boyfriend the lama. It sounds so idiotic, I utter a mocking, hyena-like laugh in the darkness, an alien laugh unrecognizable as my own.

Franka wants to run away and I'm meant to stop her. But I'm on the run too. On the run from my thinning hair, my inevitable physical decay, the end of my love for my wife, the end of my marriage.

I'm running as fast as I can.

I'm a man on a galloping horse. Where are you off to in such a hurry? a passer-by asks him, and he replies, Don't ask me, ask my horse – ask my faithful Toyota Corolla. I'm fleeing from the realization that every day is more unendurable than the last. Get a move on, gee-gee, you can't go too fast for me.

You're like a hunted man, Claudia tells me, but where do you want to go?

Not a clue. All I know is, I don't want to be where I am.

I've been the same way all my life, for as far back as I can remember. Every day of my childhood in Celle I wanted to be somewhere else, wanted to get away from the coarse red living-room carpet on which I sprawled on my tummy, or the sofa with the salt-and-pepper upholstery, or the damp little garden behind the house. Away, just away, but where to? No idea. I wanted out but stayed put.

All my life I've lolled around and dreamed of escaping – even from the beds I shared with women. From all the beds I shared with Claudia, too. I took refuge in them and simultaneously wanted out. The rock-hard futon in her tiny apartment; later on, the Ikea double bed in Schwabing's Destouchesstrasse in which Franka spent the first few months of her life; the same bed when it accompanied us to Gentzstrasse; the narrow couch in the *Seventh Heaven*'s office to which I fled more and more often because I felt like a Sing Sing lifer in the confines of our little family; all the hotel beds in the States, France, Italy, and England – places where I've been in the flesh and was simultaneously elsewhere in spirit.

Where was I really?

Where my weary body lay, or where my mind was avidly roaming? My body and mind were seldom in the same place, at all events. Question: Which of the two places was the more real?

Franka once asked me how you actually know whether you're awake or asleep. She was about four at the time.

If you pinch your arm and feel it, you're awake, I replied, quick as a flash, because I was afraid she might be fleeing from reality like me.

But I can dream I've pinched myself and it hurts, Franka retorted just as swiftly, fixing me expectantly with her huge blue eyes. I prayed she didn't detect the fear on my face, but at the same time how proud of her I was! Proud of her imagination, lack of inhibition, curiosity, intelligence. How I loved to brag about her!

Pubescence sent her intellect to sleep. All her thoughts were located below the waist – a normal development, I suppose. Chimpanzees that have been trained for years and can perform the most amazing tricks forget everything at a stroke when they reach puberty. Franka forgot all her wisdom and did nothing but comb her hair.

She became alien to me. Extraterrestrials took possession of her body and brain. She ceased to be my little philosopher with the elfin body. It disappointed me that she wasn't unique any more; she was like all the rest. I was alone again, neither here nor there. Franka had kept me anchored to the present, but now I floated pointlessly, aimlessly through life like a balloon, uncertain whether I was awake or asleep.

7

N OT A TULIP IN sight. Amsterdam was cold and grey.
Franka and Claudia got out in front of the hospital, and
Claudia took Franka's hand as if she were accompanying her
to school on her very first day. Franka meekly went along with
her. What else could she do? Had she ever expressed an
opinion or made a decision for herself? Or had we deprived
her of a decision because we simply couldn't imagine that she
might dream, at the age of sixteen, of becoming a mother?

She'd left it so late, well beyond the third month, that it
would have been impossible to carry out a legal termination in
Germany. Termination . . . The very word made me shudder.

I did nothing, just waited in silence.

As per usual, Claudia would say. But what *could* I have
done? I didn't know any gynaecologist whose advice we could
have asked, and I'd merely been a helpless, inarticulate con-
tributor to all those phone calls to Dutch abortion clinics. In
the present situation I was a dead loss; I knew it, and so did the
two women. They'd ceased to consult me – in fact they didn't
even ask if I wanted to come in when I pulled up outside the
clinic. They'd enlisted my services as a chauffeur; more than
that they didn't expect of me.

I obviously couldn't help to resolve the situation. But what
did 'resolve' mean? Eliminate it? Undo it, so everything could

be as it was? So we didn't have to change our lives? So our lives would be devoid of incident?

In the middle of one of our wordless, sleepless nights at this period, Claudia had unexpectedly opened her mouth, and the following words tumbled out like pebbles:

I wish it were mine.

Nothing more. Just that one sentence: I wish it were mine. In those five words I sensed the effort it was costing her not to misuse her daughter so as to get a baby herself. The baby I had denied her.

No, I hadn't wanted all that palaver again: the eternal caterwauling, the permanent state of fatigue, the parental fears. No, once had been quite enough for me.

Claudia had discreetly broached the subject many times, and my answer was always the same: You really want to get out of bed every night? You want to cope with the stinking nappies, the sicked-up milk, the screams? You want to drive round the inner ring-road every night, freeze your butt off beside a playground, play with building bricks, spend three years teaching it to count, put up with innumerable colds and floods of tears? Is that what you *really* want?

She never answered, but she faithfully informed me when she was fertile and I would open the drawer of the bedside table and get out the condoms. She made no comment, so I thought it was all right. She stopped asking when she turned forty, and I assumed the subject was closed for good.

I wish it were mine . . .

Well *I* didn't. I'd have liked my little Franka back at the age of five, but not another baby. No way.

I watched them from the car as they disappeared into the modern hospital building, both slightly hunched, Franka in the thick quilted jacket that always made her look like a Michelin Man, Claudia grave-faced and brisk in her smart

38

beige Armani winter coat. She would straighten out our lives again. She always straightened things out, she was so efficient. Although I often detested it, her efficiency had been my reason for taking refuge with her. My unspoken plea: Straighten out my life – and she did. No longer a disappointed and untalented artist, I was a successful businessman: Fred Kaufmann, who had become a businessman because he was too dumb to be anything else.

And Claudia would straighten out our lives yet again while I drove round the block, impotently smoking a cigarette.

I saw Franka stretched out in the gynaecological chair with her legs splayed, one nurse holding the mask to her face, another busy with stainless steel instruments. They were doing it to my little girl, my little mouse.

I gave a yell, drove the car on to the pavement in front of the clinic, jumped out and ran off down the road – anywhere, just away. I ran and ran. Abortion . . . The very sound of the word was frightful. Abortion, termination . . .

I'd never told Claudia about the French girl. She went to the doctor's one morning and came back that afternoon. Looked a bit pale, but that was all. We didn't say a word about it. Two days later she simply disappeared, took all her belongings and went. I silently drank myself into a stupor. Never saw her again.

I ran along the Grachten, ran on and on until my lungs hurt so much I had to stop short, coughing and gasping, and cling to a wrought-iron grille for support. Multicoloured specks of light danced before my eyes as I stood there coughing my lungs up. A very slim young black woman in a dark blue turban was sitting on a park bench, watching me.

I tottered over to the bench and sat down beside her. Without a word, she handed me a tissue. I thanked her in English and wiped my sweaty forehead. She eyed me serenely. When the pain in my lungs subsided the tears came. I didn't

39

care, I let them flow freely. She grasped my hand, turned it over, ran a swarthy finger over my palm, and said, Ask me a question.

A question? What question? I had thousands of them. How would Franka get over it? How would we, as a family, get over it? Would Claudia and I get over it? Would my hair fall out? Was my car being towed away by the Amsterdam police? What disease would I die of? Would I ever be happy again? I was unpleasantly struck by the fact that most of the questions revolved around myself.

I didn't speak. She held my hand and waited patiently. A squirrel hopped out of a tree in front of us and surveyed us from a safe distance. The woman beside me produced a nut from her bag and tossed it at the squirrel. The squirrel picked it up and held it daintily between its forepaws. It gave us another appraising look and scampered off.

I sobbed, wiping my tear-stained face with my free hand. I couldn't remember the last time I'd wept. The woman held my other hand and let me weep. She started to sing a song.

Row, row, row your boat, she sang, *gently down the stream. Merrily, merrily, merrily, merrily, life is but a dream.* Everything's just a dream. Cautiously, I turned my head and looked at her. She grinned.

Will my hair fall out? I asked in English.

She laughed. Of course, she said.

Will my daughter ever be happy again?

She shook her head. My heart faltered like an engine on the point of seizing up. I can't answer questions about other people, she said. It's not in your hand.

My heart came to life again. I nodded. That figured. Am I a dead loss? I asked quietly in German.

In English, she commanded.

I couldn't think of a suitable translation. I crumpled the

tissue into a ball and aimed for the litter basket. Needless to say, I missed.

Good shot, she said scathingly. She took my hand and held it up in front of her eyes.

Am I an asshole? I asked her, and she grinned so broadly I could have buried my head in her bosom.

She let go of my hand. Yes, she said, just like everyone else.

Thanks, I said.

She looked at me derisively, retrieved my hand, and studied it like a street map. I see a journey, she said. Not a very long journey, but one that will change everything.

Where to? I asked like Herr Marschall, my obliging travel agent on Kurfürstenplatz.

The big, dark blue turban wagged from side to side. Not far, she said. Europe, is my guess.

Thank you, I said, and removed my hand from hers. A journey . . . Of course, they always say that, it's a dead cert. I felt disappointed, disenchanted.

When I got up to go she caught me by the sleeve. I haven't eaten today, Mister. She didn't look at me as she spoke.

Suddenly she was calling me Mister. I gave her twenty guilders, a sum that seemed to satisfy her only moderately. I looked over my shoulder when I'd gone a hundred metres or so. She'd gone, but the squirrel had reappeared and was staring at me with its forepaws raised.

I had no idea which direction I'd come from, nor could I remember the address of the clinic. Nothing seemed familiar, every street looked the same. I was wandering helplessly around in a dream. Experimentally, in the hope of regaining my bearings, I started running again. While running I looked down at my English shoes, which struck me as the only solid, reliable things in sight. When I'd still failed to find the clinic after an hour, panic set in.

I'd lost my family.

I'd pushed off and lost them. I was back where I started. No longer young, but alone – alone in a strange city. All my options were open, anything was possible once more. If I didn't go back I could start again from scratch. Feeling dizzy, I tried desperately to think what to do.

A list of hospitals. A telephone directory – I needed a telephone directory. I dashed to the nearest telephone booth, but there wasn't any directory. Inquiries?

But what should I say? My wife and my daughter are in some abortion clinic or other, I can't remember which. Please read them all out to me.

The police? No, not the police. I might be a dead loss, but I wouldn't go to the police. Why hadn't I brought my mobile? Franka and Claudia could at least have called me. What an idiot, dead loss, asshole I was!

Exhausted, I rested my throbbing forehead against the cool glass of the telephone booth. Someone tapped on the pane from outside. Reluctantly, I looked up. There she was again: my fortune-teller.

I greeted her like a long-lost relative, blathered unintelligibly, gesticulated wildly, told her about my pregnant daughter and my wife, but nothing I said seemed to make any sense. She eyed me as impassively as she might have eyed the rotating sails of a windmill, then raised her arm and pointed. Straight ahead, she said, and turn right at the next traffic lights.

I fished a few notes out of my pocket and proffered them in a trembling hand. She crossed her arms over her chest. You really are an asshole, she said.

I stared at her, dumbfounded, then stuffed the money back in my pocket, stammered 'Thanks' in several languages, and ran off like a hunted man. Straight ahead and right at the next traffic lights.

* * *

42

They were sitting on the kerb, Franka with her head on Claudia's shoulder, Claudia with her arms round Franka, holding her tight. They were sitting just where I'd abandoned our car on the pavement. Where it *had* been, because it wasn't there any longer. Towed away.

I dashed up to them, panting hard. They glanced at me briefly and dispassionately. I might have been a total stranger. They expected nothing of me, nothing at all. They'd lost the habit a long time ago.

8

I'M DRIVING THROUGH A night like molten lead.

I adjust the rear-view mirror for a look at Franka, but all I
can see is the curve of her back as it quietly rises and falls
beneath the blanket. Who knows where she is in her dreams?
Certainly not with her father, driving along a Swiss motorway
in a silver Toyota.

Perhaps she's dreaming about her lama. All I've ever seen
of him is a photo depicting a mischievous-looking young man
with a helmet of thick, short black hair, Asiatic eyes, a dark
complexion, and a red robe like his teacher, the man with the
beer can on the back cover of Claudia's book about happiness.

A year ago I'd never heard of him. Now, Franka has
announced her intention of living with him and going off
to India with him. Is he, or is he not, a monk? Is a monk
permitted to have a girlfriend? What about sex?

Franka shrouds herself in silence and lets our questions roll
off her like raindrops on oilskin.

After long nights of strategic deliberation, Claudia and I
decided that it was better to take her to see him than risk her
running away some day. Whispering, often giggling, we sat on
our bed and concocted this plan. Franka's lovesick condition
became a new source of intimacy between us, made all the

sweeter by the despair that lurked in the background. We devised a plan for Franka but none for ourselves.

So now I'm to keep a discreet eye on Franka at the meditation centre, put my faith in the disillusioning effects of everyday life, and, after a few weeks, bring the girl home again – deinfatuated.

That's my mission. Strictly speaking, though, the lama is all Claudia's fault. It was she who dragged Franka off to the Buddhist retreat after her abortion to heal her inner wounds.

It would do you good too, she told me. Come with us.

No thanks. How to be happy when you aren't . . . What gave Claudia the idea I was unhappy? I stayed behind in Munich, and they were scarcely out of sight when I dived between Marisol's thighs like a deep-sea diver sinking into the dark depths, intent on visual and auditory oblivion.

Now, for my sins, I must go on retreat. Claudia knows nothing about Marisol, of course – nothing at all. I was very careful.

I'm going to buy myself a case of wine and several cartons of Gauloises before we check into the mediation centre, that's for sure, and every morning I'll drive to the nearest village and slurp coffee and devour thick steaks.

Franka mutters something in her sleep and turns over. Bereft of her lama back in Munich, she slunk around unhappily like a sick cat. I eventually agreed to take her to him, her lovesick heart was hurting so badly. My daughter's heart, the heart I listened to with fascination when it was still the size of a quail's egg, beating inside Claudia's belly.

Loudspeakers broadcast those heartbeats to the surgery at large. They sounded rapid and agitated, like the hoofbeats of a galloping pony. Gefuffle, gefuffle, gefuffle . . .

I couldn't get enough of them. Holding hands with Claudia in the cramped booth, I would turn up the volume every time and listen to our child's hurried little heartbeats until the doctor's receptionist came in, shaking her head, and turned it down again.

My mobile rings, and its green display lights up like an eye. 'Claudia calling,' it announces. My mobile speaks English because I want it to. Because I'm an old show-off. Claudia calling . . . It sounds like a song. Claudia calling, Franka calling, Marisol calling. For Marisol's benefit I switched it to Spanish for weeks on end: *Marisol llamando*.

She called me several times a day. *Hola, hombre*, she would say, and those two little words were enough to make me go weak at the knees.

Uh-huh? I mutter. I always answer Claudia that way. I mutter as if we're in the middle of a conversation. Uh-huh?

Where are you?

Still in Switzerland.

Are you okay, the two of you?

Are we? No idea, but I say yes. How about you? I ask.

She doesn't reply at once. She can never, never, simply say, I'm fine. That would be *too* simple. If only she'd say, just once, I'm fine, thanks. But no, never. She wants me to wonder how she is. Silence falls. I wait. At length, in a pinched little voice, she says, Oh, so-so.

A clattering sound. What are you doing?

Emptying the dishwasher.

I picture her putting away the plates we ate off together yesterday. A thought darts through my head like a poisoned arrow: Perhaps we'll never eat off those plates again, not together, and the plates already know it but she doesn't. She doesn't have a clue.

Any other plans for tonight? I ask her, all innocent.

I'm going to veg out in front of the goggle-box in my tracksuit bottoms and have a beer, she says.

I laugh. How simple life could be.

Drive carefully.

Sure.

And call me.

Sure.

And tell Franka . . .

Yes?

Oh, nothing.

In that case . . .

She abruptly hangs up, and now I miss her. I put out my hand and stroke her knee. I get on best with her when she isn't there. At the same time, I feel lonely driving along by myself in the inky night.

I turn and look to make sure that Franka's really still in the car. Her fists are clenched like a baby's and she's frowning in her sleep. I put out a hand and touch her. She snuffles and twitches like a sleeping dog.

A Mövenpick restaurant looms up on the skyline, a real place that will release me from this no-man's-land of darkness. I pull up right outside the door, adjust Franka's blanket, and lock the car in case someone steals her.

9

I LOAD MY TRAY WITH *Rösti, Zürcher Geschnetzeltes,* and two beers – albeit non-alcoholic ones – because I won't get anything like that at the meditation centre. They probably live on a solid diet of rice soup, and all Claudia's tales of fantastic vegetarian food were merely designed to reassure me. She's well aware that rice soup would have scared me off, even at the cost of losing our daughter to a lama.

In the yawningly empty restaurant I sit down at a blood-orange plastic table beneath a blood-orange light. Although I'm not really hungry, I stuff myself with *Rösti* and *Geschnetzeltes* for fear of never getting a decent meal again.

I feel like the planet's last survivor, marooned in a blood-orange 1970s disco. I pour the second beer down my throat.

You've got the emotional intelligence of a snail, Claudia says angrily. As soon as emotions crop up you crawl into your shell and don't re-emerge until you're sure nothing important is happening.

I don't believe in the power of speech.

You're incapable of communicating, you mean.

I don't think one can really talk about emotions.

One can try.

There's no point.

How would you know if you never *do* try?

It doesn't change a thing, all that talk.

Talk can prevent wars or stop them.

The language of diplomacy has nothing to do with it.

Egoist, she says, and slams the door behind her.

I hate it when she calls me an egoist, because whenever she runs out of ideas she snaps 'Egoist!' and turns away, leaving me stranded. First she gets me to talk, then she won't respond.

So I'm an egoist. I still don't know exactly what an egoist is, but I've been called that all my life. My mother called me an egoist when I didn't want to share with my friends; my father when I wouldn't mow the lawn or go buy him some cigarettes; girls when I wouldn't go for a walk with them. Fundamentally, everyone called me an egoist when I failed to do what they wanted, when I differed from their conception of me.

You're just resentful, says Claudia. Resentful because you're not so very different from the rest – because you lead an ultra-normal existence. And I'm supposed to be to blame.

There's an element of truth in that. Even so, I secretly believe I'm not quite as ultra-normal as other people.

The fried potato cake and strips of meat have combined to form a dense, malignant lump in my stomach. I'm just wondering whether to disperse it with a Fernet Branca when a family comes trooping in – a family recognizable from afar as German. Thin, pallid and red-haired, the father wears shiny lilac shorts, a sports shirt of riotous design, and the inevitable socks and sandals. (How many generations of German mothers have impressed upon their sons never to go around sockless? For fear of catching cold? For fear of athlete's foot?) He has a small, elongated leather case suspended from his neck and is carrying a pallid, red-haired, possibly three-year-old boy in shorts, socks and sandals like his own. The mother, a buxom little woman with curly fair hair, is attired in a pair of batiked trousers and a sleeveless blouse that exposes her plump white arms.

She's also carrying a child. A year old at most, it keeps putting a hand down her cleavage in search of her breast. They sit down directly opposite me. Here, Claudia, is an ultra-normal family for you.

Norbert, the woman says sternly, did you lock the car?

Norbert gives a weary nod.

Are you sure?

Another nod.

I know this is Switzerland, but you never can tell. Just some fruit salad for the children. You'd like some fruit salad, wouldn't you? The children stare mutely, blankly, at the blood-orange light.

Two fruit salads, then, says Norbert like an obedient waiter, and gets up again. What shall I get you?

Anything, says the woman, angrily plucking the infant's hand out of her cleavage.

I'm bound to get it wrong, says Norbert.

Good God, says the woman, you know the kind of thing I like.

Norbert puts the elder child down on the banquette and stands there irresolutely.

The man is probably in his mid-forties, his wife early thirties at most. He's been lucky enough to land himself a young wife, and she's presented him with two children in quick succession.

But I don't know what you like, Norbert says unhappily.

Show a bit of initiative, can't you?

Salad? Norbert suggests timidly.

Yes, but only if there's no ham in it.

He walks off.

Your flute, she calls, leave the flute here.

Norbert turns, removes the leather case from around his neck and deposits it carefully, almost tenderly, on a chair. Then he strides off to the salad counter to choose something for his family.

His wife gives me a would-be alluring smile. I politely smile back. She dabs her moist forehead.

What a summer, she says.

I nod. The little child plunges its hand into her cleavage again. This time she lets it happen, holding my gaze. If she knew what to do with those brats of hers she'd go into the loo with me like a shot. Ten to one she would, or she wouldn't be looking at me that way. That plump, boring provincial house-wife, with her batik pants, would retire to a Mövenpick loo with a total stranger, and two minutes later she'd be snarling at her Norbert for bringing the wrong kind of salad. That's the really scary thing about women.

Where are you bound for? she asks.

France, I say truthfully.

Oh, how lovely, she says, France! I'd like to go there too, some day. Paris, for choice.

She leans forward and whispers, Without the kids, mind you . . .

I smile faintly, regretting that I answered her at all because now this conversation could meander on along the same lines for ever. But she abruptly gets up and hauls the older child, who's looking very sleepy, to its feet.

Would you be kind enough to tell my husband I've taken the children to the toilets for a minute or two?

Of course, I say.

Taking the children and her handbag, she gives a last look round as though reassuring herself that she hasn't forgotten anything.

I'd like to go myself, to be honest, but I feel it my duty to inform Norbert that his entire family is in the loo.

I guard his flute case and wait.

Not long afterwards Norbert rounds the corner carrying a loaded tray. I give him his wife's message. He responds with a grateful nod.

Have a good holiday, I say.

Oh, thanks, Norbert says blithely. You too.

I walk to the exit, then notice how genuinely tired I am and retrace my steps. I buy myself a double espresso but decide to avoid Norbert and his family by drinking it on the far side of the establishment.

The coffee's hot. I wait for it to cool down, staring out of the window at the motorway and the car in which my daughter is sleeping.

Without seeing me, Norbert walks past in the direction of the loo. Soon afterwards he returns, peering around helplessly. He rotates once on his own axis, then comes over to me.

I wish I could dive into my espresso and submerge. I can't stand it when I see people bearing down on me. They usually want something, so they always trigger an escape mechanism.

She's not in the toilets, he says reproachfully.

That's what she told me.

But she isn't there.

He turns away without a word and goes over to the cash desk. He says something to the cashier, who shakes her head. Norbert stands there at a loss, a pathetic figure with his pale, spindly legs and socks and sandals. He runs a bewildered hand through his sparse red hair. His long, equine face grows still longer. He looks in my direction, and before I can escape he comes over to me again.

She's gone. He gives an incredulous laugh.

She's probably waiting outside, I say cautiously.

He looks at me without conviction. The car's gone too, he says. And the children.

I heave a vicarious sigh.

His eyes flicker, his lower lip trembles. She's gone, he repeats, just like that. He suddenly turns pale, and I can see, even in the blood-orange lighting, that he's white to the lips.

I get him a mineral water which he doesn't touch. Beside him is the tray laden with two bowls of fruit salad for the children and a plate of salad for his wife. Without ham.

He stands there like a zombie, a living corpse. I tug at his sleeve. Come along, I say, and don't forget your flute.

He gives me a grateful nod and cradles the flute case tenderly in his arms the way he held his child only minutes earlier.

IO

I COULD PLAY YOU SOMETHING, he says as we're driving past Lake Geneva. The moon, which has risen, is mirrored in its surface. Some flute music would be far from inappropriate. Why not, I say. He plays surprisingly well. It could be something by Béla Bartók, but I'm no expert. It's usually something by Bartók when I'm stumped.

Franka's still asleep. She doesn't know we're now *à trois*, and all at once this trip becomes lovely and peaceful and I'm quite content for a few moments. Until Norbert puts his flute away and starts sobbing uncontrollably.

I try to ignore him, fervently wishing that Claudia were here. Claudia would know what to do. Norbert howls like a wolf, his whole body racked with sobs, until a tissue is proffered from the back seat and held under his nose.

Norbert turns round. Thanks, he sniffs, and I see Franka respond with a sleepy nod. My daughter, who has never yet had a handkerchief handy when it's badly needed, has conjured up a tissue.

Norbert loudly blows his nose. I had an inkling of it when we set off, he blurts out. She was so silly, kept griping the whole time, I couldn't do a thing right. And then she insisted on taking the passports, hers and the children's. Normally we keep all the passports together in a plastic wallet, but she took out her own and the children's and put them in her handbag. It puzzled me at the time.

He emits a dry sob, like a child. I don't know what I did wrong, he says.

Maybe you always did the right thing, Franka suggests matter-of-factly. That can be just as irritating.

Norbert turns and looks at her, intrigued. Maybe, he says pensively. Maybe.

Sometimes, says Franks, it gets on your nerves when people keep trying to do the right thing, when they're always nice and kind. You feel like hitting them, she says, and I listen to her as if she's a stranger whose presence in my car is as fortuitous as Norbert's.

She's ten years younger than me, says Norbert. She could have any man she wants.

But she hasn't, says Franka.

Maybe she will.

No, all she needs is time out.

Time out?

A break. Everyone needs an occasional break.

You really think so?

I see Franka nod in the rear-view mirror.

Thanks, says Norbert. He blows his nose once more, opens the window, and lets the tissue fly away. Oh, so sorry, he says, looking at me as if it were *my* native land he'd just defiled.

I concentrate on the white centre line – the only dependable feature of this peculiar night, it seems.

She was so prickly when we started out, Norbert goes on. Nothing but complaints: Do you always have to drive so slowly? Can't you overtake him? Get a move on, can't you? He sighs. She's so young, that's the trouble. It's hard sometimes, being married to someone who's never heard of Bob Dylan.

I'm surprised Norbert knows who Bob Dylan is.

Wallflowers, says Franka in the gloom.

What?

Wallflowers, she repeats, not volunteering an explanation.

Bob Dylan's son's band, I say, feeling ever so slightly proud of knowing this.

Bobby and Joan's son? asks Norbert.

Bobby? Franka bursts out laughing.

Joan Baez? No idea.

He once had a thing going with Joan Baez, Norbert says like an elderly aunt trying hard to sound hip.

He's the best-looking man in the world, says Franka.

It's true. Bob Dylan's son is an incredibly handsome young man. Franka and I once saw a black-and-white video of him on MTV, walking along a wintry New York street with his band, hands deep in his pockets. He looked so much like his father on the sleeve of *Highway Revisited* that the length of time I'd already lived hit me on the head like a dislodged flowerpot. I looked up indignantly and saw myself twenty-five years younger, leaning out of the window and laughing derisively at my belief that I was still the same person. An absurd mistake.

In the waiting room of the Munich gynaecologist who refused to help us because Franka was more than three months gone, I came across a magazine containing an interview with Bob Dylan in which he said that, sooner or later, everyone has to come to terms with the fact that he isn't the person he used to be. I'd scarcely read that sentence when the blue fitted carpet beneath my feet gave way, to reveal a menacing abyss that threatened to engulf me. Who else should I be if I wasn't allowed to be the person I'd always been?

Franka and Claudia came out of the consulting room, Franka with her head bowed, Claudia white as a sheet.

Claudia looked at me and almost imperceptibly shook her head – Nothing doing – and I felt ashamed because, in spirit, I'd been with Bob Dylan and my lost youth. Egoist! Yes, it's true.

Honey, just allow me one more chance to get along with you. Honey, just allow me one more chance, sings Norbert, and I join in: *I'll do anything with you*.

I step on the gas, and we warble, *With my head in my hand, I'm looking for a woman who needs a worried man. Just one kind of favour I ask – allow me one more chance.*

We laugh, Franka groans and turns on her Discman.

Norbert puts the flute to his pursed lips and plays 'It's Alright, Ma' and 'Mr Tambourine Man' and 'It's All Over Now, Baby Blue'. I've always found Dylan unintelligible, so my knowledge of the lyrics is very sketchy.

We sing our way through all his albums. To this day I know exactly when to turn the record over. The breaks have etched themselves into my memory for ever. We used to lie on mattresses in dark party cellars, necking with girls we almost certainly wouldn't have recognized in daylight, and one of us always had to get up and turn the record over. It was always the one who wasn't getting anywhere or had failed to land himself a girl at all. Norbert must often have done that, I reflect. He's a record-turner *par excellence*.

Switzerland is asleep, you can almost hear it snore, and we go on singing together. *I ain't looking to compete with you, beat or cheat or mistreat you, simplify you, classify you, deny, defy or crucify you. All I really want to do is, baby, be friends with you.* I'd so much like to be friends with Claudia again, the way we used to be.

Franka shakes her head at us like a granny deploring her grandchildren's antics, but then she joins in herself. She grew up with Bob Dylan, after all – I took her along to his concerts when she was little more than a baby, so we sing our heads off: *. . . baby, be friends with you. All I really want to do is, baby, be friends with you.*

11

A PALE SUN IS RISING. The air on my arm, which I'm dangling out of the window, is slowly warming up. I'm feeling rather queasy with fatigue. Norbert is asleep with the flute on his lap. In daylight he has the pallid, crumpled look of a used handkerchief.

Would Claudia have taken him along? Probably not. She'd have commiserated with him awhile and given him a few practical tips, but she wouldn't have given him a lift.

I've never known her to stop for a hitcher when she's at the wheel. Her eternal argument: He'll find someone else.

Once, late at night in La Palma, we picked up three scruffy young Swedes, two boys and a girl. They hadn't anywhere to sleep. There would have been room for them in our holiday villa, but Claudia wouldn't have them in the house. She fed and watered them, then directed them to a place on the patio.

We argued all night long. I called her behaviour outrageous, reprehensible, disgusting; she called me a goddamned social romantic.

We come to the French border. Franka has taken charge of Norbert's passport because he's now asleep, tired out after all his sobbing and singing, but nobody wants to see it anyway. We cruise past the frontier huts. Is there a frontier or isn't there? I can't get used to a Europe without frontiers. Until the mid-eighties I was always beckoned out of the queue, always checked, sometimes searched. I was every frontier guard's perfect idea of a terrorist: long, dark hair, designer stubble, Ray-Ban shades, leather jacket, black Citroën, later on an old Mercedes. I looked politically subversive. It was like an accolade, in fact I almost prided myself on it. How idiotic we were!

It's been a long time since any frontier guard took an interest in me.

Oh hell, says Franka. It's his birthday today.

She waves Norbert's passport under my nose. July 26, 1960. Forty today. I stare in horror at his sleep-crumpled face. The man's only forty! Nearly five years younger than me. How the devil does he know all Bob Dylan's lyrics by heart? He must be hopelessly behind the times, another thing that suits him.

Well, says Franka, what do we do now? When he wakes up it'll be his birthday.

So it's his birthday, I say.

And that's it?

I shrug my shoulders.

But he's forty!

Indignantly, Franka extricates herself from the blanket and leans forward, studies Norbert's dormant face.

What a mess, she whispers. Wife gone, children gone, car gone – and all on his birthday. Pull up, she says.

What for?

Just pull up.

Tell me why and I will.

Have a bit more respect for me, can't you? Could you possibly manage that?

I pull up. Franka gets out and closes the car door behind her – quietly, so as not to wake our sleeping passenger. I watch her, marvelling, as she goes into the nearby field and picks a bunch of flowers. In the distance she looks like a six-year-old. I remember all the bunches of dandelions she picked me. I can still feel the sticky drops of dandelion milk on my hands, still see her gap-toothed smile as she ran up to me brandishing the yellow bouquet in the air like a little flag. She always ran up like that, expecting me to open my arms so she could hurl herself into them. She flung herself at me like a ball, and I always caught her, always. Until the day she stopped short of my waiting arms. It was over. Just like that, from one day to the next. Without warning.

She comes running back with Norbert's birthday bouquet, rosy-cheeked and out of breath. It's a long time since she smiled that way. We've got some candles, too, she whispers. In the camping kit!

12

THE FIRST CAFÉ AU LAIT at Annecy. This is where the holiday begins. We're really abroad here. Switzerland didn't count, Annecy is the line of demarcation – Annecy and the first *café au lait*. We stagger into a bistro that's just opening. It's just gone eight, and we're already a little smelly after our ten-hour drive. It's amazing how soon a person starts to whiff.

We sit down at a table covered with a red plastic tablecloth. The proprietress is an archetypal Frenchwoman: fiftyish, dyed blonde and bad-tempered, with a pretty well-preserved figure, a firm, miniskirted posterior, and a Wonderbra-enhanced cleavage in her pink crocheted sweater.

Claudia has taught me to recognize feminine beauty aids. I'm not sure I'm really grateful to her.

The proprietress deposits three huge cups of coffee and some fresh croissants in front of us. I automatically note the size of the cups. It corresponds to a large cappuccino in one of our cafés, which sells for six-ninety. Overpriced, but our customers pay up without a murmur. It amazes me. Even the teenagers seem to think nothing of spending nearly seven marks on a cup of coffee.

Norbert is blinking sleepily. I don't think he realizes it's his birthday. Franka fumbles around under the table and conjures up her bunch of flowers and three lighted candles. We hum 'Happy Birthday', which is as far as we feel able to go. We're really very shy, my daughter and I.

Norbert gives a startled grin. Then, without warning, he bursts into tears. Yet again. Franka hands him her last tissue.

These sentimental Germans, Madame must be thinking. She's polishing her long black counter with thorough little movements, as though scrubbing the back of a sperm whale.

Forty, sniffs Norbert. It sounds funny. My God, forty!

Franka shrugs. We look at each other. What are we to do with him?

Forty, Norbert repeats, and here I am, all on my own. I'd never have dreamed it.

He sobs like a baby. Madame is watching us suspiciously. I feel a urge to get up, drag Franka off, and leave him sitting there. I don't think I care for men in tears.

I ran away on my fortieth birthday, I say. Norbert stops blubbing and looks at me sceptically.

Yes, I go on quickly, I was scared stiff of a surprise party – all my friends hiding in the bathroom, something like that – so I didn't go home. I got into the car and drove round Munich's inner ring-road all night. The inner ring-road is a tradition in our family. We used to drive round it with Franka when she was a baby because nothing else would send her to sleep. Franka was a poor sleeper. She nearly drove us mad.

Franka smiles faintly, looking rather embarrassed. I stroke her head and she tolerates my touch like a wary cat about to skedaddle at any moment.

Norbert blows his nose. My kids too, he says. They both had colic as babies. We wouldn't have survived without *Sabtropfen*. He grins feebly.

Sabtropfen! I exclaim. I have a sudden recollection of those baby-pink drops and little Franka's tummy-aches. I used to carry her round the apartment propped on my forearm like a kitten.

Franka yawns without putting her hand in front of her mouth.

So I drove round the inner ring-road all by myself, I go on. Midnight, one, two, three in the morning. At dawn I came home, feeling sure I'd find the remains of my surprise party, but there was nothing to be seen. Absolutely nothing. My wife and daughter were asleep. All quiet, not a sign of a party. I was bitterly disappointed. I even looked in the fridge to see if they'd at least chilled a bottle of champagne, but no. I'd always told them I didn't want anything for my birthday, nothing at all, and they'd taken me at my word. I stood there empty-handed and unfêted. Then I sat down in the kitchen, got drunk, and started smoking again after seven years.

Dad, how childish of you! says Franka, shaking her head.

Norbert gives a crooked grin and crumples up the sodden tissue.

I've also got a little present for you, Franka says. Only a tiny one. She takes Norbert's hand, turns it over, and traces the lines on his palm with her finger like the fortune-teller in Amsterdam. Not a very long journey, but one that'll change everything . . . Is this the journey she meant?

Who do you see in your hand? Franka asks. Norbert stares at her uncomprehendingly. Gently stroking his palm, she speaks in a soft voice unrecognizable as my daughter's. This isn't just your hand, she says. It's also the hand of your mother, your father, your grandparents, your great-grandparents, your great-great-grandparents, your great-great-great-grandparents, your great-great-great-great-grandparents, and – she can't help giggling – your great-great-great-great-great-grandparents. And who do your children have in their hands? You, your mother, your father, your grandparents, your great-grandparents, et cetera. They're always with you. None of them can ever disappear.

She carefully shuts Norbert's hand like a laptop and sits back. Norbert stares at her curiously. It's as if he's trying to remember where this peculiar creature sprang from.

Who told you that? I ask.

Oh, she says casually, Buddha in person. She grins.

Got to go to the loo, she adds, and leaves us alone together.

I didn't really understand, says Norbert.

Weary and rather bemused, we stare at our palms like people reading a newspaper.

But they *aren't* there, Norbert mutters. If he starts blubbing again I'll run outside. I feel like an amputee, he says. Know what I mean?

I nod.

Oh God, he groans. Half the time you wish your family would get lost, and when they're gone you feel like shit.

I'm surprised to hear Norbert use the word. It won't be for long, I say, trying to console him.

He looks thoughtful. I'm not so sure, he says soberly. Besides, he adds, I don't have a bean. She always keeps the purse.

I feel genuinely sorry for him for the first time. A man without money is a man without a prick. Does she? I say.

Yes, it's simpler that way. She does the shopping while I'm at the school.

A teacher, what else? A music teacher, probably.

We share the work of looking after the children, he explains, and I notice that I'm transposing everything he says into the past tense: She *kept* the purse, she *went* shopping while he *was* at the school, they *shared* the work of looking after the children. I know their marriage is over. No happily married woman smiles at another man the way she smiled at me.

We could call her, I suggest.

She won't be there, he points out.

But maybe she'll be home before long.

He shrugs.

We could call her and leave our phone number.

What phone number?

Some people still don't have mobiles, I tend to forget that.

We could always call Aunt Anni, says Norbert, looking suddenly alert.

I hand him the mobile. He doesn't know how to work it and hands it back. I key in Aunt Anni's number, put the phone in his hand, and write my own telephone number on a paper napkin.

But I won't know where I'll be, he objects. He simply doesn't understand. But then it strikes me I haven't given any thought to how much longer I intend to cart him around with us.

You never think ahead, I hear Claudia say angrily. Not even two steps ahead.

When Aunt Anni answers, Norbert yells my phone number into the mobile and tries to explain the inexplicable: Gabi has walked out on him, just like that. Gabi . . . So that's her name.

Aunt Anni is totally mystified. Norbert gives the mobile a puzzled look and hands it back without a word. 'Call waiting,' says the display. It can't be Claudia or the phone would say so. The same goes for Marisol.

Yes? I say.

You'll have to explain all that again, Aunt Anni bellows in a thick Swabian accent.

One moment, I tell her like a telephone operator, don't hang up. And I take the second call.

Hi, baby, says a man's voice.

Hello?

Hello?

Yes?

Oooh . . . A long drawn-out, English 'oh'. Then: Can I speak to Franka please?

Who's calling? I have the presence of mind to ask, although I already know perfectly well.

Pelge. My name's Pelge.

I nearly drop the mobile into my coffee. It's the lama.

Oooh, I say, and then I tell a lie. I hope other fathers do so too. I'd hate to be the only one.

Franka isn't here right now.

Oooh, he says, and hangs up.

What's the matter with Gabi this time? I hear Aunt Anni bellow.

I hand the mobile back to Norbert without a word.

Just then Franka comes back from the loo. I exchange a look with Norbert, but luckily he didn't catch on.

I give Franka a fraudulent grin. Like another coffee? I ask.

She eyes me suspiciously. A child's antennae are more sensitive than a snail's horns. She shrugs.

Trois grands cafés au lait, I call to Madame behind the counter. Norbert says goodbye to Aunt Anni and hands back the mobile. I slip it into my breast pocket and surreptitiously turn it off. The lama won't disturb us again. Nor will Aunt Anni. Nor Gabi. Claudia won't either.

13

S HE HASN'T CALLED, NORBERT says despondently. We're driving along an avenue of plane trees whose tops form a roof of greenery above us.

In Antonioni's film *The Passenger*, starring Jack Nicholson and Maria Schneider, the latter stands up in a convertible and exultantly watches just such a green vault of foliage flash past overhead while Nicholson smiles behind his dark glasses.

No dialogue. That was precisely how I envisioned my relationship with women in those days: casual, unspeaking, fleeting, wistful, weightless. Such was the life I wanted to lead and the kind of picture I aspired to make.

I knew she wouldn't call, Norbert wailed. It's her way of torturing me, getting me down. She knows how to hurt me. He gives the windscreen a half-hearted thump with his fist.

Franka casts her eyes up to heaven in the rear-view mirror. I nod, she smiles. A brief moment of mute, mutual understanding. Precious as gold, rare as a snowstorm in May.

'*Camping sur ferme*', it says on a little notice board. I turn off. I'm dog-tired and my eyelids are drooping. Norbert doesn't have a driver's licence, it transpires, so he can't relieve me at the wheel. Franka's pouting. She was hoping to be reunited with her lama before nightfall.

We pull up near a lopsided little windmill overlooking a lake. Lining its shores like a herd of huge grey beasts are caravans with Dutch licence plates and flaxen-haired occupants.

Get out and take a look, I tell Franka.

Take a look yourself, she says.

I could slap her sometimes. I want to hug her like my little baby one moment and wallop her the next. I've never hit her, discounting three or four spontaneous smacks.

Claudia and I both believed in bringing up a child without punishments or constraints. We wanted to be our daughter's friends. What bullshit! Parents are parents, not friends, Franka said so herself. But we're lonely without our children, so we want to be their friends.

I stroll across the campsite. An elderly man in huge yellow clogs gives me a friendly nod as he goes by. The Dutch evidently pack their *Klompen* when they go abroad, just as we take our socks and sandals. It's a form of national ID. Outside the caravans are camping tables bearing beer bottles with flowers sticking out of their necks. The portable TVs are on. The men wear shorts, the women's fat rumps are encased in neon-coloured lurex. They're laying the tables for supper and lighting their propane gas stoves.

I stand there helplessly, watched with suspicion by numerous pairs of eyes. I don't belong here in my black slacks, black T-shirt and expensive English shoes. I go inside the dark little windmill, where a taciturn man in riding boots rents me a space for 150 francs.

Norbert shakes his head. No good, he mutters, no good at all. Not a level patch of ground anywhere. He tramps back and forth across the campsite like a property developer. Franka is still sitting in the car. I can see her in the distance, angrily twisting her hair.

Norbert is the camping expert. I might have known, he looks the part.

Know how to pitch a tent? he calls. He's getting uppity already. Yes, I can pitch my tent unaided. It's a woman's tent, that's why – the kind even a woman can put up in the dark. Claudia bought it for her Easter trip to the meditation centre. It's the type used by the first women's team to climb Annapurna. My wife is impressed by such things. It looks like a little yellow UFO.

I'll sleep outside, says Norbert.

No way, I say, and show him the icon on the flap: two matchstick children and two matchstick adults.

You'll fit in easily.

He looks at me with doggy eyes. If he had a tail he'd wag it.

For supper we each consume three paper screws of *pommes frites* with mayonnaise, which are on sale in the windmill. Unspeaking, we sit on our padded mattresses outside the tent. The scent of grilled fish assails our nostrils from all directions. Across the way a young man is scratching his girlfriend's back in the glow of a paraffin lamp. We can't hear her, but she seems to be saying 'Up a little' and then 'Down a little – no, not there, *there*! No, up a bit . . . no, lower, *lower*!'

Norbert and I sigh deeply and simultaneously. We're envious. The young couple's love still seems as fresh and pristine as a new shirt. No creases, no worn patches, no stains.

At ten o'clock Franka and I crawl into our sleeping bags and Norbert pulls the car blanket over himself. We've positioned the two mattresses diagonally so we all have at least a little of them under our backsides, but the ground is diabolically hard.

Norbert wedges himself tightly against the side of the tent for fear of invading our space. Music from transistor radios is squawking all around us, and people walk past so close to our tent that the ground vibrates. I won't sleep a wink all night. Norbert whispers something.

Did you say something?

Goodnight, he replies. A few minutes later he starts snoring.

Oh God, Franka groans, a snorer on top of everything else. Did you hear him praying just now?

No.

He did, though.

Silence.

He's got three balls.

What!

So he told me.

When did he tell you?

Earlier on, while you were looking for a space.

He actually told you he had three balls?

Yes.

Did he make a pass at you?

Franka groans. No. Some one-track mind you've got!

Why would he tell you a thing like that?

How should I know?

Three balls, eh?

We both giggle in the dark, and I enjoy it – I breathe in great lungfuls of Franka's giggles. How long it is since that happened!

Moments later I hear her regular breathing. She's fallen asleep in mid-giggle.

Once, ages ago, I saw a woman with three breasts. Franka wasn't even born then.

I was helping Claudia occasionally in the *Seventh Heaven* and had started to revolutionize her sales concept. I'd just introduced 'Indian Week' and 'Tao Cuisine'. Both had been a big hit. Our customers had gone home. Claudia locked the café door and lowered the blind. There were just the two of us plus Ralf and Mirja, Tav and Sabine.

Tav then owned the hottest disco in Munich. Today he's a property consultant with the Hypo-Bank. His girlfriend Sabine was a nice, plump girl with lovely auburn hair.

Tav fetched a couple of cans of beer from the fridge and opened one with a hiss. Here's to Tao, he said, and tossed me the other.

Your eyes are all red, he said, did you know?

I went swimming this morning.

Swimming? said Tav, shaking his head. Looks to me like you've been smoking grass all day.

The Chinese say you can eat anything as long as you cut it up small enough. Ralf tittered as he chopped up a big hunk of Black Afghan with our best Japanese kitchen knife.

I saw Claudia's jaw muscles tighten. She briskly turned away and started to clear the tables. She didn't care for our pot-smoking sessions, but she couldn't complain, the till was overflowing tonight: 'Tao Cuisine. Admission DM25.' An assortment of locally celebrated culture vultures, a few journalists, a sprinkling of film buffs, and the joint was jumping by six o'clock. They fought to get at the food, especially the sweet compounded of poppy-seed purée and pannacotta to symbolize yin and yang – another of my ideas.

I was arrogant enough to feel sorry for them. I sensed how they despaired of their lives, which subsisted not in their bodies but somewhere outside them – precisely where, they didn't know. They believed in money and success and Mercedes Benz.

Claudia, who had worn a bland, artificial smile all evening, kept stroking her long white apron as if her hands needed wiping. She thought it immoral to give people what they wanted and earn a lot of money by doing so.

I went over and put my arm round her shoulders. She looked pretty with her hair pinned up. So serious, so adult.

Hi, everything OK? Her shoulders twitched almost imperceptibly. It was a gas, wasn't it? I said.

Her friend Mirja came up to us, licking the last of the yin-yang off her plate. Well, Fred, she said, which would you say I am, a yin type or a yang?

I looked at her. A beanpole of a girl with a thin, interesting face. The kind that raises the roof in bed.

I pinched her wrist between finger and thumb as if taking her pulse. Too much yin, I said. Far too much yin. Tired, listless, lethargic, unimaginative, earthbound, timid, narrow-minded, gutless . . .

She laughed. Oh dear, she said, what am I to do? She draped my free arm around her shoulders. The other was still holding Claudia, who released herself and went on clearing away.

You look as if you've got conjunctivitis, did you know? asked Mirja, peering deep into my eyes.

Leave it, Claudia, can't you? I said. We'll do that in the morning. Claudia shook her head.

Sabine sat down on the floor and propped her back against the dishwasher. Ralf sat down beside her and passed her the spliff. Before long, Mirja, Tav and I were also sitting on the floor.

The fridge was purring away behind me like a big cat. Mirja plucked at Claudia's apron. Give it a rest, can't you? she said.

Claudia smiled and went on clearing the tables.

What am I going to do about my lazy yin temperament? groaned Mirja.

You must eat plenty of garlic, Claudia said coldly. That'll yangize your excess of yin.

Yangize, chortled Tav.

Yes, Claudia said, still coldly, that's what it's called.

Careful, I said, Claudia takes it very seriously, all that stuff.

More seriously than you do, that's for sure, snapped Claudia. You only sell it.

A brief, startled silence fell.

I was talking to someone earlier on, said Sabine, who can't

stand altercations. He told me he always keeps some lemons handy, no matter where he goes. He works for Ikea.

Ikea, huh? Mirja guffawed and passed the spliff to Tav.

Yes, Sabine went on, he often has to go to Sweden for refresher courses.

Refresher courses, Tav sniggered. I suppose they get those ridiculous furniture names drummed into their heads; Klippan, Billy, Töftan . . . He aimed a ladle at our kitchen cabinets.

Büllebröd, said Ralf.

Tav pointed to the stove.

Smörre, said Ralf. What about the dishwasher? Upsala, said Tav. And the bar stools? Tröntworm, said Ralf. No, Köttbullar, cried Tav.

No, said Ralf, you're wrong! Not Köttbullar.

Mirja laughed. Köttbullar is Ikea's name for those frightful little meatballs, she said.

Köttbullar, everyone shouted, clutching their sides.

I know people who only go to Ikea to eat salmon, said Mirja.

You can't be serious, said Tav, handing me the spliff at last.

No, honestly, said Mirja. I've got a journalist girlfriend who can't afford a babysitter, so she goes to Ikea, dumps her child at the crèche, and does her writing in the cafeteria.

And eats Köttbullar, said Tav.

We laugh like maniacs again. All except Claudia.

What were you saying about that guy from Ikea? she asked soberly.

Oh, him, said Sabine. He takes some lemons with him everywhere he goes because he thinks travelling depletes his yin.

Oh man, giggled Ralf, the things people do. That's sick, isn't it?

He does it to be happy, Claudia said coldly. Just to be happy.

We all looked up at her simultaneously. With a vigorous gesture, she tucked an errant strand of hair behind her ear.

I handed her the spliff. She took it but passed it straight on to Sabine. Claudia doesn't smoke grass, doesn't drink, never lets her hair down or loses control.

There's something I'd like you all to tell me, Claudia said slowly. When were you happy today and why? Genuinely happy, I mean.

Ah, Mirja said loudly, then clapped a hand over her mouth as if she'd uttered an obscenity.

She took off her high-heeled shoes and put her feet on Ralf's lap. Ralf absently took hold of her feet and started massaging them.

Happy? said Sabine. Here, for instance – this evening. It was a pretty good party, people enjoyed themselves. I was happy, sure I was.

That's not what I meant, said Claudia. I meant real, true, genuine happiness.

Hey, Claudia, said Tav, stop bugging us with shit like that.

I grabbed Claudia's ankle and looked up at her. She took a dishcloth from the sink and made to wipe the tables. I hung on tight, but she lashed out at me like a pony.

What's the matter with you? asked Tav. Claudia shrugged her shoulders.

You men, said Mirja, you don't have a clue.

And you do, I suppose, said Ralf. The atmosphere threatened to disintegrate like a clay pigeon.

Well, I said loudly, I felt really happy while I was shaving this morning. Don't ask me why, but I did.

Claudia glanced at me and went on wiping.

And again when I made my first yin-yang purée and it looked perfect, I went on.

It *was* perfect, said Mirja, nodding, simply perfect. Ralf was rolling another spliff. He was doing his national service as a hospital orderly and spent most of the time high as a kite. Mirja worked for the Holiday Inn health club, which was why I could swim and use the sauna for free.

I'd gone there early that morning because Claudia and the kitchen were getting claustrophobic and I developed a sudden yearning for the pool's pale blue water.

Must you go swimming *now*? Claudia had demanded as she de-seeded the melons for the starter. An anahata dish for the fourth chakra, the heart chakra. Anahata dishes nourish emotions, moods and premonitions, according to the Taoist cookbook we'd read aloud together, giggling. Eat a melon and open your heart.

Yes, I said, shoving a slice of melon into my mouth. I'm feeling terribly nervous, believe it or not.

Then go, said Claudia, but don't be back too late. The sweet is your department. I took my jacket and kissed her lightly behind the ear.

It was strange, lying beside a hotel pool in one's home town and watching an Arab father teaching his obese children to swim.

I lay on a lounger in my white towelling bathrobe, shut my eyes, and dreamed myself into their world while they disported themselves in mine. Veiled women leant over me with whispered offers of sex and grapes. Palm fronds nodded confirmation above their heads. Camels were overtaken by bulky black Mercedes limousines with sheikhs at the wheel.

I was roused by a tug at my bathrobe. Standing beside my lounger was a short, stout woman in an apple-green swimsuit too small for her. Water was dripping on to me from her black hair.

Please, she said, in an accent that sounded Hungarian or Russian, can you help me? I blinked and sat up. The Arab family had disappeared. I was alone with the fat little woman in the green swimsuit. There was something strangely alluring about her ample figure. She raised a plump hand and pointed at the pool's turquoise water, which was gently lapping against the sides.

The key to my clothes, she said, it fall in. Her eyes were black, the lips in the round, smooth face were full, and the swimsuit barely held her substantial bosom in check.

I lose it, the key to my clothes in the cupboard. I cannot dive, she whispered sadly. You, please.

I felt cold and disinclined to go in again, still less dive for a tiny key and get a lot of chlorine up my nose. I looked around for a stand-in, but there was no one else in sight.

Marta my name, she said, and put out her hand, which I instinctively took. It was cold and wet. I come from Budapest, she added with a smile. I nodded and slowly got to my feet. Thank you, she said before I'd done anything. German men so friendly. Her smile widened.

There was nothing for it. I gave another curt nod, then dived in and let myself drift down to the bottom. I tried to open my eyes but couldn't see a thing and soon had to surface. The little woman was standing on the edge of the pool, hands on hips.

More in middle, she called imperiously.

Obediently, I performed another header and groped my way along the bottom, but without success. I returned to the surface, gasping.

Middle! she called, pointing downwards with her fat little arm.

I dived again and again but still failed to find the confounded key. By now my eyes were on fire. I clung to the edge of the pool, breathing heavily. The woman crouched down until her ample bosom rested on her knees. No key, no clothes, she exhorted.

I was ready to give up. She must have spotted this, because she gingerly stroked my wet head like someone stroking a seal.

77

You strong, she said. You good-looking man. I smiled despite myself.

There, she called. I see something.

She stood up and pointed at the far side of the pool. Flash like silver, she said. Like key.

She scuttled quickly round the pool on her short, fat legs, beckoning me to follow.

I swam over to her and duck-dived several times. Sure enough, I could see something metallic glinting on the pale blue bottom. My fingers closed on it. It was the key! I shot to the surface with my fist raised like a heavyweight champion. She uttered a cry of joy so loud and genuine, I couldn't help grinning.

Oh, thank you, she said, thank you! She took the key, hugged it to her outsize bosom, and hurried off to the changing room.

I got out of the pool, dried myself, and went off to change as well. Behind me, the wavelets were gradually subsiding. For one brief moment I felt strangely weightless, as if I'd quietly but happily drowned and no one had noticed.

I hadn't the least desire to drive back to our café and embark on preparations for the evening's shindig. I didn't want to re-enter my life. All at once, it was all I could do to put one foot before the other.

Claudia is a stranger to that sensation. I've tried to explain it to her, but it's futile. She doesn't know how it feels when there's no difference between motion and rest. When one state is no more active than the other – when immobility is really the more active of the two. Claudia thinks you have to be on the move to find happiness. She thinks you must never come to rest. Her constant search for happiness through activity tires me. I realized that for the first time beside the pool.

Slowly, step by step, I made my way across the slippery tiles to the stuffy, cubicle-lined changing room. The little Hungarian woman was standing all alone in front of her locker wearing a fluffy pale blue jumper, but her legs were still bare.

She beamed at me. Thank you, she said again. I made a dismissive gesture and was walking past her to the men's section when she caught me by the arm.

I have secret, she said in a low voice. You like see?

Surprised, I came to a halt and stared at her. She looked prettier than before. She seemed to glow, and her hand wasn't cold any longer.

Little thank-you present. I show you secret. You like see? she repeated.

I gave a little shrug, then nodded.

She smiled contentedly, released my arm, and, in one quick movement, whipped the jumper over her head.

She had three breasts.

Three round, white, identical breasts. Three side by side: one, two, three. Simply three instead of two. I blinked, but there were still three.

She smiled gently and beckoned me closer with her pudgy little hand. To my own surprise, I tottered towards her like a child in need of consolation, fell on my knees and buried my face in her trio of breasts.

She took hold of my hair and drew me closer still. I could hear her heart beating. My own heart had stopped, I think, because here it was: a feeling of perfect happiness induced by contact with a Hungarian woman's three breasts. Nothing more needed to happen. I was dissolving. I never wanted to be anywhere else. Nirvana.

Were you really happy with your yin-yang sweet? Really, really happy? Claudia looked at me dubiously. I nodded.

Okay, said Ralf, lighting the new spliff. Shall I tell you all when I was happy today? But Mirja, you mustn't feel hurt.

Mirja shook her head and drew up her knees.

Ralf dismissed his own suggestion. No, no, it's too risky.

This is getting silly, Tav grumbled, opening fresh cans of beer all round. First you wind us up and then you cop out.

Claudia stacked some plates in the dishwasher. Well, when *were* you happy today? It can't be all that earth-shattering.

Ralf tittered.

Come on, tell, said Sabine.

You really want to know? Ralf surveyed us all in turn. I wasn't so sure, myself, but the rest nodded eagerly. Claudia closed the dishwasher and stood up. Stop making such a meal of it, she said.

Well, Ralf drawled, the hospital day shift came on at six this morning. When I came off duty I locked myself up in the little treatment room, smoked a joint, and jerked off.

Oh God, Mirja groaned.

Tav gave a dirty laugh. Claudia turned away. I kept quiet.

You're a pig, said Mirja, but I don't feel hurt.

Ralf looked at Sabine. What's more, he told her, I thought of you while I was at it. Sabine's eyes flickered in surprise. She crossed her arms and stared at the floor. The luxuriant hair flopped over her face like a curtain.

A disagreeable silence fell. We could hear each other breathing.

And it made you feel happy, Mirja said quietly.

I told you you'd be offended, said Ralf.

Another silence. Sabine continued to stare fixedly at the floor's pattern of black-and-white tiles.

Good God, don't be like that, Ralf protested. Don't act like none of you ever thought of someone else occasionally. I just happened to think of Sabine. Big deal! I only *thought* of her, and then only for a minute.

And what, in your opinion, is the difference between thinking and doing? Mirja demanded sharply.

Jesus Christ, groaned Ralf, what is this? An epistemological debate or something?

Thoughts and reality tend to conflict, I ventured. The more you think, the further reality recedes.

What's that, said Tav, some more of your yin-yang shit?

I saw a woman with three breasts at the Holiday Inn pool today, I said. No one reacted.

Tav went over to Ralf. My friend thinks of my wife while he jerks off, he said. That's great, really great. I ought to smack you in the kisser.

I really did see a woman with three breasts, I said, a Hungarian. No one took any notice.

Oh man, Ralf groaned, I wish hadn't told you all, but you did ask. He left Tav standing there and went over to Claudia, who was leaning against the dishwasher playing with a spoon. She kept tossing it into the air and catching it.

No, said Ralf, *you* were the one who asked me. Now let's ask you for a change. He took the spoon from her hand.

Well, come on, he said, it's your turn now. When were *you* happy today?

Claudia chewed her lower lip.

You owe me one, Ralf said in a low voice.

Well, Claudia said slowly, I think I've forgotten how it feels to be really happy, that's why I asked the rest of you. I wanted you to tell me you're happy. That you're almost bursting with happiness – that you feel like a pod when it opens to reveal those perfect little green peas that have only been waiting to display themselves in all their perfection. Seems I can only think in terms of food these days ... She grinned rather forlornly. I'm not talking about contentment. I'm contented when the place is full, when the stove behaves itself and Fred calls me when he promised to. I don't mean that, I mean *happiness*. Just that one little word. It sounds too short, as if you've swallowed it before you've even got it out. You probably haven't a clue what I mean. I mean the feeling you get when your heart jumps out of your chest for joy, and you have to run after it, giggling, for fear of losing it. Or when you suddenly seem to consist of nothing but shimmering air and might just as well be a sunbeam on the wall. Or a note, a long, low note like a ship's siren. Or a high C. Or when something inside you sings or glows, she said softly.

She looked at me with narrowed eyes. But you've no idea what I'm getting at, probably.

She fell silent and whipped off her apron with a sudden, fierce movement.

Yes, I said slowly, I know just what you mean.

14

T HE CAMPSITE HAS GONE quiet. The Dutch have retired to bed. Franka's warm breath is fanning my hand. Three peas in a pod: Claudia, Franka, and me. That's what we used to be: three perfect little peas in a perfect container. Our little family.

What's happened to us? We're in danger of tumbling out of our pod, one pea after another. We'll be scattered to the winds, and, if we're unlucky, squashed underfoot.

I'm wide awake. The interior of our tent smells like a damp plastic bag. I unzip the flap and worm my way outside like a caterpillar, stagger over to the nearest tree and turn on my mobile.

The green display blithely lights up, but no one has called or left a message, no one wants any news of me. I sit there all by myself, keeping vigil over the slumbers of the Dutch, Franka, and Norbert. Norbert of the three balls. I don't believe him.

But nobody believed my story about the three-breasted Hungarian woman, either.

The leaves above me rustle, stirred by a warm breeze. Cicadas are busily sawing away as if to prove I'm really down south. The lake stretches away in front of me, dark and silent, its shores fringed with tall clumps of fern. A narrow strip of pale blue sky is gradually taking shape on the horizon.

It's beautiful, I suppose. Hundreds of Dutch campers spare no effort to come here, braving long, arduous queues of traffic. But I can't *feel* the beauty, only perceive it. I can see the personal soap bubble in which I'm imprisoned, but nothing, nothing has ever burst it. It almost burst once, when Franka was born. I had a shortlived feeling of oneness with the whole of humanity when that gory infant painfully, laboriously emerged from my wife's body like a butterfly leaving the cocoon. I simultaneously laughed and cried as I held Franka in my arms like a fragile figurine. I sensed all the sorrow and happiness in the world, but not for long.

That's because you're incapable of thinking of anyone but yourself, says Claudia. Egoist.

I must have nodded off against my tree trunk after all, because the campsite is as busy as an anthill when I wake up. A loud '*Hop, hop, hop, hop!*' comes echoing across the lake. A riding class consisting exclusively of fair-haired Dutch girls is being chivvied around a rectangular paddock by the proprietor of the establishment, who's stationed in the centre with a riding crop. He keeps bellowing '*Hop, hop, hop, hop!*' without a break. This being France, the H is silent.

My back's aching. I feel grubby and exhausted.

Our little yellow UFO tent stands there mutely. Franka and Norbert must still be asleep.

I was hoping to buy myself a coffee at the windmill, but no such luck. The vending machine sells cola only. Meantime, issuing from every caravan, comes an aroma of coffee and eggs and bacon. I'm tempted to plant myself outside the nearest one, looking pathetic, and wait for an invitation. I return to our tent, cursing. I'm going to wake Norbert and Franka at once, strike the tent, and drive to the next village for a coffee.

I unzip the flap, and the smell of sweaty feet hits me in the face. Norbert's snoring. Franka's place is deserted, but there's a slip of paper on her sleeping bag: *Dear Dad, have gone on alone. See you.*

I've only just finished reading the note when my mobile bleeps. *Claudia calling.* A mother's seventh sense. I stare at the flashing name and decide not to answer. I've failed to look after our daughter even for twenty-four hours.

It bleeps reproachfully seven times, then falls silent. The little envelope in the top right-hand corner lights up: Claudia has left me a message.

Norbert, roused by the phone, rubs his eyes and gives me a broad smile.

I leave the tent without a word and stand there at a loss, mobile in hand. *Bonjour*, calls a passing paterfamilias with a heavy jerrycan of water on his back. Three flaxen-haired children trot sleepily in his wake.

Norbert crawls out of the tent with Franka's note in his hand.

I didn't notice a thing, honestly, he says. He tugs at his sparse red hair. Another bolter, eh?

He looks round. Nice here, though, isn't it?

I nod. He's looking quite composed, almost happy, this morning. Now I'm the one whose nerves are in shreds. He puts his arm round my shoulders, but I brusquely shake it off the way Franka does mine.

We dismantle the tent in silence. Norbert wants to roll it up neatly, but I, to his horror, stuff it into the boot, chuck the poles in after it, get behind the wheel, and start up. Norbert jumps into the passenger seat as if scared I'll drive off without him. His reaction makes me realize how much that idea appeals to me.

I calm down a bit after the second *grand crème*. We sit in the village square under some red-and-white striped umbrellas. The sky is blue, the sun hot, and the village square transforms itself before our eyes into a toy model of a French scene. A little old man walks across the square with a baguette under his arm, a shiny red fire engine rounds the corner, a little madame in a floral apron stares after it, a mother emerges from the *pharmacie* across the way with a little girl in a white lace dress. Toy people in a toy country. They're all resolutely leading their own lives, and I envy them like mad. Why don't they go on the rampage? Why don't they yell? Why are they all so content with their little model lives?

Perhaps I'm the real teenager, not Franka.

Where were you making for? Norbert asks diffidently. He hasn't asked that question before – advisedly, since it could spell the end of our journey together.

Curtly, I tell him about the meditation centre. Not a word about Franka's lama. That's a point of honour.

Norbert sighs. It sounds just what I need right now, he says. Somewhere to concentrate on myself, regain my equilibrium . . .

Stop it or I'll be sick.

He stares at me like a bewildered hen, then cautiously pursues the subject. Do you think . . . Do you think it's expensive?

Dole out rice and tofu three times a day and charge through the nose for it? That would really take the cake.

Do you think . . . Do you think you could possibly . . . . I mean . . .

I cut him short. Lend you some money?

He blushes, and his cheeks clash unpleasantly with the red of his hair.

I keep him on tenterhooks for a bit, then nod. He almost flings his arms round my neck.

OK, I say, let's tuck in.

I order an enormous slab of meat and a bottle of wine. Norbert, like a child, only asks for some *pommes frites*. And a Fun Tea, he adds shyly. His frugality makes me feel aggressive.

Gabi's a lactovegetarian, he says, as though in explanation.

I really don't want to hear anything about Gabi, not now.

Know something strange? he goes on brightly. We were together day and night for seven years, and now she's been gone forty-eight hours I can't really remember her. I *think* of her all the time, but I can't really remember what she looks like. Know what I mean?

I look into his ingenuous, pale blue eyes, feeling angry that this nerd, this flute-playing carrot-top, of all people, should have hit the nail on the head so accurately.

Not really, I say with a shrug.

Norbert sighs. I'm not much good at expressing myself, he says. Sometimes, when I'm not thinking about her for once, she shows up in my head. The way she really is.

His lower lip trembles. How I've grown to hate that!

The waiter brings my wine and Norbert's Fun Tea, a liquid of oceanic blue. *Prost*, says Norbert. Or rather, *santé*!

He smiles at me happily. My meat arrives. It reposes on my plate, a massive, bloody lump of dead cow. I shoo away a fly. Norbert leans forward and studies my steak with the critical eye of an abattoir inspector. If he utters one word, one little peep about his lactovegetarian Gabi, I'll slap him around the chops with it. I saw off a piece, thrust it into my mouth, and chew it apathetically. I'm not enjoying it. It's a precautionary measure, really, because there won't be any meat at the meditation centre.

I lay my knife and fork aside and pour myself some wine. The fly triumphantly touches down on my steak again.

After a few minutes' silence Norbert asks timidly. Don't you want any more? When I shake my head he pulls my plate towards him – cautiously, as if scared of getting his hand slapped at the last moment.

I thought you were a vegetarian.

Gabi, he says, munching away. Gabi's a lactovegetarian. So are the kids.

Great. My condemned man's last meal has been a flop. I don't even enjoy the wine, not really. I tell Norbert to get a move on. I've got to find Franka before I'm compelled to account for her whereabouts to Claudia.

Norbert is chewing faster now. He's almost choking on my steak.

The roads are getting steadily narrower. Norbert wrestles with the map, incapable of piloting me. I'm beginning to sympathize with Gabi.

We drive past endless expanses of sunflowers, fields of stubble dotted with bales of straw so huge that human hands could never shift them. In this part of the world everything seems to be on the big side. Plastic wine bottles six metres high sway briskly in the wind, marking the entrances to vineyards. An ideal location for a teetotal meditation centre.

And suddenly we're only five kilometres away. I develop palpitations the way I did when consigned to summer camp as a ten-year-old. I don't want to go there. I don't!

In a godforsaken little village I pull up outside a grocery store to buy some cigarettes and chocolate and a few cans of beer. No one'll be able to stop me taking refuge in my car to drink, smoke and use the phone.

Immediately ahead of me in the queue at the cash desk is an attractive young mother with a baby in a sling. Her T-shirt has slipped down on one side, revealing some tanned bare skin. I lean forward, inhale her scent, feel an urge to sink my teeth in her shoulder.

A rather squalid-looking man with a two-litre bottle of cheap red wine in his hand elbows his way to the fore. The fat teenager behind the till shakes her head and calls, *Maman!*

Maman, evidently a hip sufferer, comes waddling out of the back room. She relieves the man of his bottle, and a flood of invective descends on him like an icy cascade. I can pick out only a few words: *docteur, aucun alcool, malade.*

The man kicks up a fuss, knocks over a crate of apples. I grin delightedly: ructions in Toy Land at last. Madame dresses him down. The young mother ahead of me nods approvingly. Pity, I could have gone for her.

Norbert picks up the apples. When the young mother turns and I see her full-face, she ceases to be a source of regret. Her mouth is grim and thin-lipped. She'd probably send you out on the balcony to smoke and insist on showering before *and* after.

15

ANOTHER FOUR KILOMETRES. ANOTHER three. A deserted tract of land stretches away in front of us. No more gargantuan wine bottles. Nothing.

Another two kilometres, another one. I feel condemned to do something I haven't trained for.

Aren't you scared? I ask Norbert.

What of?

Well, meditating. Getting up at the crack of a sparrowfart, never having a decent meal, keeping mum the whole time.

He shrugs. No, he says cheerfully, I'm looking forward to it.

Me, I'm the loneliest man on earth.

Bear left, bear right, and now I know we've come to the right place, because we're already passing some of them.

They're worse than my wildest dreams. Men with long, sparse hair in pale green tracksuit bottoms, women with massive buttocks in baggy lilac pants, their pendulous, braless boobs wobbling beneath faded pink T-shirts, children with fringes in front and page-boys behind. So these are the Enlightened Ones – or the candidates for Enlightenment.

They welcome us, waving joyously, and escort us to the parking lot. German licence plates from Bergisch Gladbach, Neuss, Peine, Füssen – very few big cities. French, British and

Dutch plates as well, and an old Mercedes from Madrid like the one I used to own. Norbert jumps blithely out of the car and slams the door.

A woman with hennaed hair and a flowing, pastel green robe smilingly puts a finger to her lips. Norbert makes a series of apologetic, sweeping gestures, like a puppet gone haywire.

I sit in the car and light a last cigarette. Norbert, beaming, points to a notice in several languages: YOU'VE ARRIVED. ENJOY YOUR BREATH. KEEP SILENT.

I inhale deeply. Best to view the whole thing in a sporting light: anyone who survives this experience earns a place on the victor's rostrum. I stub out my cigarette and exit the car. I'm feeling like the stranger who rides into town and dismounts with his hand on his six-shooter, ready for anything. I look around for Franka but fail to see her anywhere.

Norbert, who was already located the reception tent, tows me toward it.

Steady, I tell him. Take it easy.

Norbert puts a finger to his lips. Aha, silence. Amazing how adaptable he is. Any chameleon would envy him.

It's swelteringly hot inside the reception tent. Hand-carved wooden signs divide us into different linguistic groups. Patient queues of varying length are waiting behind every sign. The longest in the German, the shortest the Spanish.

I toy with the idea of insinuating myself into the Spanish group, but I probably wouldn't get far with the Spanish obscenities Marisol has taught me, not in this place.

Nobody speaks apart from the nun receptionists seated at rickety little tables at the head of every queue. Each table is equipped with an Applemac, which I find reassuring. 'Think different', the Applemac ad depicting the Dalai Lama, brought him closer to me than all his public speeches could have done. I took an instant liking to that man with the insurance salesman's glasses and the big vaccination marks on his bare, flabby arm.

The Germans – no surprise – are the least attractive people here. This is partly because of their batik pants and billowing dresses, and partly because of their carroty fair hair.

Norbert fits in here the way fish goes with chips. It's his scene, even if he didn't know it before.

I'm getting rather overheated in my black outfit. If I belong with any group, I feel it's the Americans. Though not necessarily any better-looking than the Germans, they're cooler. They don't look so nerdy and docile to the point of self-sacrifice. They haven't completely switched off their shit detectors.

The handsomest, as usual, are the Italians. They just can't help it. It's their genes plus Armani. From the look of them, they might be queueing up for opera tickets.

There's a smell of sweat and garlic – the last garlic we'll exude, because there won't be any of that either, not here. Garlic stimulates desire, apparently, and happiness is dependent on the renunciation of desire. Of course, Claudia told me reprovingly, you're only thinking of sex, but desire in this context means a desire for all you don't possess and think it would make you so much happier if you did.

Speaking for yourself, a cigarette would make me very happy right now.

We shuffle forward at a snail's pace.

At last it's our turn. We're processed by a young, shaven-headed nun. She looks up from her computer – and I almost levitate. I've never seen such a perfectly limpid face. She's an Asian, so her cheekbones are naturally sloping, her nose is small, and her eyes are almond-shaped, but that's not it. Her beauty is only secondary. I'm overwhelmed by the *clarity* of her face. It's as limpid and serene as the surface of a lake when the wind drops completely.

She puts her hands together and bows to us. Norbert, ever the eager beaver, promptly follows suit. Her German is soft and fluent. She finds my name in the computer in two seconds flat.

I'm looking for my daughter, I say, almost guiltily. Her first name is Franka.

She smiles and consults her computer again. Oh yes, she says, Franka's working in the kitchen. She arrived here last night.

I heave an audible sigh of relief.

Yes, everything's fine, says the beautiful nun. Franka is staying in the House of the Lotus Blossom. You're in the House of the Full Moon. A room for three. Second floor, third door on the left.

I'm flabbergasted. They're better organized here than Lufthansa. It's on the tip of my tongue to ask her for a window seat.

Do you have any questions? She smiles, revealing pearly white teeth.

Yes. Do you absolutely have to be a nun?

We register Norbert, who will also inhabit the room for three. The third bed is already occupied by a stranger. I shall keep the tent as a secret place of refuge and retire to it when I can't endure the others any longer. It's an age since I shared a room with strangers.

I always disliked it, even as a ten-year-old in summer camp, but it's some people's idea of heaven. Norbert's, for instance.

Jovially, he drapes an arm round my shoulders. I find it hard to part from the beautiful nun. In conclusion she hands us a leaflet bearing the daily schedule:

5.00 Getting-up time
5.30 Meditation
7.00 Breakfast
9.00 Lectures
12.30 Lunch

14.00 Working Meditation
18.00 Supper
19.30 Meditation
21.30 Lights Out
And, at the foot:

Please observe noble silence. We request you, during your retreat, to abstain from tobacco, alcohol, drugs, and sex.

You won't find that too hard, I say to Norbert.

Not where three out of the four are concerned, he replies with a grin, and this time *I* get a chance to put an admonitory finger to my lips. Norbert gives a start and peers round anxiously, as if scared of being arrested on the spot.

16

P UFFING AND BLOWING UNDER the weight of Franka's bag and my own, I toil up a steep hillside dotted with wind-blown, tumbledown stone buildings – just the sort of Provençal ruins the *Süddeutsche Zeitung* advertises for sale as 'rustic farmhouses'.

How often we've flirted with the idea of buying ourselves a modest house in Italy or France, forever haunted by the dream of leading another life and becoming two quite different people. Better, happier people. We always scoured the 'Foreign Properties for Sale' section when we were feeling more than usually depressed. Why not move to a little village in Italy? To the Majorcan mountains where no other Germans live? To Ireland, where the light is reputed to be so beautiful?

We haven't talked about a life elsewhere for quite a while. Why? Because we've given up hope. That dawns on me now, as I look for the House of the Full Moon, panting and loaded down like a donkey. I must be out of my mind.

Norbert skips ahead of me on his spindly legs like a young goat, pausing now and then to bow reverently to some batik-trousered woman and ask her the way. Below us lies the campsite, a huge field of stubble. The tents, barely two metres apart, are drawn up in rank and file like soldiers on parade. An equally unappealing sight. Not far beyond them are a circular pool, an orchard, and some woods.

Long tables and benches are set out on a stone terrace in front of a squat building. That must be the kitchen. I can't imagine Franka working in a kitchen of her own free will. At home she can hardly bring herself to put her plate in the dishwasher.

Norbert has found the House of the Full Moon. Being unable to call out loud, he hops up and down with excitement. 'Noble silence . . .' What a fatuous expression!

In the hallway we have to remove our shoes. My handsome brogues look rather bizarre among the sandals and flip-flops, like a pedigree dog in a pack of mongrels. I spot a lonely pair of white Pradas and feel instantly drawn to the unknown woman in question. The women sleep downstairs, the men upstairs. Couples who prefer to cohabit have to creep into a tent. They mustn't have sex, though, or one of those females in flapping dresses would doubtless poke her head through the flap and wag a prohibitory finger.

Norbert beckons me up a narrow flight of wooden stairs. I crack my head on a projecting beam.

I shall hit my head on these stairs several times a day, especially at half-past five in the morning. That stupid beam is my very own, personal alarm clock.

Norbert taps cautiously on the door of our room, opens it, and bows the way he learnt from the nun.

So the third occupant is already in residence.

At a generous estimate the room measures two metres by four. Three thin, skimpy foam rubber mattresses are butted tightly up against the walls. Suspended above each is a bamboo pole – in lieu of a wardrobe, presumably. Lying asleep on his stomach on the mattress beside the window, the best position, is a man with a bald patch fringed with wispy fair hair.

I sit down on my mattress and sniff it. It smells.

This mattress stinks, I say. Norbert hisses at me like an adder.

Surely we can speak in our rooms, at least! I hiss back.

He shrugs.

You don't know, I whisper angrily. Admit it: you've no idea when we're allowed to speak. Anyway, I couldn't care less what the rules say. I'll speak whenever it suits me.

Noble silence till lunchtime, during working meditation, and after sunset, murmurs the bald-headed man, without turning over. He has a faint accent I can't place.

He rolls over on his back. Welcome, he says. It's Theo, the man we met at the airport on our way to London. The man who faxed Claudia the address of this dump. The man who's to blame for my daughter's infatuation with a lama.

He sits up and regards Norbert with a smile. When he sees me the smile fades like a flower wilting in time-lapse.

I think we've met before, he says slowly.

I prompt him: Munich Airport, the London flight, the steps jammed . . .

He nods. Fred, he says.

I'm surprised he remembers my name.

Theo, I say.

You remember my name, he says without smiling.

Are we allowed to speak now? asks Norbert.

No, says Theo, not really.

I set off in search of Franka, but the kitchen building is shut. I wander aimlessly down to the pool. It's a mass of lotus blossoms. The first time I ever saw any was in Saigon, where Claudia and I were attending a cookery course at the Floating Hotel. I was thinking of opening a chain of oriental snack bars. Cheap, good, healthy food straight from the wok, guaranteed glutamate-free.

The cookery course had little bearing on this, because we cooked Bocuse dishes *à la vietnamienne* in the company of some immensely rich American dowagers.

Better than the cookery course was the hotel's so-called health club, where beautiful girls administered massages in the traditional fashion by walking over your back on their dainty feet. They genuinely were massages, not sex, but no one ever believes you. The girls hung on to straps while they walked over your back, looking like colourful blossoms in their classic *ao dais*, bodies as slender and supple as flower stems, faces like petals.

Their beauty made Claudia jealous – she felt fat and ugly in Vietnam – and their gentle manner infuriated her. She thought it was all an act and claimed they were really as hard as nails.

Perhaps they were, I didn't care. I delighted in their graceful ways and wanted nothing more of them. Besides, like Claudia I felt ugly and monstrous with my huge, well-fed frame, my pallid skin and European body odour.

I lay on my stomach and relished the feel of those little feet on my back while dramatic tropical downpours descended from the sky like a theatre curtain and raindrops beaded the lotus leaves like diamonds. They're almost unearthly flowers with immense, artificial-looking petals and leaves as big as loo lids.

I bend to scoop up a handful of water and sprinkle it over the leaves. Every drop becomes a sparkling precious stone; some of them lodge in the middle of the leaf and roll to and fro like marbles. A never-ending source of wonder.

Batik pants are circling the pool in slow motion, as if trying to float in mid air. Ridiculous.

On the other side of the pool stands a huge white tent, its canvas walls flapping in the breeze. I peer through a crack: no one there. Incense drifts out to meet me. At the far end is a big, flame-red Tibetan shrine surrounded by butter lamps and ancient pictures, sacrificial pyramids of fruit, photographs of lamas, flowers, and sacred objects unfamiliar to me, the whole thing as colourful as a child's nursery. In the centre of the shrine is a podium painted sunflower yellow, a kind of throne.

Arranged in a semicircle in front of the shrine are hundreds of little rectangular mattresses. Lying on them are cushions of every conceivable hue, blankets and knitted sweaters, towels, notebooks and vacuum flasks, and behind them stand several rows of white plastic chairs like the ones you find in every pavement café. The tent's wooden floor is entirely covered with a spider's web of cables and headphones, and erected in the corners are the familiar hand-carved signs in various languages.

I'm not alone after all, I suddenly realize. A fair-haired woman in a white summer dress is sitting motionless on a cushion with her eyes shut.

For a microsecond I think it's Claudia. Of course! She went on ahead, she wanted to surprise us, she doesn't trust me to handle things on my own, she wants to check up on me. She wants to be with us, not alone, she's come to tell me how much she still loves me, to tell me she wants a divorce – but no, this woman has short, thin plaits, she's younger and thinner, she isn't Claudia at all. Worse luck, I think, and thank God – both at the same time. How can I endure it, how can I go on living now that nothing between us is simple and straightforward any more!

The unknown woman is running a mala, a Buddhist rosary, through her fingers. I can hear the wooden beads clicking faintly. It really worried me the day Claudia came home from her meditation hour with one of those things around her wrist. Her mala didn't bear a picture of her guru like a sannyasin's, admittedly, but it still looked to me like the insignia of a club, and I don't care for clubs because they all exist to exclude outsiders.

Claudia blathered something about the healing powers of reciting mantras, of letting the sounds and syllables resonate within you in an age-old sequence and restoring the universal, cosmic order – something like that. When I expressed my doubts, she reproached me for being an eternal sceptic. My life, she said, was a constant 'Better not!' instead of a 'Just do it!' She was trying to defeat me with the slogan on my own sneakers.

How tired I am of being absorbed by your negative aura! she said angrily. It's like being sucked into a black hole.

Claudia's knowledge of black holes was derived from the Deutsches Museum, our refuge on countless grey winter weekends when Franka was still an inquisitive little girl – when she still wanted to know how the world worked. The astronomical section contained a simulation of a black hole in the form of a whirlpool that looked like a miniature tornado when you pressed your nose against the glass. *A black hole is a space having a gravitational field so intense that neither matter nor radiation can escape*. I knew that by heart, after all our visits. Was I inescapable? Was I Claudia's gravitational field? I felt almost flattered.

Do you know what I feel like?

She didn't wait for an answer, fortunately, because I hadn't a clue how she felt.

I feel like that little astronaut in the Deutsches Museum who falls into a black hole. First of all he's horribly stretched like a rubber band, and then—

Then he snaps, I broke in.

Yes, she said.

I burst out laughing and crossed my arms. And I, I said, am sick of feeling like I'm choking to death on your positivistic whipped cream!

She gave me a startled look and fiddled with the mala on her wrist. Her sharp nose looked sharper than usual.

I'm glad you finally got it out, she said quietly. With catlike tread, she retired to the living room and proceeded to prostrate herself on the carpet a hundred and eight times.

I followed her in, sat down on the sofa, and counted along with her. Down on your knees, then flat on your stomach, then up on your feet and begin again – a hundred and eight times. The mala has a hundred and eight beads. Claudia once told me why, but I've forgotten. By degrees she turned puce and beads of sweat erupted on her forehead. I suddenly loved her for the effort she was making to escape our measly, mediocre existence.

Black hole and whipped cream, I said. Black and white, yin and yang. Just like us.

She looked at me as she fell on her knees for the fifty-eighth time.

Oh Fred, she panted, you and your confounded cynicism. Anyone who comes too close to you gets swallowed up. They vanish.

So saying, she slid across the carpet on her stomach and lay still.

Hey, I said, but she didn't move. Her back twitched. She was crying.

I was amazed at the power she credited me with. The way I looked at it, we were more in danger of being stifled by her enforced optimism and depressed by her constant injunctions to enjoy life. But that was what had originally attracted me to her. I, the gloomy film student, had fallen in love with the radiant goddess of the kitchen.

There was nothing I could do, nothing at all. Perhaps that was what she meant by a black hole. I couldn't save or redeem her any more than I could Franka or myself.

She slowly got up and wiped the tears away.

I must do what I'm doing or I'll kill myself, she said. She drew a deep breath and resumed her prostrations.

17

THE WOMAN IN THE tent has thin blond plaits. They give her a rather girlish look, though she must be late-thirties or older. Very little younger than Claudia, at a guess.

She has a narrow, Modiglianiesque face – so narrow there's scarcely room in it for her long, straight nose – but the lips that are muttering a mantra are full and curved in an interesting way. She looks forlorn, all by herself in the big tent, like a babe in the woods. I christen her Gretel. She opens her eyes and sees me but goes on muttering. I hold her gaze for a moment, then drop the flap.

A gaggle of Tibetan monks in yellow and dark red robes walk past. I've no idea if they really are monks, because their heads are thatched with dark stubble, not shaved. They're laughing and chattering like kids on a school outing. Pelge could be one of them.

They make for the kitchen building, where long queues have formed in the past few minutes. Batik pants are well in the majority, three hundred of them at least, interspersed with more monks and nuns from various Asian countries. The ones in grey and brown seem to be from Vietnam – I can recall seeing their costume when we visited Saigon. They were as much a part of the street scene as the Vespa riders with their long white gloves and Calvin Klein baseball caps. The yellow robes probably hail from Sri Lanka and Thailand, and the one in a black kimono with a kind of lilac bib round his neck must be from Japan. They look like slim, elegant question marks among all those ugly Westerners, with their utter lack of gravitas and sloppy, shapeless attire.

I'm really hungry, so I reluctantly join a queue. Standing in line seems to be a permanent occupation in this place.

Small children whimper to themselves, older ones race around yelling and are gently shushed by their parents. Gentle parents are like a red rag to me. I don't believe a word they say – I think they're weaklings who allow their offspring to terrorize them.

The queue moves forward at a snail's pace. At long, long last it's my turn. Arrayed on the wooden refectory tables are some huge, battered cooking pots. Plate in hand, I expectantly home in on them. One contains brown rice, another some watery vegetable soup.

My heart sinks. I had secretly been hoping that all my dark forebodings would be dispelled. A third pot evidently contained salad, but all that's left of it is one lousy lettuce leaf.

Disappointed, I ladle rice on to my plate and look around for some soy sauce, but there doesn't appear to be any of that either.

Hello, Dad, I hear someone whisper. I look up, and there's Franka, standing behind the table. I should have seen her before, but the cooking pots were monopolizing my attention. She's wearing a long white apron and a white T-shirt. They almost dazzle me, because she wears nothing but black as a rule. Her hair is freshly washed and pinned back. She looks completely different, like a waitress in a restaurant.

Franka! I exclaim, but she, too, puts an instinctive finger to her lips. I lean forward, hoping at least to kiss her across the table, but she draws back, fits her palms together, and bows.

My daughter greets me with a bow! I can't take it in. People are jostling me from behind. Franka waves me on like a policeman on point duty.

Soy sauce? I whisper. She shakes her head. Salt? No such luck. I cast my eyes up to heaven. She chuckles.

Plate in hand, I stroll over to one of the long wooden tables, sit down, and start on the dry rice. It tastes like wrapping paper, but I wolf it down because my stomach's rumbling. A minute or two later it dawns on me that I'm the only one eating. All the rest are sitting there in silence, like statues, with their plates and bowls in front of them. The children are whining and bawling, but that's all.

A young European nun in a brown habit sits down opposite me. She has a shaved head as round as a billiard ball and the big blue eyes of a china doll. Twenty at most, I estimate. She bows to her bowl, then stares straight ahead, quite motionless.

What are they all waiting for? I put my spoon down as unobtrusively as possible. Turning, I see Norbert and Theo sitting beside each other. Norbert raises his hand and gives me a slow, condescending wave. Needless to say, he knows the routine yet again, the conformist asshole.

My rice, which was only lukewarm in the first place, is getting cold. We continue to wait, no idea what for.

In slow motion, a Vietnamese monk goes over to a big gong hanging outside the kitchen, bows, strikes it three times, and bows again. Everyone starts eating at last, but eating, too, proceeds in slow motion. They chew in a leisurely way, like cows. The blue-eyed nun shuts her eyes at every mouthful she takes, smiling ecstatically.

I bolt the rest of my rice. My stomach is still rumbling, so I get up and help myself to some more. It's an opportune moment, because no one else has finished. Franka is presiding over the cooking pots.

Dad, she whispers, you have to wait for the second gong before getting up for another helping.

I help myself nonetheless. Can't you organize some ketchup or some salt, at least? I ask her. Franka shakes her head and goes back into the kitchen. I open a few rickety cupboards. Even Buddhist meditation centres buy their equipment from Ikea, I notice. Not a sign of salt or soy sauce, though.

Franka comes back with a few grains of salt between finger and thumb. She sprinkles them on my rice.

I give her a kiss. Where's this Pelge of yours? I whisper in her ear.

She points to a bench occupied by some Tibetan monks.

Which one? I ask. She smiles. Guess, she whispers, and turns away. I rejoin the ecstatic nun, whose bowl looks as full as ever.

It's like a blow in the solar plexus, the realization that Franka may decide to stay here and become a nun. She may become meek and holy. That would be terrible – far worse than rebellious and refractory. She could take it into her head never to have sex again, and that would distress me more than if she had several lovers concurrently. She may simply want to become the diametrical opposite of her parents, her father in particular.

The ecstatic nun smiles at me, gentle as a lamb. I count: she chews every mouthful thirty times precisely.

Claudia, I think, do you know her, that little Joan of Arc with the sanctified expression?

I hear Claudia laugh. The one with the clear blue eyes and the seraphically fluttering eyelids? Of course, she says.

There was nothing I enjoyed more, once upon a time, than chatting with Claudia, discussing things and pulling people to pieces. Her world was so different from mine, so much more colourful. She saw things to which I wouldn't have paid the slightest attention on my own, and when Franka arrived her powers of observation intensified.

The two of them were adept at discovering marvels. They

alerted me to the fantastic patterns in red cabbage, to the rainbow colours of patches of oil in the road, to old ladies' peculiar hats and gold-lacquered fingernails. They showed me the wealth of shapes in cornflakes, the sense of order manifest in raindrops on a window pane, the mini-tornadoes that occur when a bath runs out, the wide world of Barbie footwear.

They invented a game called 'Five Wonderful Things'. Every night you had to list five wonderful things you'd seen or experienced during the day. Claudia and Franka were always bubbling over with them, whereas I was hard put to scrape five marvels together. They would eye me with indulgence and wait patiently until I came up with them at last, but I was often stumped even for one. *They* never failed. The milk-and-chocolate swirls in cocoa, four raindrops in a straight line on a stalk of grass, a snowflake on a sleeve, a one-legged pigeon, the sound of Rice Krispies popping in milk, the smell of new coloured crayons . . .

Without them I felt blind – I, who had wanted to depict the world on film. I didn't observe the world and its inhabitants, I felt observed by them. Maybe that's the real reason why I always talked about making a movie but never made one.

I had no real talent, that dawned on me after only a few weeks at film school. There were fellow students who could think in images, who converted the world into a kind of permanent storyboard in their mind's eye and knew at once where and how they had to position the camera.

I, by contrast, was irresolute. I never knew what would make a good camera angle and could never shake off my dull, all-round vision, which was so random and unspectacular, boring and devoid of mystery.

A friend once asked my advice on his graduation film. He needed to cut it and didn't know where. It was utterly assured and perfect in its timing, simultaneously comic and tragic, lucid and mysterious. I was envious of his ability and knew I would never be able to narrate with the camera as he did. So I deliberately disconcerted him, laughed in the wrong places, feigned inattention during the best sequences. He implored my advice, so I finally, with spurious hesitation, advised him to cut two of the best scenes. To my surprise he did so. He trusted my judgement.

The film was out of the ordinary even then, but I'd thrown it out of kilter. From then on it went downhill, becoming more normal, more commonplace and colourless. It became like me.

After fifteen minutes the monk strikes the gong once more. Everyone jumps up at once, chattering, and goes to get a bit more brown rice.

I get up too, intending to take my plate over to the plastic sinks, when the telephone in the kitchen rings and something quite extraordinary happens. They all come to a halt in mid-movement and fall silent as though transfixed, as though the sound has put them into a Sleeping Beauty trance. I see Franka standing there with a broom in her hand, more erect than I've seen her for years, because she usually keeps her head down so her hair hides her face.

Nobody seems to be going to the phone. I don't know what to do. Embarrassed to be the only one in motion, I also halt with the plate in my hand. At children's birthday parties in the old days we used to play a game in which we had to freeze suddenly, whatever we were doing at the time. If someone in the big tent were fucking – which God forbid – would they have to stop short and wait?

After the phone has rung seven or eight times, everyone abruptly comes back to life and carries on as if nothing had happened. I make a beeline for Franka.

You might at least have explained the rules, I say reproachfully. I feel like an absolute idiot. What the devil happened just now?

You'll find out, Dad, she whispers.

This eternal whispering is getting on my nerves, I say loudly.

She simply laughs and turns on her heel.

It seems we each have to wash up our own plate at the series of sinks. We dip it in the malodorous, lukewarm broth and hand it to our neighbour, who dips it in some slightly less malodorous broth and hands it on in turn. Meantime, we go to the end of the washing-up queue, take our plate, and dry it on an already sodden and not particularly clean drying-up cloth. The local hygiene leaves a lot to be desired. In my bagel cafés I'd have had the health inspector breathing down my neck a long time ago.

A bacterial paradise, I mutter to myself.

Beside me is a grey-haired, bespectacled man whose white jeans and white T-shirt make him look like the camp doctor. He nods. Best not to think about it, he says in a thick Swiss accent.

It and most things in this place, I add.

He eyes me with amusement. Are you new here?

I nod unhappily. Where can one get a coffee?

He beckons me over to a table round the corner. On it are some cups and a cauldron of boiling water. No coffee that I can see.

The rose-hip tea's good, says my guide.

No coffee, huh?

He laughs. I can also recommend the monk's-hood tisane. My name's Ueli, by the way. I'm from Berne, ninth day.

You count the days here, like in prison?

Sometimes. Have you only just arrived?

I nod.

I might have known, you're still so quick off the mark.

How many days before you turn into a snail?

Somewhere between the third and the fifth, Ueli replies gravely.

He must find it easier than most of the others, being Swiss.

Does it get easier when you're a snail?

He laughs derisively. Yes, but that's not the point.

What is, then?

Stopping, he says firmly.

Stopping?

Switching off, he explains. Doing nothing.

And then?

Not being afraid. He nods to himself, sipping some hibiscus tea. What family do you belong to?

I don't understand the question.

He eyes me suspiciously, as if he has just unmasked a spy, an infiltrator. Then he leads me over to a white notice board on which all the participants are listed in groups beneath coloured pictures of birds and insects, like children in a kindergarten. I find my name, together with those of Norbert and Theo, beneath a grasshopper.

You belong to the Grasshopper Family, says Ueli. The Grasshopper Family's job today is preparing vegetables.

What are you?

A Dragonfly, he replies gravely. I'm on latrine detail today.

I giggle hysterically. Ueli gives me a look of concern. It gets better, he says. It gets better on day three. You feel worse again between days five and seven, but it gets much easier from day nine onwards.

A bit like skiing, I say. Why are you here?

Ueli sips his hibiscus tea. Just when I've given up hope of an answer he startles me by blurting out, My wife's menopausal and my firm went bankrupt. We were both scared. He stares into his cup. I, too, fill a cup with hot water and dunk a hibiscus tea bag in it. Old Nick himself would drink hibiscus tea in a pinch. The water blushes faintly.

We sip our tea, gazing out across the lotus pool. One or two figures are strolling around it in slow motion.

I'm trying to learn that everything must change in order to survive, sighs Ueli.

But does one have to be so snail-like about it? I ask.

That's walking meditation, he explains. One step per breath. It looks a bit silly, I admit.

We laugh. Ueli has a booming, hearty laugh. A gong sounds. He stops laughing, and everyone freezes as before. The blue-eyed nun, in the act of taking her plate to the kitchen, stands transfixed like a deer caught by headlights in the middle of the road.

Norbert and Theo are already carrying wicker baskets full of potatoes, carrots and courgettes out on to the terrace. Norbert already looks as if he's been here for ever. Franka hands out some kitchen knives. Working meditation, she whispers in my ear. That means peeling potatoes and keeping your trap shut. She grins.

What's the matter with the girl? She's looking so cheerful. What's behind it? Or is it simply the presence of Pelge? I'd like to meet him face to face at last, so I can look deep into his eyes and convince him, once and for all, that he can't whisk my baby off to India just like that.

It's time I met your lama, I whisper.

She nods. Ssh, she says.

Extremely practical, this silence, from many people's point of view.

I sit down at a table, sighing, and Norbert tips out a mountain of potatoes in front of me. Reluctantly, I start peeling them. The smell and the sand between my fingers remind me of my early years at the *Seventh Heaven*. Claudia and I used to peel potatoes until far into the night, side by side, for our celebrated spinach-and-potato *au gratin*, price seven marks eighty. They were happy days, it strikes me now. Peaceful and carefree.

I can peel potatoes pretty fast. Efficiently, too, keeping the skins very thin. The next time I look up, Gretel from the tent is sitting opposite me. My heart gives a little jump as though vaulting over a puddle.

Gretel, head bowed and plaits bobbing, is scraping carrots. Her hair is either expensively tinted or Scandinavian blond. Her white dress, I note to my relief, is fairly close-fitting, and she's wearing a bra. Bra-wearers are as rare in this place as tulips in the desert. Gretel is different. Like me. My English lace-ups and her bra: not a bad basis for a relationship.

I shake my head. I'm amazed at the ideas my brain generates of its own accord if I don't watch out. She looks up, but only for a fraction of a second. Little silver dolphins are dangling from her ears. She has wonderful honey-coloured eyes. Acacia honey – no, darker, more like chestnut honey. I'm an expert on honey. Sugar was naturally taboo at the *Seventh Heaven*. She looks down at her carrots again.

Everyone is preparing vegetables – slowly and intently, as if devising a new Olympic discipline. Theo is slicing courgettes with surgical precision, Norbert literally fondling a cabbage. He strips off the outer leaves more tenderly, I suspect, than he ever undressed his wife.

Seated beside him are two fifty-something women with identical henna-red perms, one dressed in orange, the other in apple green. They could be twins. They're slowly and humbly cleaning leeks.

I feel I'm imprisoned in a slow-motion dream. I'd like to chuck the potatoes around, hurl them at the others' heads, rouse them from their dream, make them yell.

Gretel, look at me, I implore. Look at me and tell me they're all insane.

But Gretel doesn't look at me. Come on, spare me a glance. I need an ally with all these loonies around, or I won't survive this place.

But no, she goes on staring at her stupid carrots. Scrape, scrape, scrape.

She doesn't want to. She doesn't want to look at me because she finds me unappealing, unattractive, smelly. I haven't been able to take a shower since we left Munich. I'll go look for a shower and shampoo my hair as soon as we've finished the vegetables. I'll go as soon as you look at me.

She doesn't raise her blond head by so much as a millimetre, the stupid cow. OK, suit yourself. Go on scraping carrots till you turn blue or attain Enlightenment, it's all the same to me.

I put down my knife and scoop the potatoes back into their basket. After all, I never promised to stay the course. I stand up – and she looks at me with those chestnut-honey eyes of hers, quite calmly and steadfastly.

I resume my seat at once.

Could we swap? she whispers in an accent that must be Dutch. Really cute – it makes everything sound so much nicer. If she'd asked me in Swabian or Hessian, not a chance.

I'm glued to my seat by a linguistic coloration she can't help. That and her honey-eyed gaze.

I hate carrots, she whispers.

And I hate potatoes, I whisper back, though it's a barefaced lie.

She gives me a smile minuscule enough for its detection to require a magnifying glass, but detect it I do. She has a little gap between her teeth, which gives her a rather sexy look. She starts peeling potatoes vigorously.

Claudia's standing beside me with her arms crossed, watching her. Gretel's not much good at it, she says. All else apart, she removes far too much skin and doesn't dig out the eyes. Get lost, Claudia! I'm indulging in a little flirtation so as to survive this confounded place, that's all. Didn't you do that when you were here?

Theo is watching me appraisingly from afar. I give him an

exaggerated grin. No idea what you told him about me, Claudia. He was here at Easter too, wasn't he?

I scrape pounds and pounds of carrots in the hope of another honey-eyed smile, but no. Gretel immerses herself in her potato-peeling as if it were the most interesting activity under the sun.

I could kill for a cup of coffee, I whisper. She goes on peeling.

I'd been hoping she would whisper 'Me too!' I could already see us jumping into the car, racing off to the nearest café, sitting under the plane trees, and slurping coffee out of great big cups, but no such luck. Nothing of the kind. There's a blister developing on my forefinger.

When the gong sounds at last, Gretel freezes in the usual way – I'm already within an ace of joining in – then gets up and clears away the debris without giving me another glance.

I sit there like an idiot, and all at once I'm seized with such a fierce craving for a cigarette, I nearly pass out. This stupid vegetable-peeling session has almost made me forget about smoking. Incredible. I haven't smoked a single cigarette since I got here over five hours ago.

18

I SPRINT TO THE PARKING lot, dive into my red-hot car, and light up. Telltale smoke drifts out of the window. I crank it shut, almost asphyxiating myself in the heat, but I've no desire to be reprimanded by some well-meaning, batik-clad cow.

It's like smoking in a sauna. Sweat trickles down my neck. It must be well over a hundred in here. YOU'VE ARRIVED. ENJOY YOUR BREATH. KEEP SILENT. If I had a gun I'd shoot that notice. I turn up the radio loud and wonder what other forbidden things I can do. Of course, telephone!

I extract the mobile from my pocket, key in my PIN, and stare in horror at the two little words that show up on the glowing display like a sarcastic message from the Buddhists: *No Network*. My mobile is out of range!

I'm cut off. Reception-wise, this accursed Buddhist camp is situated in dead ground. My contact with the world has been severed.

With what world, though? With Claudia? With Marisol, who never calls me anyway? With my work? With a handful of acquaintances? My world can well do without me. It won't miss me, won't give a damn that it can't get in touch with me. Dejectedly, I play an aimless tune on the keys of my disabled mobile.

I could drive to the nearest high ground, where I'd probably get some reception, and call Claudia. I experience a sudden longing for her. The stupid law of nature that turns us men into a pack of Pavlovian dogs: an inaccessible woman is always more attractive than one who's there in the flesh. It's a biological reflex, because we seem fated to hunt and grow bored once we've killed our prey. I sometimes find my own sex insufferably predictable, not – of course – that any woman would believe me.

Just as I'm inserting the key in the ignition there's a tap on the rear window. No peace for the wicked, not even for five minutes.

Reluctantly, I turn to look. It's Theo. He's mounted on a red racing bike and miming a smoker. I take a while to realize he isn't admonishing me; he'd like a cigarette himself.

I nod. Visibly relieved, he gets off his bike and slumps into the passenger seat. He looks ridiculous in his cyclist's red pants and the matching, skintight vest that shows off his potbelly to full advantage. I know his aftershave. It's the same as mine: *L'eau d'Issey.* Pronounced correctly it sounds like 'Odyssey', but not even Odysseus would have come here, he'd have sheered off in time. He wouldn't have lent himself to this crap.

Theo takes a long drag and sighs contentedly.

My first little cigarette for nine days. It's great. Almost as good as a spliff.

His faint Dutch accent, which I found so enchanting in Gretel, makes him sound strangely girlish. 'Little' cigarette . . . This absurd penchant for the diminutive. He has blue eyes and sandy lashes. A shapely mouth. Women probably find him sexy in spite of his corpulent figure and bald patch. He makes a self-assured impression. They like that, heaven knows. He's probably got a nice 'little' pecker too. Could you do me a favour? he asks. Could you tell our family I won't be coming today?

Coming to what?

The discussion.

What discussion?

He looks at his watch, a gold Rolex with a red dial. Seven minutes to go, he says. The family's daily get-together.

The Grasshopper family, you mean?

He laughs. All this noble silence turns you into a kind of pressure cooker, he says. If you don't let off a bit of steam once a day, you blow your top.

I'd love to have a little punch-up with some of these imbeciles, I say.

He regards me with a smile. Yes, he says, I can tell. That's why I go for bike rides – and why I keep our tent pitched. It's in case I need to go to ground.

So as not to get into a fight?

Can I have another little cigarette?

If only he wouldn't say 'little'! I offer him the packet and we both smoke another. We sit there in the smoky, diabolically hot car, staring at the wooden sign on the grass in front of us: YOU'VE ARRIVED. ENJOY YOUR BREATH. KEEP SILENT.

It isn't until you're here that you notice how often you have violent thoughts, Theo says with a grin. It's like an endless tape unwinding in your head.

You're right, I say, and I can't find the knob to turn it off.

I'm learning not to listen to it, he says. Not to lash out when I'm feeling low.

Theo a slugger? Does he beat his wife? His child? His girlfriend? Does he get drunk and go on the rampage? He doesn't look particularly violent, but appearances can be deceptive.

When my little niece learned to walk and kept falling over, he says, she got so mad she used to hit the person nearest her.

I laugh. I can remember my daughter doing that, I say.

Theo blows a smoke ring. We never change, he says. When

117

something hurts us, we lash out at the first available person. We swear at other drivers, reduce our secretaries to tears, yell at our children . . .

Well, I point out, sometimes we're right.

Theo looks depressed. Not often, he says. Very seldom. How, er . . . how's Claudia?

The question is so unexpected it floors me. Good, I say. Fine.

He nods and plucks at his cycling pants.

Were you also here at Easter? I ask.

He looks startled. Yes, of course.

Really.

Meaning what?

Claudia never mentioned you, that's all.

Oh, he says, looking out of the window, we didn't see much of each other. Because he looked out of the window as he said it, I know he's lying. Was Theo Claudia's Easter beau? I grin to myself. So this little Edam cheese flirted with my wife . . .

Ah, he sighs, a little glass of red wine and I'd really be happy. There he goes again.

I've got a little can of beer in the boot, I say, but it's probably boiling.

He shakes his head and looks at his watch. You'd better get going, he says.

I don't know if I feel like socializing with a dozen pressure cookers.

He gives me a fatherly pat on the shoulder. Go on, he says. Sometimes it does you good to see you aren't the only asshole in this world.

I'm not sure how to interpret this remark. I watch him get out, mount his bicycle, and pedal off.

I stay behind in the car like a fly in a preserving jar. I could smoke another 'little' cigarette.

I've got nothing to discuss with the Grasshoppers. But doesn't Gretel belong to our 'family' as well?

I toss the butt through the window, then get out, guiltily retrieve it, and drop it in the ashtray. Five minutes late already. I break into a run. The blue-eyed nun is heading my way. She bows to me and smilingly gestures me to slow down. Enjoy your breath, she advises, the stupid cow, but I meekly comply.

19

THE GRASSHOPPERS ARE SITTING in a circle on white plastic chairs under a big oak tree. Maya, an ageing hippy with a lilac sari and a gnarled, deeply tanned complexion, introduces herself as our mother. Great, I've always wanted a mother like Maya. Our family has acquired two new members, she trills. Please introduce yourselves.

Norbert stands up, bows, and states his name in a reverently tremulous voice. The ugly twins in orange and apple green are Renate and Ilse from Stuttgart. Nhiem is a lanky stick insect of a Vietnamese monk, and beside him sits a pallid young couple from Hanover, Tim and Sabine, both of whom look twelve. Then comes fat Giovanni, a thirtyish doctor from Bolzano; Ingeborg, a wiry little yoga teacher from Cologne with close-cropped red hair; and finally me. The two chairs beside me are still unoccupied. I present Theo's apologies, which Mother Maya silently acknowledges, but where is Gretel? I look round uneasily. She's my only reason for being here.

And then, as if I'd conjured her up, she comes walking across the grass like a margarine commercial, a blonde in virginal white with swinging plaits.

Sorry, she says, and smiles her sexy, gap-toothed smile. She sits down beside me and shuffles her feet around on the grass. I recognize the white Prada sandals from our heap of shoes on her slim brown feet. Better and better. So she's also staying in the House of the Full Moon.

It's my turn to introduce myself. For one brief moment I wonder whether to give a false name so no one will ever recognize it, but I can't think of one, and anyway, it's completely illogical. So all I say is, Fred, Munich.

And this is your first time here, Fred? coos Mother Maya.

I nod. She leaves it at that and turns to Gretel

I'm Antje from Amsterdam, says Gretel.

So Gretel's name is Antje. Antje from Amsterdam. It sounds like a song, *Antje from Amsterdam*. You could link arms and sing it, swaying from side to side and brandishing tulips the way other people hold up cigarette lighters.

How are you all today? asks Maya, surveying the circle with motherly solicitude. I howl like a dog inside, feeling like someone at an AA session. Like someone with a *problem*.

To my surprise Antje announces, in her entrancing accent, that she's had an awful twenty-four hours. Last night the rain came through the skylight into her room, so she hardly slept, and mosquitoes attacked her during morning meditation – just her, no one else. She fell asleep during Tubten Rinpoche's lecture, at lunch she was so hungry and impatient she went to the children's table and filched two lumps of tofu, and this afternoon she couldn't keep her mind on the vegetables she was preparing. *Me*, I tell myself – she was thinking of *me*! If I were a dog I'd lick her white Prada sandals.

Antje concludes her tale of woe with a bow. Everyone grins. Maya asks who else is in the same state, and – surprisingly enough – they all put their hands up.

All, that's to say, except Norbert. Mother Maya looks at him inquiringly, and already he's inflating his lungs like an airbag.

Speaking for myself, he trumpets, I haven't felt so good for a long time – not for ages, even though I've been here only a few hours.

The brown-nosing eager beaver! I wonder how soon he'll get out his flute and play them all a tune.

I feel meaningful for the first time in ages, he goes on. I don't have a bad conscience, don't feel scared of making a mistake, of being criticized and rejected . . .

His lower lip trembles alarmingly. I know what comes next: the Gabi saga. And, sure enough, Norbert's eyes gush tears as if he's turned on a tap.

The group waits in silence. Apple-green Renate produces a tissue and hands it to him. He sobs into it.

I look over at the children's playground, which is situated a little out of the way beside a bamboo thicket. Some youngsters are tussling for possession of the swing while three girls of around twelve brush each other's hair and a couple of monks play volleyball with the older boys. The robed monks move with the grace and precision of dancers.

I'm strongly tempted to get up and join them, but Norbert has at last resumed the thread of his remarks. I've been out of work for a year, he sobs. There was an accident at my school. The painters left a can of cellulose thinners in my classroom. I put a notice on it – 'Caution, highly inflammable!' – but some boys held a cigarette to it out of sheer high spirits . . .

We all freeze, waiting for the inevitable explosion. Three, two, one . . .

Norbert draws a deep breath. Then he says, very quietly, Three children died. Two boys and a girl. I've been charged with manslaughter – I'm still awaiting trial. He pauses briefly. And the day before yesterday my wife left me.

He bows. He's through. The group preserves a shocked silence.

I'm hopping mad. I rescue this man from Mövenpick, drive him to the South of France, sing Bob Dylan songs with him, and celebrate his fortieth birthday – and he tells me nothing. Absolutely nothing. Only that Gabi always kept the purse.

I've lost everything, Norbert says flatly, blowing his nose. I've no work, no children, no wife, no home.

Silence. They all stare sheepishly at the ground. Then Nhiem, the scrawny monk, bows and says, As long as you remain in the present, you've a home.

He bares his big yellow horse-teeth in a smile and bows again.

Norbert nods as if he's understood. I've no idea what Nhiem means. It won't be long before this esoteric guessing game brings me out in a rash.

I fled from Vietnam to Canada at the age of seventeen, Nhiem goes on. I worked there as a waiter in a Chinese restaurant for twenty years. After work I would go home and watch television. I had no friends, no family, only my television set. One day, on September 17th, 1997, I suddenly realized I was more dead than alive. I was never where my body was. I was in Vietnam in spirit, but my body was sitting on a sofa in Canada, watching television. I wanted to get back inside my body, so I gave away the TV – he gives a boyish giggle – and everything else I possessed and went into a monastery.

He smiles at Norbert, then lowers his eyes like a bashful fifteen-year-old. I'm sure Nhiem is as queer as a two-dollar bill, possibly without being aware of it, but I'm astonished that someone apart from me knows what it feels like to be permanently out of one's body and elsewhere in spirit.

Nhiem bows once more. It's really time for some applause and a commercial break.

Neither materializes. Instead, orange-clad Ilse from Stuttgart takes the floor. Television destroyed my marriage, she says reproachfully in the thickest of Swabian accents. All my husband did, day in, day out, was sit in front of the box. I implored him to turn it off. I begged, threatened and argued, but the television was stronger than me. That black box squatted in our living room like an evil spirit, sucking in all there used to be between us. I couldn't enter the room in the end, I was scared of being swallowed by the thing.

Apple-green Renate nods, but Ingeborg and even Gretel/Antje regard her sympathetically. I feel I'm on a roller coaster. Though dismayed by Norbert and touched by Nhiem, I could slap Ilse for her stupid TV story. I picture her husband taking refuge, night after night, with his television set, a good friend who willingly and unquestioningly keeps him company while Renate stands in the doorway, reproachful and utterly un-comprehending.

Television is what staring into campfires was in the Wild West, or leaning on a cushion and looking out of the window in the nineteen-fifties. Watching television is meditation. When you concentrate on that colourful rectangle, time stands still and nothing matters any more. Like Ilse and Renate, Claudia simply doesn't understand that.

Underwater documentaries are my favourites. Luckily, they show one nearly every night. The pale blue of the water, the gurgle and hiss of the divers' breathing and the resonant tones of the commentator as he tells of crayfish that take eight years to mature, or yellow-tailed mackerel that swim far across the Pacific in the Humboldt Stream, or moray eels that never shut their voracious mouths – that's pure relaxation. An absolute drug.

Fish are incapable of regulating their body temperature independently of the ambient water temperature. It's just the same with me when I'm watching the box. I merge with whatever programme is on, transcend my boundaries, cease to be myself, become no more than an electromagnetic wave. Isn't that exactly the same as meditating?

No, snarls Claudia, it's autism.

The truth is, men need little more than sex, something to eat, and peace and quiet. Women think that's autism.

To save us, Claudia enrolled us on the Spanish course. Enter Marisol.

But what should you do when all your partner does is watch television? young Sabine asks shyly, blushing. There's a trace of fear in her voice. Her boyfriend Tim stares guiltily at his shoes.

Maya ponders her answer. Well, she says, I think you should try to turn it off. Television only distracts us from ourselves.

But of course, I feel like shouting, that's what it's there for! That's the beauty of it!

An ancient Vietnamese nun with a face like crumpled parchment comes gliding past. Maya waves her arms excitedly. Sister, she calls, sister, we've got a question for you.

The nun glides up, but her snail-like movements don't annoy me. In her case they look elegant. Her majestic bearing lends her a beauty irrespective of youth and age.

She listens to the question intently, strokes her shaven head, cogitates, and then laughs till her little eyes almost disappear.

Oh, she says casually, I think one should sit down beside one's beloved and enjoy his presence because he's alive. Television can be like silence . . .

Exactly, sister! I want to shout. Thank God, you've hit the nail on the head! Television is like noble silence! Noble television, you could call it!

The nun smiles, bows, and glides off.

The others are shocked. Renate and Ilse scan our faces in bewilderment. They never expected the nun's advice to take that form. A subdued silence falls. I'm the only one who's inwardly jubilant. Just then the mosquitoes attack.

Whole squadrons of them pounce on my ankles, my neck,

my hands. Almost as one, the women produce some mosquito repellent – it smells revolting – and feverishly rub it in.

Antje hands me her bottle without a word. Before long I smell like all the rest, but the mosquitoes couldn't care less. I flail around wildly, and blood spurts as I flatten one on the back of my hand. The others stare at me in dismay. I'm a butcher – I've slaughtered a mosquito.

I'm a killer and everyone saw it. I lower my murderous hand, feeling guilty but wanting nothing so much as to lash out again. I fan myself impotently, ears filled with the high-pitched whine of my tormentors' wings.

Out of the corner of my eye I see Nhiem sitting there quite still with his hands in his lap, smiling as he suffers a mosquito to land on his bald pate and make itself thoroughly at home there before biting him. I want to draw back my arm and crush it, I want to kill, kill! I try to draw Nhiem's attention to his head and succeed at the third attempt. He smiles, nods – and does nothing. Absolutely nothing. Nothing at all.

He's deliberately, purposely, allowing himself to be bitten. I stare at him in bewilderment, as I would at a fakir.

As a boy I once looked on, with equal bewilderment, as the proprietor of a flea circus fed his performers by letting them bite him. I knew just how much flea bites itched because I'd occasionally brought a flea home from school, so I found it incomprehensible that anyone would voluntarily subject himself to such torment. He seemed mysteriously strong to me, stronger even than Hercules, the world's strongest man, who bent iron bars in the tent next door. I might be able to train my muscles and become like Hercules, but I would never manage to resemble the owner of the flea circus. Simultaneously fascinated and repelled, I stared at the fiery red flea bites on his fleshy arms, and every additional bite he tolerated made me more and more angry because I knew that the will-power required for the endurance of pain was not in my nature. I was a coward.

It later transpired that I couldn't even endure problems, let alone pain.

So Nhiem infuriates me just like the proprietor of the flea circus. I itch to grab the gay waiter from the Chinese restaurant in Canada and shake him, yell at him to be a man, for God's sake, and lash out. I can't stand it any longer. I jump up, bow briefly – to my own surprise – and vamoose. That's to say, I try to glide, not run, but glide as fast as humanly possible. Along the gravel path and past the bamboo thicket and the lotus pool to the parking lot. The stupid lotus pool must be to blame for that accursed plague of mosquitoes.

I dive into my car and slam the door. I'm safe in my fortress. Safe from mosquitoes and Buddhists. Gleefully, I watch mosquitoes swirling around the outside of my car in the purple twilight. I light a cigarette and sigh with relief.

When my eyes happen to fall on the notice board – YOU'VE ARRIVED. ENJOY YOUR BREATH – I start the engine. Aimlessly, I drive along the little country roads. The air is pink, the fields of stubble glow like gold. It's beautiful here, I suppose, but I want out. Just out of here.

My mobile bleeps while I'm breasting a rise. Reception! I'm back within range! I pull up at once and extract the phone from my breast pocket. The little envelope is winking. I've got mail! CALL ME, it says.

The mail's from Claudia, I can tell by the phone number. I've only to press a key to get through.

Claudia, I fume without preamble, I hate it here! I want out! I think it's awful! You can't get a coffee! The food's appalling! The people are stupid and ugly! There are mosquitoes!

Claudia giggles. She actually giggles!

And they all move so slowly, like they're on Valium, and

they chew their food a hundred and fifty times. I could go berserk—

That's normal, Claudia breaks in.

What's normal?

You do go berserk the first few days. I longed for a pump-action shotgun for a week at least.

You did?

Why not me?

You've been practising this crap for so long.

It doesn't help much.

So what's the point of it all? I feel like saying.

How's Franka?

Franka's OK, I tell her. That's the really odd thing. She's fine. She grins the whole time and works in the kitchen. In an apron.

Oh, Claudia says softly, and I seem to hear her heart disburden itself of a sack of cement. In that case, she says, you're welcome to rant and rave. It's paid off after all . . .

I still haven't seen Pelge, I object.

Oh well, says Claudia. She's fine, that's the main thing.

What? What does that mean? I thought I was here to make sure she doesn't run off with her lama . . .

It'll do you good too.

Don't you believe it. I'll be eternally grateful to God if I don't become a serial killer in this dump.

Claudia laughs. I don't think I've heard her laugh for ages.

And all you can do is laugh yourself sick.

I was just trying to picture you munching brown rice at thirty bites a minute.

You lied to me, what's more. All that stuff about salad and Vietnamese cuisine . . . She giggles again. What are you doing right now?

Lying on the sofa talking to you.

I'd like to lie beside her, inhale the scent of her, bury my face in her bosom.

128

Was the Dutchman here when you were?

What Dutchman?

What Dutchman! The one that gave you the address of this place – the one who's to blame for everything, strictly speaking.

Oh, you mean Theo.

Yes, Theo. Was he here too? I ask this as casually as I can, blow it into her ear like a puff of wind. She hesitates for a hundredth of a second only, but her hesitation isn't lost on me.

Yes. Why?

He's here now.

Oh . . . Pause. Give him my regards.

OK. If I see him.

We preserve a silence costing DM1.15 per minute.

Have you already learnt Buddha's first noble truth?

No, only noble silence, and that's already getting on my tits. Feels like a kindergarten, the way they keep scolding us. Enjoy your breath! I can hardly breathe at all, it infuriates me so much.

Are you smoking at this moment?

I don't answer.

You could take the opportunity to give it up.

So what's the first noble truth?

That life's no picnic, she says in a flash.

Says Buddha? I ask.

Yes. Life's no picnic. Suffering is quite normal.

I suffer even when it *is* a picnic.

Do you know what that means?

No.

It means there's no point in getting upset about it. You suffer like everyone else, so you can take life more easily – laugh at it, even.

Don't talk nonsense, Claudia. Do *you* take life more easily since you learnt it was no picnic?

129

Yes, she says. It's just that you haven't noticed. Kiss Franka for me.

OK.

Bye, darling.

OK.

Oh, and don't forget to enjoy your breath. She chuckles and hangs up.

Instantly, unhappiness envelops me. I feel lonely. My daughter is happy – my wife too, apparently – but I'm not. Without thinking, I dial Marisol's number.

Yeees? she drawls in her husky Spanish voice, which still hits me plumb in the underpants. I feel Marisol's white flesh, the black hair that falls over me like a curtain, the sexual desire into which I could subside, like a big, soft cushion, at any hour of the day or night.

I hang up in alarm. No, no additional complications.

Instead, I reach into my underpants and proceed to jerk off. The sky above my Plexiglas bolthole is turning lilac. I get bored, wait impatiently for the conclusion. I shut my eyes and summon up a vision of provocative, lethargic Marisol. It doesn't work. Not even that works these days. When I open my eyes again the sky is duck-egg blue. The evening star has risen.

Straightening up, I see a bicycle approaching in the wing mirror. The road is dark now, and the beam of the bicycle lamp flits to and fro across its surface.

It's Theo, toiling up the hill at a walking pace. I wonder whether to drive on quickly, so as not to get involved with him, but he's already too near. If he recognized my car it would look as if I were running away. I crouch down and watch him go by in the wing mirror.

Fifty metres beyond the car he comes to a stop, gets off, lets go of the bicycle, which falls to the ground unheeded, and stands there doubled up, holding his sides. From the violent way his back heaves, he's breathing heavily.

My wing mirror bears the following legend: *Objects in mirror are closer than they appear*. Toyota's simple warning seems to epitomize my perception of the world. I keep it at a distance, but it's harder on my heels than I think, and I keep running to escape it. *Objects in mirror are closer than they appear*. Could be a Bob Dylan lyric.

I lie back and gaze up at the steadily darkening sky overhead.

Night has fallen by the time I wake up. Theo has disappeared. The dashboard display says time: 22:00, outside temperature: 78 degrees. I open the window, and the warm night air streams in like a dark, heavy cloth. My stomach is rumbling. I've missed supper, but it was bound to be brown rice again.

On the back seat I find one of Franka's squashed muesli bars and half a bottle of lukewarm water. Does the meditation centre shut sometime? I drive on feeling bemused, almost drunk.

I follow the beam of my headlights as if they're guiding me. I drive too fast and nearly overcook the bends, but I don't want to drive any slower. I simply don't want to.

A small, dark animal is crouching in the middle of the road. It's too late to brake or swerve. There's a dull thud. I've no idea what it could have been. A cat, a rabbit? Franka would badger me into turning back. Claudia too. So I do turn back and search until I find a little grey heap.

With my headlights on the heap I get out and prod it with the toe of my shoe. It's an owl. I've never seen an owl close up before. It stares at me calmly with wide-open, lemon-yellow eyes, then slowly, very slowly, shuts and opens them again like a doll. I hunker down beside it. The owl stares at me intently. Its body is a twitching grey, feathery mass.

You've killed me, you schmuck, says the owl.

My heart almost stands still.

I'm so sorry, I whisper.

It stares at me. Schmuck, it says.

I really am so terribly sorry.

Shut your trap.

It shuts its eyes again, and just when I've given up believing it will ever open them again, it does so for the last time, the pupils like sharp little knives in the yellow irises. Be happy, you schmuck, says the owl, and takes its leave. Its body is just a heap of feathers, nothing more.

I stand up, my heart hammering as if I've been running. I'm ripe for the funny farm, and an owl bids me be happy.

Shaking my head, I tow the grey heap of feathers to the side of the road, pluck a few stalks of grass that cut my palms unpleasantly in the dark, and scatter them over the owl. I crouch down beside it, feeling utter despair spread inside me like a squirt of ink in a glass of water.

What's the matter with me? What's making me so sad? My ultra-normal, botched little life? Be happy, you schmuck.

Happiness is where you find it, I can hear my mother saying. It's an age since I thought of her. She lives near Frankfurt with an ex-heating engineer of choleric disposition. We seldom phone each other. The heating engineer is jealous of her past. Happiness is where you find it, says my mother, that's my motto.

Mother, Mother, how far shall I go? I whisper into the darkness.

I've definitely gone mad at last. First I talk to an owl, then to my mother. But my mother doesn't answer. I repeat my question: Mother, Mother, how far shall I go?

I feel her stroke my forehead as if I've got a temperature, and then I hear her, hear the smile in her voice. Freddy, she says, oh Freddy, where do you want to go to all the time?

No idea, Mother. That's just it, I've no idea.

I put my head back so she can stroke my forehead again, but

there's nothing there, just the dark, sultry night and a few solitary stars that no longer exist, though their light continues to impinge on my retinas one night at the start of the third millennium, on a deserted country road in France.

The other two are asleep by the time I stumble into the room and – needless to say – hit my head on a beam. Norbert is snoring, and I'm almost grateful for that familiar sound. Theo sleeps beneath a mosquito net. The pro, I think, burning with hatred. He probably picked up that tip at Easter. Tomorrow I'm going to have it out with him, ask him if he made a play for my wife. Actually, the hesitation in Claudia's voice and the way he looked out of the car window are all the proof I need.

I get undressed without turning on the light and lie down on the thin mattress. It's hot and stuffy in our cell. I twist and turn, conscious of every bone in my body.

The whine of a mosquito grows louder. I hit out wildly, imagine it's already bitten me, and scratch, though scratching only makes me itch the more. But the mosquito isn't through with me, far from it. Its whine steadily increases in volume close to my ear. It returns to the attack again and again. I jump up and switch the light on.

Theo turns over with a grunt. I scan the walls in the dim glow of the bare bulb. Nothing. No mosquito, nothing. They probably secrete themselves in the cracks between the rough-hewn stones of the window embrasure, the swine.

I snaffle Theo's Dutch edition of *How to be Happy When You Aren't*. The back cover displays the lama with the yellow can in his hand, just like the German edition. I use the book to fan the stones, and, sure enough, a mosquito comes whirring out. I chase after it, perform a leap worthy of Michael Jordan, and capture it in my hand. Got it! I clench my fist, trying to squash the beast, and don't open my fingers until I'm sure it's a goner. But no, off it flies again. I briefly lose sight of it, then rediscover it on the white door frame. Great, now I can see it clearly. I steal up on it, draw back my arm, and clout the door with the flat of my hand, producing a sound like a pistol shot. Hurrah! My quarry is adhering to the white doorpost in a little smear of blood. Euphoria!

What the hell are you doing? whispers Norbert.

I turn round. Norbert and Theo are sitting up in bed like a couple of kids, glowering at me critically. Theo's mosquito net resembles my grandmother's fine-meshed cheese cover.

I'm slaughtering your reincarnated relations, I whisper back. Because they attacked me first, I add, as if compelled to defend myself.

Norbert puts out his hand and levels an accusing finger. There's another, he says.

Excitedly, he points to my jacket, which is draped over the bamboo pole. There's a monster of a mosquito perched on the sleeve. I creep up on it. Norbert hands me Theo's book, but just as I raise it the mosquito takes off.

Norbert gives a groan of disappointment. He, too, gets up and pursues the mosquito with a feverish eye, babbling like a baby. There – no, there, there! On the ceiling! Lift me up!

I hoist Norbert eighteen inches off the floor – he's startlingly light – and hand him the book. He draws back his arm and slams it against the ceiling with all his might. There's a crash that shakes the whole building. The thin, plasterboard partitions shudder.

Norbert holds up the book in triumph: the mosquito is stuck, dead centre, to the lama's stomach. Theo peers out from under his mosquito net.

How to be happy when you aren't, he sniggers.

We all burst out laughing, desperately trying to stifle our amusement for fear of waking everyone else. Theo splutters into his pillow like a elephant sneezing, Norbert flops on to his stomach and sobs with laughter, I squeal like a stuck pig. We can't help it, we laugh till it hurts.

Norbert buries his head in his sleeping bag to smother his salvoes of mirth, his whole body shaking. I watch him, convulsed with hilarity, and try to remember all I know about him: his boundless sorrow, his despair, his tears. None of that is perceptible now. He abandons himself to laughter as self-forgetfully as a man engaged in an orgiastic sex act.

Someone next door bangs angrily on the wall, and off we go again, purple-cheeked and panting like communal masturbators. Oh God, oh my God, help, oh, oh, oh! Exhausted, we lie on our mattresses with streaming eyes and relish the sense of emancipation that laughter has conferred on us. Better than sex, actually, I reflect before falling asleep.

20

I N THE MIDDLE OF the night Norbert gives me a shake. It's a quarter-past five, he whispers. Get up! Meditation!

I turn over with a grunt, but once awake I can't get off to sleep again. I sit up, swearing. Theo, seated on his mattress, is pouring hot water into a cup from a vacuum flask. He produces some Nescafé from his bag. Coffee! I inhale the scent longingly. He sees the look on my face. Like some? he asks, and holds out the cup for me to take a sip, a sublime, glorious sip.

He signs to me to follow with a jerk of the head, so I climb into my trousers and stumble down the stairs in his wake, not forgetting to give my head another crack on the beam.

I put on my shoes, which are proving to be very impractical because I have to keep tying and untying the laces. Blearily, I shuffle outside into a dawn light as soft as a teenager's first kiss.

Gliding along in slow motion, figures are converging on the white tent from all directions. I hear a bell ring and a nun singing in Vietnamese. The combination of her singing and the baby-pink sky is sweeter than sugar, simply entrancing, so all at once I, too, glide slowly down the hill to the tent.

Shoes off again. I get in everyone's way because it takes so long to undo my laces. Maybe I should have acquired a pair of stupid sandals for this trip.

They all make for their cushions. I park myself on one near the entrance, so I can escape. It's terribly flat and compressed by long use, and the mat beneath it smells of sweaty feet. A gong sounds, and from then on nobody moves. Except me.

The cross-legged position I've adopted proves extremely uncomfortable after a few minutes. I surreptitiously try to adjust it, but the resulting noises are embarrassingly loud. My joints creak, the planks beneath me groan, the cushion rustles. The others are quiet as mice. No idea how they manage it. I could cry out, my knees hurt so much after another five minutes. I readjust my position, but now my back hurts instead. By the time I've more or less relieved that discomfort, my right foot has gone to sleep. It's all I can think of until a mosquito comes whining round my ears. I try to blow it away, but even that sounds loud in this reverential hush. The pain travels to my upper thighs, my left foot imitates my right foot and goes to sleep too. I swivel my wrist for a glance at my watch. Less than ten minutes have elapsed. I can't stand this. I know from Claudia what one has to do: simply let one's mind wander.

But how can I, if all I can think of are my various aches and pains? At best, the mosquito will distract me from my numb feet, the pain in my knees from the mosquito, and my numb feet from the pain in my knees.

Interesting, really, that one pain should take my mind off another and one torment be replaced by the next. Is there ever an interval between them?

That thought itself was the interval, it seems, because I forgot about my knees, my feet and the mosquito while thinking it. Now that it's gone, the whole process starts again: cramp in the shoulder muscles, another mosquito, a sudden urge to sneeze, an unendurable itch in the balls. If I don't scratch them this minute, I'll have hysterics.

Just before I reach that stage my left knee becomes so painful, I forget about the itch.

Meditating is sheer torture. How will I be able to stand an hour and a half of it?

Furtively, I glance to right and left. Antje is sitting two cushions away. She's looking delightfully drowsy. What's going on in her head? What are they thinking about, all these stoically motionless people? How can they bear it?

Not me. That's it, I'm off. Just as I'm about to get up, however, the gong sounds again. They all stretch and get to their feet. Great, it's over. In slow motion – so slowly I almost tread on the heels of the person ahead of me – we shuffle around the tent in single file. Making for the exit, I think, but no: at the next gong, they all halt in front of their cushions and sit down again.

I stand there fractionally longer than the rest, uncertain what to do. I could perfectly well thread my way through them and leave the tent – nothing to it. Except that I'd be a failure, a weakling. So I sit down again, and the next bout of torture takes its course.

The whole procedure is repeated four times, and I stay with it only because, during the second session, I experience a tiny, wholly unexpected moment of time that opens up before me like a treasure chest on the seabed.

I see a blackbird hopping around on the grass outside, where the light is growing stronger by degrees, and suddenly I hear the dawn chorus.

I hear it as if I'd only just been equipped with ears. I don't know anything about birds, so I can't identify them, but I hear them not in the usual way, as an incidental twittering sound, but as a unique occurrence unrepeatable in this particular form. This dawn chorus will only occur once – now, this very moment – and if I don't hear it now I'll never hear it again. I'll have missed it once and for all.

Euphoric as this realization makes me feel, I'm simultaneously shattered because it means I'm forever missing my own, unique life – because I'm blind and deaf.

After an hour and a half I totter out of the tent like a zombie. It's an effort to stoop and put my shoes on. Once again, being the only one who has to tie his laces, I'm jostled on all sides.

Although the shower in the communal bathroom yields only a trickle of lukewarm water, I feel as if I've performed some mighty feat. I'm a hero. I've sat cross-legged and motionless – or almost – for an hour and a half without screaming and running away. My whole body hurts, my head is a void. I let the water trickle over my scalp and stare at a handwritten, trilingual notice hanging on the door: *Brothers and sisters, kindly remove any hairs from the plughole when you're through.*

While cleaning my teeth I read: *Brothers and sisters, use water sparingly.*

On the loo: *Brothers and sisters, kindly refrain from putting paper in the toilet. It can cause blockages!*

If there's one thing I hate about loos in southern Europe, it's those little waste bins brimming with shit-smeared toilet paper. I refuse to observe that revolting custom. My used loo paper goes down the pan, and that's that.

When I emerge I see Norbert, with a hand towel around his waist, disappearing into a shower cubicle. Norbert of the three balls, charged with manslaughter and deserted by his wife. He catches sight of me and raises a cheerful hand in greeting. I'm about to open my mouth – I feel it incumbent on me to make some belated comment about his terrible predicament, to react in some way, but how?—when, just in the nick of time, I'm reminded of noble silence. So I raise my arm likewise, and we exchange a majestic wave.

I'm too late for breakfast. Meditation hasn't done much for my fellow inmates' looks. Grey-faced and exhausted, they sit shivering over their muesli in fleeces and trousers, staring at me like a herd of cud-chewing cows. The children are unwashed, fretful, and food-bespattered. The breakfast table has been thoroughly grazed, the muesli bowl scraped almost clean. There's nothing left but a slice of wholemeal bread – wholemeal bread in France!—and a smidgen of jam, plus soya milk or herb tea. Although I know there's no coffee, I seek it like the Holy Grail. An equally hopeless quest.

I sit down and munch my slice of bread, overcome with melancholy. Where the devil is Franka? Without her I feel as forlorn as if I were soaring through space on my own. It's not even eight o'clock yet.

An interminable day lies ahead of me.

I feel a draught on the back of my neck. There she is at last! Laughingly, without turning round, I reach behind me two-handed and grab a pair of firm, slender thighs. Unfamiliar thighs. Franka's they certainly aren't. To her mother's chagrin, Franka has legs like Doric columns. Hastily releasing them, I turn to look.

Antje is standing behind me.

So sorry, I say, I thought you were—

She puts a finger to her lips and signs to me to come with her. I give the cud-chewers an apologetic smile, get to my feet, and follow her, afire with curiosity.

We've barely rounded the kitchen building and are out of sight of everyone when Antje breaks into a run. Along the gravel path, past the lotus pool, to the parking lot. I catch her up, panting hard.

Which is your car? she asks.

I point it out and open up. She flops down on the passenger seat, produces a lipstick from her bag, lowers the sun visor, and paints her lips bright poppy-red in the courtesy mirror.

Then she smiles at me and says, *Un grand café au lait, s'il vous plaît*. I turn the key in the ignition.

21

WE STROLL ACROSS THE sun-drenched marketplace like a couple on vacation. Normal people pass us in normal clothing. They haven't been mediating, haven't chewed their food umpteen times, they walk too fast, don't enjoy their breath. They're like me. I sigh with relief, back among my own kind at last.

Two days ago they weren't my own kind, they were bourgeois French play people.

I make for the nearest café like a homing pigeon. Then the church clock starts to strike and Antje freezes. She stands motionless with downcast eyes, rooted to the spot. I look round to see if anyone's watching, but the little town is observing its own special rhythm and doesn't have time to worry about deranged tourists. At the last stroke Antje comes to life again. She smiles at me and walks on as if nothing had happened.

What's the point of this cataleptic fit whenever a bell rings? I ask.

Oh, she says gravely, when a bell chimes or a phone rings, we simply take the opportunity to switch off and abandon all our plans and emotions – all our thoughts about other people and ourselves.

Abandon all our human perceptions? I ask indignantly. In that case, what's left of us?

No, she says with a shake of the head, I only mean our conception of the world.

I like the way she pronounces the word 'conception' in her Dutch accent, as if it were hot and she might burn her lips on it.

I wish I could speak a foreign language as fluently as you do, I tell her. Please say 'conception' again. Explain it to me. What's the difference between my perceptions and my conceptions?

Resolutely, she makes for a café beneath some plane trees whose leaves are casting decorative shadows on the white tablecloths. She sits down and regards me sceptically, as if gauging whether I'm bright enough to merit an answer. Most of the time, she says, we form an opinion about things without really perceiving them.

She points to an elderly woman waddling across the square laden down with plastic bags. For instance, she goes on, I look at that woman and I think, How bow-legged she is, and that skirt! A ghastly colour and far too short for her. No one should wear short skirts at that age. Are my own legs still good enough for short skirts? I used to have a blue skirt myself. Where is it, I wonder? I wish I was wearing that blue skirt right now. But if I looked like that woman there . . . She props her head on her hands and regards me with a twinkle in her eye.

I laugh.

I haven't really 'perceived' the woman, she says, I've merely pondered on skirts and legs and the ageing process. I'm a prisoner of my own ideas – my conceptions, in other words. See what I mean?

I say yes, but I'd say yes to a whole host of things when she looks at me that way. A waitress of Franka's age takes our order. She's wearing a white crocheted sweater over her enormous breasts and a white apron tightly knotted around her prominent little tummy. Her platform-soled sandals, which are reminiscent of hoofs, give her a clumsy, foal-like appearance.

Now it's your turn, says Antje.

French teenager, I say. Probably bullied into passing up an apprenticeship and working in her parents' café. Dreams of being a beautician.

No, Antje protests, that won't do. You must say what's really going through your head.

I hesitate.

Come on, do.

I sigh.

Please, she says.

OK, but I take no responsibility for my thoughts.

Deal!

Sexy little mam'selle, I say. Great boobs, probably an easy lay, wouldn't refuse a few francs for a new sweater. She'd be bound to feel good and holler *Maintenant, viens!* That song of Jane Birkin's, haven't heard it for years. I wonder what Jane Birkin's doing these days. She used to be the woman of my dreams. Still, I'm sure that girl doesn't like German men, and besides, I could easily be her father, I've got a daughter her age. I wonder what my daughter's doing at this moment . . .

I dry up. Phew, I say. Sorry, that was my head, not me.

Antje nods contentedly. She leans back so her plaits dangle over the back of the chair. Nothing torments us worse than our heads, she says, closing her eyes. You've got to hand it to the Buddhists, they've got the knack of switching off. It's simply wonderful.

Except that they don't approve of coffee.

Buddhism *and* coffee, she sighs. That would be perfection.

As though on cue, the sweater girl comes trotting over with our coffee. Antje shuts her eyes again and sniffs hers with a blissful smile.

I slurp mine greedily, even though I burn my tongue.

She straightens up, cradles her cup in both hands, and takes little tiny sips like an American movie star in a romantic comedy. All she needs to complete the picture are some thick socks and an outsize sweatshirt.

I'm really only here because of my husband, she says, staring into her cup. He's having an affair. She looks up and fixes me with her tawny eyes. I fall into them like a wasp into a honey pot, unable to extricate myself.

I had one too, I say. An affair, I mean.

Antje doesn't bat an eyelid. I must be crazy. She's still looking at me. Her nose is freckled and there's a little scar on her cheek. I'm blushing, I can feel it. I can't remember the last time I blushed. She cocks an eyebrow, looking intrigued, and I've no choice but to go on. An affair with a twenty-five-year-old, I say in a low, faltering voice.

Great sex? she asks, just as quietly.

I nod. That's all it was, sex. Like a sudden, overpowering hunger I couldn't control. And my marital relations are pretty normal. It's nothing whatever to do with my wife.

She gives a mocking laugh.

I didn't recognize myself any more. All at once, I was behaving like a demented chimpanzee. And I still don't know why.

My husband knows why, she says dryly. With him it's love.

I'm sorry, I say. But I'm not sorry in the least. On the contrary, I see light on the horizon: her old man isn't just having an affair, he's in love. But wasn't I in love too? How often did I whisper *Te quiero, te adoro* in Marisol's ear? Of course I was in love.

He got to know her here, with the Buddhists, says Antje, sipping her coffee. He came here to cure his professional stress and fits of depression – and bingo!

I'm sorry, I repeat like an idiot.

She looks at me absently.

Is she here? I ask.

She shakes her head. I came here to find out what made the woman so interesting. Silly of me, wasn't it?

I give a cautious shrug.

She's so . . . so relaxed, so broadminded, so liberated – a genuine Buddhist, Antje says scathingly. It's true I haven't learnt to be like that, not yet, but at least I can enjoy a cup of coffee in a completely different way.

Oh yes, I say, thankful to have left the subject of love and affairs behind us. The pleasures of the poor and disadvantaged. They need so little.

She stares into her cup, and I sense that she's withdrawing. I've said the wrong thing, scared her away like a startled deer.

The silence persists. I wonder how to lure her out of her shell again. She orders another cup of coffee without looking at me, without asking if I want one too.

He'll get over it the way I did, I say in an attempt to console her, glad of her obvious need for consolation. One day the craving simply left me, as if I'd overeaten. (That's completely untrue. I called Marisol only yesterday.)

That's the trouble, she whispers.

The deer is cautiously re-emerging from the forest and venturing back into the clearing. What is? I ask in a voice like silk, so as not to scare it again.

Love doesn't just stop. Oh, I . . . She clenches her fists. That woman, I could . . . I'd like to slaughter her and stuff her into little tiny cans.

Very Buddhistic of you, I say teasingly.

Oh yes, she says, narrowing her eyes, I also kill flies and spiders. And mosquitoes.

That makes two of us.

She gives a fleeting smile, dips her finger in the sugar at the bottom of her cup and licks it, then firmly pushes the cup away. He's so hung up on her, she says. He clings to her like a

146

burr, even though Tubten Rinpoche is always telling us we mustn't hold on to anything or anyone. He illustrates it this way . . . She picks up her coffee spoon like a club, extends her arm, and clenches her fist till she's puce in the face. Holding something like this is quite a strain, she says between gritted teeth, whereas this would be so much easier . . . She turns her fist over, opens it, and balances the spoon on her palm. She sighs.

I remove the spoon from her hand. Except, I say, that someone can take it away from you.

But I can't hang on to my husband either, she says. Not indefinitely.

I carefully deposit the spoon on the table, wondering which of us it represents, Claudia or me.

Hell, she mutters with a dismissive gesture, as if shooing away a fly. What about you? What brings you here?

I tell her about my daughter and the lama.

She laughs. We're probably the only two people who aren't here of our own free will. There are times when I feel like screaming and running away.

Me too.

We exchange a shy, silent smile. Then I ask a stupid question:

What about your husband? Where is he?

She stares at me in surprise. But you know him.

What?

You're sharing a room with him.

I run a hand over my hair and quickly look away, trying to conceal my dismay. She's Theo's wife! Theo from Amsterdam. Antje from Amsterdam. Of course! How incredibly obtuse of me!

Oh yes, of course, I say lamely. All at once I notice how sultry it is. The air seems to be draping itself over me like a wet handkerchief, and I'm suddenly very tired.

We don't speak for a long time. Then Antje slides her hand across the tablecloth like a foreign object. With the instinctive reflex of a frog snapping at a fly, my own hand pounces on hers and settles on top of it. Got her!

Antje leans over the table, gazing at me intently, and I try to look simultaneously interested and interesting, profound and sensitive. Her hand lies beneath mine like a little trapped animal, and it's only now, as we stare at each other, that a terrible suspicion burgeons within me, sprouting from the pit of my stomach like a fast-growing, poisonous plant and coming to full flower in my head: Who is she, this woman Theo's in love with?

22

FRANKA TAKES ME BY the hand and drags me into the big tent. She tugs at me impatiently while I remove my shoes. The place is already chock-full. At least four hundred people are sitting in a reverent, cross-legged semicircle, waiting for the head lama. I try to locate Antje, but without success.

I toss my shoes into a corner and am picking my way across the mats behind Franka when a fat man with a grey ponytail taps me on the shoulder and points to my abandoned footwear. Arms crossed, he watches me retrieve and neatly align them with hundreds of other pairs of shoes. That hasn't happened to me since my schooldays. I'm beside myself with rage. Buddhist Gestapo, I think irately.

Franka shakes her head at me and tows me over to a tiny cushion barely big enough to accommodate both buttocks. I draw up my legs like a fakir, kneeing the back of the man in front of me. He turns – slowly, of course – and gives me a look of contempt.

A suspenseful silence reigns. Flies drone through the hot air like tiny aircraft, the tent's canvas walls billow gently in the breeze. The four hundred are quiet as mice until a sudden murmur runs through their ranks. Then they scramble to their feet and freeze with their heads bowed.

Standing on tiptoe, I see Lama Tubten Rinpoche, the man

with the (beer?) can on Claudia's book, come gliding through the crowd. Not like the batik ladies beside the lotus pool – no, this man positively *floats* along. His body doesn't rise and fall as he walks, it glides slowly, like a ship, past his reverently bowing disciples.

Following him with a tea-mug in his hand is a young monk with a black crew cut. Franka raises her head a little and beams at him, and I know he must be Pelge. At this distance he makes a pleasant but extremely youthful impression.

Tubten Rinpoche glides over to his yellow throne and sits down cross-legged. Having gathered up his red robe and arranged it in neat folds, he raises his hand an inch or two.

It's the signal to be seated. All my neighbours prostrate themselves three times in succession, panting and sweating, while I stand rooted to the spot like an absolute idiot. I'm vaguely reminded of those agonizing school concerts in which I had to take part because I was learning the violin. I regularly stuck out like a sore thumb because my bow was on the upstroke when all the rest were down. I had no chance to correct this mistake: my bow kept stabbing the air while every other one was down and out of sight. It's the same now. I can't possibly fling myself to the ground because I'd be bound to be out of sync. Everyone else would be on their feet when I was on my knees and on their knees when I was on my feet. I shrug apologetically, but Lama Tubten Rinpoche just gives me an affable smile.

At last they all sit down, holding their breath. He continues to survey them with a smile. Nothing happens. Nothing at all. I yawn behind my hand. Tubten Rinpoche looks at me. He fixes me with his smiling gaze – *me* out of all these hundreds of people – and asks me a question in mellifluous, Indian-tinged English:

The best moment of your life – have you experienced it yet?

The words speed toward me like an arrow. I instinctively

duck, but they've already found their mark. Smack in the middle of my weak, vulnerable flesh. Have I experienced my life's best moment? The best moment of my entire lifetime? I hope not. Sure, there have been a few good moments to date. Catching frogs as a boy, sitting on my mother's lap, driving through the night with music playing, being in love, fucking and smoking thereafter, the birth of the person who's sitting beside me, whom I only occasionally recognize as my daughter.

When Franka slithered out I thought it was the best moment in my life. That tiny, age-old but brand-new being seemed to have come from far away to tell me what life was all about. The night she was born I thought I'd understood it at last, once and for all.

My best moment? When a frog hopped up and down on my palm, when I drove to France in my very first car, a green 2CV, with a Gauloise-laden hand dangling out of the window and the warm breeze on my arm and the feeling that everything, but everything in my life, was going to be bigger and more exciting from now on. A kiss from Claudia, right at the outset – sweet as baklava. Lying on a Spanish beach with hot sand under my back and Led Zeppelin's *Stairway to Heaven* on the transistor radio. That's just how I felt at the time: that I was making for heaven in seven-league boots. My first major disappointment: dropping out of film school. In return I got Claudia, my saviour, and Franka: Franka in the washbasin as a tiny baby, Franka the little, sleeping-suited alien in our bed at nights, Franka scampering towards me in a little red velvet dress with a bunch of dandelions in her hand. I'm inundated with snapshots of my life, but I can't put my finger on the very best, most sublime moment of all. And that's fine with me because, to be honest, I'm hoping that the happiness in my life hasn't already been used up – that my lifetime's finest moment is still to come, still ahead of me.

Many people imagine, Tubten Rinpoche goes on, that their life's best moment must lie sometime in the future. At this he gives a full-throated laugh, as if someone has just cracked a good joke.

They think it will come tomorrow, he chuckles, the day after tomorrow, next year. When I've qualified, when my health improves, when I've had a child, when I find the right husband or wife, when I've earned enough money – ah, then, then . . . He's convulsed with laughter. He's laughing at us, at me–me personally. I feel myself cock my head critically and raise my eyebrows.

When, when, when, he says, still laughing, then, then, then . . . Is that the way it looks inside your heads? Yes?

Mmm. Well? What's wrong with that?

Tubten Rinpoche stops laughing. Your life's best moment, he says softly, is now.

Now?

The best moment of your life is right now, he repeats, and sits back.

What's so sublime about now – about sitting in a hot, overcrowded tent with hundreds of neurotics?

Why? asks Tubten Rinpoche. It's quite simple. Because it's the only one of its kind in your life. The present moment will never return, and if you miss it, you'll miss your life.

I'm astonished to note that tears are welling up in my eyes like little springs.

Stop running, Rinpoche says quietly. He might be telling a child not to play with its food. Stop running after the future. The past is past, the future has yet to come, your home is the present.

Quite unaccountably, tears are running down my cheeks. A slim hand reaches for mine and holds it tight – my daughter's hand. There he sits, the ageing father who's supposed to protect her from Tibetan abductors, and all he can do is weep.

She grins. Sheepishly I grin back, hoping she won't let go of my hand. In that big, almost grown-up hand I sense the incredibly tiny baby hand, with its perfect, miniature finger-nails, that gripped my forefinger like a little monkey clinging to a vine; later the plump little paw she sometimes laid against my cheek just before I woke up; later still the slender hand of the tall, thin six-year-old who trustingly placed it in mine at every traffic light; and now that soft, tender, vulnerably childish hand that seeks to protect me, her big, stupid father.

I don't really take in the rest of the lama's address. I'm feeling rather dizzy, what with the heat and the idea that I've got to enjoy every goddamned moment of my life. Every last one? Really?

A great deal of singing in Tibetan follows. Franka opens a kind of hymnal and joins in with fervour. Does she understand what she's singing? Isn't it rather bizarre for four hundred Europeans to break into Tibetan? Imagine four hundred Tibetans singing German hymns without knowing a word of German.

I try to hum along a bit, not wanting to be embarrassingly conspicuous, but I feel such a fool I give up. I spot Theo's back a few rows in front of me, and the sight of the blue T-shirt enclosing his soft, flaccid flesh makes my blood boil as abruptly as the tears came a short while before. May he roast in hell, that fat little Dutchman who fucked my wife – of that I'm now convinced. That flabby dwarf made up to her with his Buddhistic pearls of wisdom. This is the best moment of your life, he probably whispered in her ear. Now! Yes, yes, now!

My forehead is beaded with sweat, I can feel it, and it's all I can do not to jump up and punch him on the nose. There, that's the present, don't miss out on it, you obese little asshole!

His back is quivering reverently, and he's singing with all his might. His sloping shoulders rise and fall in time to the music.

Claudia can't seriously have . . . No, it's out of the question. But the next moment I visualize her long legs wrapped around Theo's paunch, see his red, porcine moon-face bathed in sweat and hear him panting. She's staring up at the ceiling, feeling bored. She's not enjoying it, definitely not. Theo hasn't a clue who Claudia really is, after all. In this place she played the long-legged, spiritual blonde, I'm sure, but *I've* spent seventeen years of my life with her. For every beautiful woman in the world there's a man who finds it pretty boring, over the years, to fuck her. At this very moment, even the pussies of Cindy Crawford or Naomi Campbell, or whatever they're called, are losing their appeal for some guy somewhere in the world.

Anyway, Claudia isn't as beautiful as all that. Attractive, yes. But it takes plenty of fortitude, stamina and patience to put up with her. And I put up with her with positively Buddhistic serenity. Try emulating me, Tulip Bulb!

But what if she did enjoy it after all? What if she enjoyed it more than I can imagine because it's so long since she enjoyed it with me?

Fun . . . Yes, Claudia smiles and keeps saying what fun she's having and how happy she is. Always nice and positive, but the truth is, she never does have any fun. In her mind's eye she's already tidying up. Stripping off the sheets, washing and ironing, folding and stowing them neatly in the linen cupboard. While you're trying to give her pleasure, she's already tidying things away. You dance with her, and she's taking your shoes to the repairer's. You go abroad with her, and she's writing postcards in her head. You sit on the beach with her, and she's already shaking the sand out of everyone's clothes and sweeping it into little heaps. And because you sense this you hurry, secretly aware that she won't have any fun until everything's nice and tidy again, and because you hurry you don't have any fun yourself. I hope it was like that for you, Theo.

Neatness . . . She's a neatness addict. Her T-shirts in the chest of drawers are arranged according to colour and the flowers in the window boxes all have little nameplates. If there were a Tidiers' Anonymous I'd like to send her there for daily sessions. At regular intervals she tours the apartment. Anything lying around gets thrown away, she announces loudly. It's all going to the tip! Franka and I hurl ourselves on top of our belongings and wait for the paroxysm to subside, but we can't save everything from her mania for discarding things. Barbie horses with three legs have to go, and so do my beloved spiral binders and my old overcoat from Istanbul, vintage 1973. Only Claudia's notion of neatness counts, and she decides what neatness is.

She once got so carried away, she told Franka the state of her room was symptomatic of her state of mind. And, while Franka was screaming at her for being a fascist, I thought to myself, Yes, that's precisely why I fell in love with you: you had your little apartment, your little vegetarian snack bar and your little brain well under control. You could be tidy for both of us, and it was bliss for me to find my bearings at last. Even in the middle of the night I knew where I was and who I was – who I was with Claudia. She took me in hand and made a thorough clearance of my room in this world, which pleased her, because she likes tidy rooms. My weakness is her strength. But her weakness isn't *my* strength.

I'm now finding her idea of a tidy world more and more suspect because it has little to do with the truth. But Claudia doesn't want the truth, she wants neatness. Did she ever tidy *your* cell, Tulip Bulb?

Emotions . . . Oh, emotions are her favourite topic, and if I've got your number, you plump little Dutch tomato, you talked plenty about them with her. She likes that better than sex. It lasts longer, too. Best of all, though, she likes to talk about her own emotions. How she feels when someone has done or omitted to do something in particular: Have you any idea how I feel? Or, when addressing Franka and me: Have you any idea, the pair of you . . . ?

We're sternly interrogated like suspects at a police station. Standing there, mute and motionless, we have to admit we've no idea how Claudia is feeling. Our one certainty is that everything we do, absolutely everything, has an effect on her emotions.

So she asks, Have you any idea how I feel when you just watch television, when you fall asleep at once after coming, when you omit to call me, when you don't look at me, when you play no part in our family life? At first, of course, you wait tensely for her to answer her own question, but she never does.

Instead of that she stalks out of the room and sleeps on the sofa, or goes off to the health club, or meditates. But she never answers the question of how she really feels.

My desire for an answer has dwindled, to be honest, because Claudia's world seems to consist of a multitude of different emotions that succeed one another as rapidly as radio stations when you twiddle the knob like a madman. You're sitting back, relaxing to some tranquil classical music, when she abruptly switches to hip-hop, but no sooner have you adjusted to the rhythm than it's replaced by some easy listening, followed immediately by a jazz programme. So you never know what's coming and always do the wrong thing. And then it comes again: Have you any idea how I'm feeling . . . ?

Did she never ask *you* that, Tulip Bulb? If not, it's only because you're the great exception and have absolutely no effect on her emotions.

Dieting . . . You probably didn't get that far, the two of you, because the food in this dump is a slimming course in itself. Me, I've had to spend years putting up with the hundreds of different diets Claudia tackles whenever she's feeling unloved by me and, consequently, ugly and overweight. So every new diet she embarks on is really a veiled attack on me. She never announces them, just sits down at the dining table with Franka and me, looking studiously cheerful, nibbles a lettuce leaf, rabbit-like, and swears she isn't hungry. Meantime, Franka and I guiltily wolf our pizzas. She stirs sachets of powder into glasses of water and eats nothing but tofu or fruit, or no fruit at all and only potatoes, or separates carbohydrates from proteins, or eats proteins only. Whatever was previously essential is bound to be strictly prohibited the next time around.

It would be all the same to me if she decided to eat nothing but paper on the grounds that it's wholesome and environmentally friendly, as long as she didn't contrive to make me feel guilty every time.

She opens hostilities by declining to eat with me, and I fall into the trap again and again. I buy her a box of her favourite chocolates because I know she develops a craving for sweet things just before she menstruates – and suddenly she won't touch them any more. I get used to soya milk, and all at once protein is banned, even protein from soya beans. I stop grumbling at having to eat nothing but *crudités*, and suddenly only cooked vegetables are allowed. It can't be about losing a few pounds (which is absurd in any case, because she's got a good figure, and I never notice whether she's feeling fat or thin at any one moment), nor is it her health she's ostensibly trying to preserve with her diets – no, every diet is a declaration of war on *me*. I've failed. I haven't loved her sufficiently and correctly.

But you certainly didn't get that far either, the two of you . . .

Sleeplessness . . . How did you sleep? Unless that's your very first question each morning, you're insensitive and egocentric. Claudia always has an answer to that inquiry, for once, even if it tends to be the same one: Badly.

She's had disturbed nights ever since Franka was born. It's biological, she says: women sleep less soundly so that they hear their babies whimpering with hunger. Is it my imagination, or is she secretly reproaching me for having slept too soundly during Franka's infancy? When I think how often I cradled that fretful, querulous baby in my arms, walked it up and down the apartment, drove it around in the car . . .

Not enough, not often enough, Nothing I did was ever enough.

Claudia can't get off to sleep. She hears every sound, even our upstairs neighbours switching on the light – and I'm not joking. Consequently, she's dependent on earplugs, which muffle the click of the light switch but not my snoring. Nothing is proof against that, absolutely nothing. She's tried a white-noise machine, played non-stop waterfalls, oceanic surf and rainstorms of varying volume; for a while she stuck anti-snoring plasters on my nose; she's taken sleeping tablets and given me homoeopathic opiates; on my advice she's dissolved a little hashish in warm milk before going to sleep, worn acupressure plasters on her wrists, swallowed vast quantities of valerian, meditated, cut out protein for supper, listened to Mozart, loaded her thoughts into little ships and let them sail away, but no dice, nothing helps.

The awkward thing is, I don't share her sleepless nights. Nor does Franka. We both sleep like the dead. My conscience pricks me every morning because I've slept well and Claudia hasn't.

Being permanently tired, Claudia finds everything an effort. Her constant fatigue is as burdensome as an insidious disease because one always has to defer to her. All right? Can you manage? Not too tired? And gamely, oh so gamely, she replies, No, no, no problem, and smothers a yawn with difficulty.

But you two probably never feel tired when you're together. That's because you're the Enlightened Ones. I wish you lots of fun with my wife, you little gouda-gobbler – lots of fun. You've got a big surprise in store.

Theo's T-shirt is a blue blur rising and falling before my eyes in time to the Tibetan chant. I'm still swimming through a toxic sea of rage and hatred when I see Claudia walking naked through the apartment with a towel around her head and a cup of coffee in her hand. I see the dimples in her buttocks, see her long back and slender neck, see her lying on the lounger on our balcony, looking up at me, see her beneath me and above me. I smell her, and the next thing I know my prick is straining against my underpants.

Tubten Rinpoche stops chanting. Hell, he says, is yourselves, not other people. It's in your head – your mind, your mind . . . A long pause. Flies whizz through the air like thoughts running amok. But if your mind can create Hell, he goes on, why not Paradise? You must simply decide if you wish to be happy. And, when you've decided, you must simply practise happiness. He smiles, then rises abruptly. His disciples scramble to their feet in surprise and prostrate themselves three times, joints creaking, but he's already glided out of the tent.

I'm about to refocus on my hatred and jealousy and go look for Theo in the crowd because now's the time to have it out with him, when Franka excitedly grabs my arm and hauls me off, so I lose sight of him. She leads me around the shrine, and there is Pelge, collecting up Tubten Rinpoche's tea things. She nudges him gently. He straightens up, and we look into each other's eyes. His are alert and dark, wholly ageless and serene, damnably serene. I blink agitatedly.

My Dad, Franka says with a beaming smile.

I put out my hand. Instead of shaking it Pelge bows deeply, so I also incline my head a little. He looks at me intently and smiles. What's going on under that crew cut? What does he see in Franka? Does he admire her white skin? Her clumsiness? Her vociferousness? Her moods?

He makes a strangely dependable impression. I'd trust him like a shot with my wallet, but my daughter?

I nod at him shyly – this twenty-five-year-old Tibetan is actually making me feel shy! I grin, Franka grins, we all grin a little. There's obviously nothing to be said, so we go on grinning in silence. I listen to my breathing, and, whether or not it's the effect of the heat inside the tent, everything slows down a trifle and I'm quite content merely to breathe in and out and grin to myself. It's rather as if I'd smoked my head full of grass, which I haven't done for ages. So we stand there like that, calmly and contentedly, and after a while we all give another bow and go our separate ways.

Well, I really gave him a piece of my mind, didn't I? Claudia will chew me out. Instead of forbidding the youngster to make a play for our daughter, I bowed to him! I never even asked him if he's really a monk and where he stands from the vow-of-chastity angle. I simply stood there like a sheep, a contented sheep!

I stumble out of the tent into the dazzling sunshine and look around for Theo, but he's long gone, of course. It's a bit of a mental effort to rediscover my rage and jealousy. I seem to have mislaid them during that brief encounter with Pelge.

23

I KICK OPEN THE DOOR of our cell, action-movie fashion, and stand poised on the threshold *à la* Clint Eastwood. Theo is lying curled up on his mattress like a baby, fast asleep. The knotted mosquito net swings gently to and fro above him in the draught from the door. Bending low over him, I catch a faint whiff of my aftershave. Sweat-beaded forehead, freckled nose, fair stubble sprinkled with white. His bald patch is dotted with little moles like fly dirt. He must be roughly my age, no longer young but not yet old. He looks innocent and ageless in his sleep. I could throttle him, suffocate him with a pillow. His breath tickles my chin. He's snoring – almost inaudibly but unmistakably snoring. I feel relieved. Claudia would find it as hard to sleep with him as with me. He smiles. Perhaps he's dreaming of her.

I sit down on the floor. It's very quiet. It's always so quiet here. I feel my heart pound unpleasantly, feel thoughts and emotions stir within me like ants. They're conveyed along hidden channels to my brain, and from there back to my heart, my stomach, my mouth, my hands. I can even sense emotions in my feet. They feel singularly numb and unconnected to me.

My body has long been convinced that Claudia has had or is having an affair with Theo, I've only just noticed. I was blind and deaf like most cuckolds, but my body knew, and now it also knows what must be done. Only my brain still baulks at hitting a man while he's asleep.

I'll wake him first and then hit him. I've a sense of honour, after all. Theo's hands are in front of his face, but one side of his fat belly is exposed and unprotected. I experiment to see which would be better, a right or a left, and throw a couple of punches in the air. He must have felt the draught of them, because he opens his baby-blue eyes and stares at me in surprise.

I dive on to my mattress, fuming. He sits up and rubs his eyes. Got the time? he whispers. What time is it? Instead of yelling at him and beating him up, I obediently look at my watch and tell him, whispering likewise.

God verdomme! he exclaims. He pulls on his trousers and dashes to the door. Before leaving he turns and says, Explanation of the Five Precepts, and I, like a fool, put my name down for the third.

What's the third precept? I ask, though I really want to hit him.

Chastity, he replies with a grin, and he's gone before I know it.

The Five Precepts, he? I've no idea what that means. I'm only here to keep an eye on my enemy. The tent reeks of sweaty feet and mosquito repellent. Even the flies have wearied of the midday heat.

Mother Maya, Ueli, Theo, and two unknown women are sitting in the midst of the German group, reading loudly and emphatically from some rather tattered little books. The same thing is happening in English and French to right and left of me. Norbert raises a hand in greeting and the ugly twins from my Grasshopper Family give me a cheerful smile, as if I were really related to them. I reluctantly sit down again cross-legged, all my joints groaning in agony.

Mother Maya draws a deep breath and begins: Precept No.
1: You shall not kill. Take every opportunity to preserve life.
Engage in no activity harmful to human beings and your
natural surroundings.

Yes, well . . . Mother Maya goes on. Then I'll kick off. And
she describes how seven years ago she came back from India,
ill and all mixed up, and went to stay in Heidelberg with a
woman friend who had a dog she idolized. But the dog
detested Maya and Maya detested the dog. One day it jumped
up on Maya's bed, and Maya lost her temper: she grabbed the
animal and hurled it at the wall. When her friend came home
that afternoon, the dog started vomiting. She took it to the vet,
who diagnosed a fractured skull. How on earth had the dog
fractured its skull? Maya didn't breathe a word. The dog lived
on for a week or two, then died. The friend was inconsolable.

I killed it, and I've never told her to this day, Maya whispers,
fat tears rolling down her furrowed, hippy cheeks.

Everyone else stares at the ground in dismay. Me, I nearly
explode with mirth. I'm an evil man – totally devoid of
compassion for the little dog with the fractured skull and
Maya the murderess.

Maya hands the mike to Ueli, who mumbles in Swiss
German that he's a thief. He once filched a Swissair blanket,
cheated a restaurant over the number of bread rolls he'd eaten,
and actually pinched a yellow Ricard bottle from a bistro en
route to the meditation centre. It was so pretty, he pleads in
mitigation.

The Five Precepts appear to be a Buddhistic version of the
Ten Commandments. Killing and stealing we've already had.
What comes next? Thou shalt not covet thy neighbour's Golf
GTI, nor his wife, nor his detached house with swimming pool
and sauna? Ueli passes the mike to Theo, and I reluctantly note
that my heart is beating faster.

Theo reads aloud with his head bowed. Precept No. 3: Sex

must not be devoid of love and long-term commitment. Be aware of how much suffering your actions can cause.

He inserts a long pause for effect, and his bald patch turns lobster red. You tomato, I think. You Dutch hothouse tomato, you!

I'm obsessed, he says. Obsessed with a woman. I think it's love, but I wonder where in my body that love resides. Sex without the head would be little different from picking your nose. Everything happens in the head – the mind, the mind, he says, smiling faintly. For the last four months or so, my head has been filled with this person. I want her more than I've ever wanted any woman.

I hear myself snort like a bull. My immediate neighbour glances at me anxiously.

This woman, says Theo, is not my wife. She belongs to someone else. I've got a wife myself. We've been married a long time – happily married. That's why I don't understand how this other woman could have entered my head. Not a second goes by that I don't think of her, yet she's no better-looking than my wife, no younger, no more intelligent. No better in bed, either.

My neighbour lays a hand on my arm. Everything all right? she whispers. Idiotically, I blush as if everyone's about to point at me, laugh at me for being a cuckold. Everything really okay? asks my neighbour. I nod and shut my eyes to keep her at bay. Eyes closed, I listen to Theo talking about my wife. His Dutch accent sugars all he says in a repulsively cloying way.

I don't know what it is about this woman, he says, but when I think of her I'm torn apart with desire. I'm hurting my wife, but I can't help it. My head does what it wants with me. Biochemists claim we're attracted to each other by certain olfactory substances, and that when we fall in love or commit adultery we're only going in search of the best possible genetic material; psychotherapists would probably tell me I was going in search of my mother . . . I only know I want to be with her come what may.

Opening my eyes, I see that Theo has gone pale as death. I beg my wife's pardon, he says quietly, and bows his head.

I can't follow Buddha's advice to sever all attachments and quench all desires, to hold on to nothing so as to reduce the suffering of all, he goes on, breathing heavily, because I *want* to cling to that other woman. I want to hold on to her with all my might, so I cause suffering. What am I to do? He scans our faces as if asking us to help him change a tyre.

I hate him with fervour, because he's making me suffer as well as Antje, and I'm unconsoled by the fact that my thoughts were the same as his precisely four months ago, during my daily sessions in bed with Marisol. This obsession, I said to myself at the time, where does it spring from? What corner of my brain produces it and why, when the end result is suffering for all concerned? It was an almost masochistic pleasure, like the sensation when your tongue keeps probing a painful tooth although you know it only aggravates the pain.

My neighbour – the one who has just been so concerned for my welfare – puts her hand up. A woman in her early thirties with long brown hair, she could look pretty if she removed her incipient moustache, wore a bra, and used a bit of make-up. The sun irradiates her shapeless green smock as she stands up, and I can clearly see her thighs.

Well, she says with a bright smile, I haven't had sex for three years, and I feel much better and more liberated without it. If I ever do miss it once in a while – she giggles and puts her hands over her face – I go out on my balcony at night, stark naked. I live in a Berlin high-rise. When the wind blows and caresses my body, it's better than sex.

She nods to Theo and sits down. Theo gives her a feeble smile, and I'm surprised to feel a surge of sympathy and affection for him. We're comrades in misfortune. No one here understood what he was talking about. What's he supposed to do, stand naked on a balcony in Amsterdam?

Me too, perhaps? Are the big-city balconies of the Western world destined to be thronged with naked men and women? Are we all to do it exclusively with the wind from now on? They're living in a dream, these people. Life without sex? Come on, Theo, let's go and drown our sorrows in a glass of red wine – a little glass, as you would put it.

Theo reaches under his T-shirt and my spark of solidarity is extinguished in a trice because I suddenly feel Claudia's hand on my chest and then on his, feel her squeeze my nipples and then his. With a smothered cry I spring to my feet, inadvertently treading on the toes of my neighbour from Berlin, who also gives a yelp, and then, to the utter amazement of all present, dash out of the tent.

24

I FIND ANTJE ON THE terrace. She's sitting over a mug of hibiscus tea, looking small and tearful. I'm glad the ban on speech prevails outside the tent so I don't have to say or explain anything. I sit down opposite her and mutely put out a hand to comfort her and myself at the same time. We're alone. Everyone else is sitting in the tent, listening to our common story as an instance of sexual aberration. Outside here, none of it seems true. Bees hum, a cat saunters slowly past, followed a little later, with equal silent grace, by the preternaturally beautiful nun from the reception tent.

I instinctively try to withdraw my hand from Antje's as an indication to the beautiful nun that I'm still available – what a libidinous, sexist pig I am! – but Antje hangs on tight. So we sit there like an item, and the beautiful nun gives us a friendly nod and glides off.

After a while it gets a bit sticky and sweaty under Antje's hand, so I turn it over and take hold of hers instead. Construing this as an invitation, she gets up and tows me behind her to the camp site.

We lie down on the bare ground inside a tiny sky-blue tent. I can feel every pebble in the small of my back. Antje clearly has no time for padded mattresses. The stuffy little tent smells of rubber and deodorant, and I find it hard to concentrate.

Antje's plaits swing to the rhythm of her movements. The lovely, honey-coloured eyes that lured me here are shut. She bites her lips and growls like a dog.

I myself do nothing. She has fended off my hands and folded them under my head. I watch her, completely detached from the whole proceedings. She hasn't disrobed. Still in her white dress, she rises and falls above me like a cyclist toiling up a steep hill. All the Dutch ride bicycles, after all. My mind's eye is haunted by images of Dutch people flitting past tulip fields on bicycles.

I'm Antje's bicycle. I'm working all right, that's not the problem. Everything's working the way it should, yet it isn't. Her husband would probably call it nose-picking. Lack of 'commitment', maybe that's the trouble. I feel sorry for her, toiling away on top of me all alone, and since we're making no progress I clasp her round the waist and, with considerable difficulty, manoeuvre her on to her back. This doesn't appeal to her in the least, judging by her little grunt of disapproval. Gravity ultimately prevails, however, and I end up aboard her. Now it's my turn to get cycling, which I don't feel like doing in this heat. What's more, little pebbles are digging painfully into my kneecaps. But the friction intensifies notwithstanding, and light looms at the end of the tunnel. She looks up at me mistrustfully. My every thrust propels her head a little nearer the wall of the tent, which begins to bulge. I redouble my movements. She shuts her eyes again and leaves me to it.

I yearn for the moment when I'll forget about the pebbles and cease to think altogether, and while I'm pumping up and down with my eyes shut, sweating profusely, it occurs to me that I've already forgotten what she looks like, this person I'm inside. I've got two choices: I can either find this fact titillating and carry on, or behave like an enlightened modern man. The latter course of action doesn't appeal to me, to be honest, but I've already acquired a bee in the bonnet – a forbidden subject

I can't help thinking about – and I know that the whole performance will come to nothing. I dutifully persevere, though. I open my eyes and look down at Antje, whose head is being rhythmically thrust against the side of the tent. She looks up at me and says, in a down-to-earth voice, It's no good.

I roll off and lie panting beside her, mop my sweaty forehead on my T-shirt. It's like being inside a blue balloon, lying there wedged together side by side. Life is going on around us, but we're prisoners of the craving to be liberated from ourselves by someone else.

I'm sorry, I say.

She flaps a hand in the air. Oh well, she says vaguely.

We listen to the surrounding noises. Footsteps crunching on gravel, a child bawling, a bumblebee buzzing round the tent.

The nearest you get to a state of enlightenment, says Antje, is when you're sneezing, dying, or having an orgasm. During those brief moments, you cease to hold on to anything.

And you can do all three on your own, I say.

True, she says, sounding surprised.

A philosophy for autists, I say.

She sighs. It just didn't work.

I'm sorry, I say again.

It was my fault, she says sadly.

No, mine, I say quickly, and long for Marisol. She used to liberate me, at least for brief moments.

A figure approaches the tent's blue wall in silhouette and taps on it. Antje?

She replies in Dutch. I recognize the voice as Theo's and hold my breath. She opens the flap a crack and puts her head out. I glimpse a patch of Theo's bare leg and red cycling shorts and some wheel spokes. He can't see me. With a pounding heart I wonder whether to make my presence known and do to him what he's done to me. It would hit him harder than any

169

fist. Is that my only reason for being here, sheer vindictiveness? And I didn't even manage it? What a miserable failure I am!

A brief exchange in Dutch. Then Antje withdraws her head and I hear him pedal off.

He rides that bike of his so as not to explode with lust for that woman, Antje says contemptuously. He rides it all the time – it's absurd. And I loathe those shorts he wears, she blurts out.

She regards me thoughtfully for a bit, then pulls her dress up over her head. I'm scared. She unhooks the cheap white bra she's wearing and shakes it off, then lies down beside me and takes my prick in her hand. Squeezes it like the bulb of a cycle hooter. Nothing happens. Why not? Why not with her? With Marisol, the very idea would have been enough. Maybe because Marisol was so young and so free from the wounds that gather on ageing people like a personal garbage dump on which we crouch all our lives, forever rooting around in it like vultures. That really hurt me, we say. I'll never get over this or that or the other. And we crane our long necks and peer enviously at those whose garbage dumps of sorrow are still small, or who have made some mysterious deal with the refuse collectors.

Maybe that's what makes the nuns and monks in this place seem so weightless: renunciation of the past and abstention from hopes for the future. Maybe that's it.

Happiness is where you find it, that's what my mother always says. I've never really understood that. I understand the words but I fail to understand how you *do* it.

Happiness is where you find it, I say aloud.

Antje stops short and lets go of my prick. What?

Do you understand that?

She thinks for a moment, then sits up and puts her bra on again. When you're happy, she says, the next dose of happiness comes by itself. And if you aren't, you won't be. Something like that, maybe, she says.

She turns and looks down at me, the abject failure. Her gaze travels from my genitals, via my chest, to my face. She tosses back her plaits and sighs.

I run my hand gently over her back, but she shrinks away and buttons up her dress. I'd so much like to be happy again, she says softly, but my happiness depends on Theo. She smooths her skirt down.

I put my T-shirt on again. I'm furious, furious with all of us. Why should we be so unhappy? What an idiotic luxury! What self-pity!

Listen, I say fiercely, grabbing her by the arm, that Theo of yours is screwing . . . . . . my wife! I want to say, but at the last moment I bite my tongue because she'd be bound to construe the fact that I've been lying naked in her tent as a lousy little attempt to get my own back, nothing more.

So I say, Theo is screwing around a bit, that's all. He still thinks it's love, but it'll soon be over, believe me. Nothing lasts.

But I can't wait for everything to be over, not for ever! she cries angrily.

I know what I'm talking about, I say.

But if nothing lasts my love will also be over some day!

Probably, I say coldly.

Oh, you . . . she fumes. You . . . you're a cynical asshole.

All unsatisfied women take it out on you. They start off being sympathetic, but you only have to count to ten, slowly, and out it comes.

She unzips the flap, crawls out, and stomps off in a huff.

25

I WRIGGLE OUT OF THE tent, which is near the edge of the woods, and go behind a tree in my bare feet. I'm about to take a leak when I see Norbert and the celestial blue-eyed nun walking in slow motion along a forest path. They're so close together it looks like they're holding hands.

Putting one foot before the other, slowly and in step, they glide out of sight.

They're doing the right thing, I tell myself angrily, gliding through the woods instead of screwing. At least they're immune to disappointment. Norbert's white legs gleam in the dimness under the trees. Norbert the Man of Sorrows seems to be radiant with happiness. Envy gnaws me like a voracious rat. Everyone else is doing fine; I alone am a sexual and spiritual zero. I'm so disconsolate I feel I'll never get over it.

Claudia, I hear myself whisper, help me, Claudia.

But she isn't here, and I'm so unhappy I don't know what to do with myself. I scuff my bare feet on the pine needles, feel them gently prick my soles, feel the sticky resin. Maybe I ought to try that idiotic, gliding walk.

I turn to see if anyone is watching, but the only person in sight is tinkering with his tent in the distance. Cautiously, I put one foot before the other. The forest floor is soft and yielding.

No one's watching, so I grow bolder. One step, one breath. In, out, one step at a time . . .

I think I was a boy the last time I walked barefoot through a wood. Dry leaves and little twigs crackle beneath my feet, the moss is cool and moist, but sometimes my soles detect sun-warmed patches. In, out . . . It's far from difficult, except that at this speed I sway like a drunk. It's better if I concentrate on breathing alone. I make my way slowly into the wood, step by step, and all at once I genuinely feel I'm floating a little.

I chuckle, I'm so surprised, and float on. One step, one breath, after another. Thoughts and emotions fall off me like flakes of old skin. I let them lie, make no attempt to retrieve them, leave my garbage dump behind. One step after another . . .

I go on and on. After a while I cease to think about coordinating my lungs and my legs. I simply walk. Nothing exists but me and this wood. Before long, all that's left is the wood, the yielding ground, the air's variations in temperature depending on the density of the trees, the silvery threads of backlit spiders' webs, bird calls, the hum of insects. I walk on, oblivious of myself, and notice to my amazement that I'm happy – happy for no reason, which suddenly strikes me as the greatest happiness of all. It has no provenance other than the fact that I'm *here in the present*.

I've got it, I think, I've grasped it at last! But that thought is like a quicksand that swiftly swallows up my new-found happiness. It seems that thinking spells the end of happiness. Each thought tows another in its wake, and already I'm aware of a varicose vein in my calf, mindful of my body's inexorable decay, of my age, my ever-increasing misery. I've lost my wife and my daughter, and I've been racking my brain for the name of our tax consultant for days. I'm just a scrapheap. I belong on the garbage dump. My happiness of a nanosecond ago is as remote as the North Pole. Your mind, your mind . . .

Tired out, I flop down in a grassy clearing. There's a little road in the distance. I can hardly remember the happiness I felt just now. I went shuffling through the wood like an idiot. I fell for their tricks. It hasn't helped at all, not really. All I feel now is depressed and lonely.

I've never managed to develop a liking for solitude. It always seems to be creeping up on me. I find it eerie and unpleasant. I don't like it. It sits down beside me and regards me derisively. Well, it says, am I making you feel uneasy? Don't you know how to cope with me on your own?

Solitude has always made me try to distract myself. In the old days with women, later with work, now with women again. This seems to be the normal thing with most men of my age, and we all know it doesn't work. I need a cigarette. Now, this minute. I jump up, light one, and make for the road.

A decrepit Renault drives past with a nun at the wheel. Like a schoolkid I hide the cigarette behind my back. The nun raises a hand and gives a little bow. I bow likewise, quickly and clumsily, but she's already gone by. The hot asphalt burns my bare feet, compelling me to walk faster.

I take refuge in the shade of a plane tree and lean against its silvery trunk. A cyclist comes speeding along the road. I recognize him by his red cycling shorts. It's Theo. I dodge behind the tree, hear him pant and change gear with a click as he rides past.

The sight of him promptly makes my blood boil, as if I'd replaced my saucepanful of rage on a hotplate.

The rubber tyres make a sucking sound on the hot asphalt. Rubber . . . Did the bastard at least use a condom? My brain seizes on every opportunity to torment me. It never occurred to me to use one with Antje, not for a moment. I can't bring myself to use them with certain women, it's such a peculiar form of mistrust. Yet I always carry a couple in my wallet and replenish my stock at once whenever I've used one, in case

174

Claudia finds out. Carrying condoms is simply prudent and sensible in this day and age, but it's just as *im*prudent to have two in your wallet one day and only one the next.

When Theo is out of sight I trot back along the road to the meditation centre. I'm bragging. I'm bragging to myself, just because Theo came by. I've only once used a condom from my stock (discounting Marisol, who always keeps some of her own), and that was at a fastfood conference in Berlin. A Burger King representative with silicone breasts that felt unpleasantly like tennis balls and were highly uncomfortable to lie on.

My future is becoming ever more predictable. I may only use another twenty-three condoms in my life; clean my own teeth another twelve thousand times or so, if all goes well; lose my front-door key some forty-eight times more before I'm finally relieved of it; survive thirty-nine colds; and cop another hundred and fifty-six parking tickets. My emotions will wear out like my joints, my scrotum hang lower and lower until it dangles against my knees, and the rest of me, too, will cease to do my bidding any more. *What goes up must come down*, sings Tom Petty. I've rediscovered that here with the Buddhists: what was high will be low, what was plenty will be scanty, what was full will be empty. Great prospect.

I'm afraid, and all that has ever dispelled my fear from time to time is Marisol. Fucking, the only remedy for death. Maybe it's as simple as that.

I'm slow to catch sight of the bicycle in the road, and even slower to see the figure beside it. I recognize the red cycling shorts. He's down on his knees with his forehead touching the asphalt like the Pope on a world tour, motionless. I debate whether to turn and run, but my legs are already propelling me towards him.

Hey, Theo! I call. What's this, performing your devotions in the middle of the road? I laugh, but my voice sounds forced and uneasy. I can hear my own breathing. It sounds unnaturally loud, in, out, in, out. One step, then another. I reach his side and tap him on the shoulder – very gently, but he topples over like a log, slumps on his side with a dull thud, legs bent and eyes wide open, staring at me in surprise.

Mort, I tell the truck driver, *mort*. I say that one word over and over, *mort, mort, mort*, until the young man in the greasy blue overalls gives me a cigarette. My hand, the one that's holding the cigarette, is trembling. It's a Gauloise, and it tastes strangely different, unlike any cigarette I've ever smoked in my life. I inhale the smoke avidly.

The young man watches me for three drags, then jerks his head at Theo, goes over to him, and grabs him by the ankles.

All my thoughts are subject to a time lag, as if they had to circle the globe before returning to me and becoming comprehensible. I take hold of Theo's wrists, and together we carry him to the grassy verge. Theo's hands are warm, his body is as heavy as a sack of potatoes. A little book falls out of his windcheater. I stoop and pick it up. We lower Theo gently on to the grass. There's no need to treat his body with care, we know that perfectly well, but we're too solicitous of our own bodies to admit it to ourselves.

The truck driver summons an ambulance by radio.

I crouch down beside Theo, who isn't Theo any longer. I can remember this feeling. I was there when my father died. My father was no longer in my father's body, but elsewhere – liberated and redeemed. It was fundamentally beautiful, that moment, for my dead father and for me, the living. Gravity, time and space were all suspended for that one brief moment. Past and future were no more. For one tiny instant we were both free.

So too, here in the South of France, time now stands still – time that contains all we crave and flee from. We're rooted to the spot, Theo, time, and me, and reality enjoys a momentary respite from suffering.

I don't understand a word. The truck driver is saying something in French. He's got bad teeth and big hands with which to gesticulate against the unnaturally blue sky. He goes over to Theo, bends down, and briefly, firmly, closes his eyes with a big paw that's bound to reek of tobacco smoke.

Oh God, I really might have thought of that myself. I feel ashamed. My normal human instincts have atrophied completely.

The young man walks back to his truck and climbs into the cab. He puts his arm out of the window and give me a cursory wave, then starts up and drives off. I call after him, feeling bewildered and rather nervous. He waves again, then disappears round the next bend.

I look at Theo lying there in the brilliant sunlight. Biting into his thick neck is the red woollen thread, the benedictory thread that Claudia wears too.

Will she weep, will she break down? I pull off my T-shirt and drape it over Theo. I feel an urge to call Claudia, but only to have her comfort me, not to have to hear her weep aloud.

Theo, I say, you stupid idiot. I wanted to beat you up, and you wanted to love my wife – and your own, a little. You can't just check out and leave me alone with the two of them. They don't like me the way they like you. I can't give them what they want. What do you do to women? What can you do that I can't? What *could* you do, I mean. What was it? Whatever it was, it's beyond me. I'm lonely and I make other people lonely. You should sympathize with me. I'm an asshole.

I fall silent. The sun is scorching my shoulders. I ought to put my T-shirt on again, but then Theo would get sunburn, and that strikes me as macabre. I grope in my pocket and extract the little book that fell out of Theo's windcheater. It's an edition of Shakespeare's Sonnets.

My mistress' eyes are nothing like the sun; coral is far more red than her lips' red, I read. *Such is my love, to thee I so belong, that for thy right myself will bear all wrong.* Did you read that aloud to Claudia? Why do you believe in love so much, Theo? I lie back on the grass and read Theo one sonnet after another, and after the sixth the ambulance comes at last.

The fat, sweating driver talks volubly at me and brandishes various forms under my nose for me to fill in. What was my relationship to the deceased? *Ami*, I reply, feeling magnanimous. *Un ami*.

They heave Theo into the vehicle and insist on my accompanying him. I'll have to, I suppose, or no one will know where he is.

I'm thrown around, we take the bends so fast. The other ambulance man, who's very much younger, points to my shoulders, which are red with sunburn. They've removed Theo's windcheater. The young man feels in the pockets and hands me a mobile phone, Theo's mobile, and a key.

Mechanically, I toy with the mobile. I access the menu, and before I know it I've brought up the numbers most recently called. The very last one, timed at 15:00 this afternoon, looks familiar. It's mine – my own Munich phone number. But it may be a mistake – it's only a number, after all. I press the selector button and the display blithely lights up: *Claudia calling*, it announces, just like mine.

And there she is. Hello, she says, breathlessly as usual, as if she's only just come in. I kill the connection. A moment later I start retching. I sit there beside my wife's dead lover, vomiting, while the young ambulance man, with a practised hand, holds a green plastic bag under my chin.

26

A TOTALLY UNHERALDED HEART ATTACK. Antje can't believe it. She laughs. Theo never ate red meat, she says.
He always went in for sports, used to swim every other day,
then took up cycling. He meditated, didn't drink, didn't
smoke. There must be some mistake.

I forbear to tell her that he cadged a couple of cigarettes off
me and probably only abstained from smoking in her presence. She seems to be in shock, prattles away cheerfully to
herself. The rest of us say nothing because it's late by now, and
the silence curfew is technically in force. Like a little covey of
conspirators we sit cheek by jowl in our cell in the House of
the Full Moon, listening to Antje: Norbert, Franka, and I –
plus Pelge. Tubten Rinpoche has decreed that Pelge mustn't
budge from Antje's side, so Norbert and I have been politely
requested to move into her tent while Pelge – and Franka, it
seems – take over our cell and look after the widow.

Franka has fetched Antje's rucksack from the tent, gathered
Theo's clothes and books together, and stacked them neatly in
a corner. She has also remade the bed and placed a small
bunch of flowers beside it.

In Pelge's presence my daughter makes a mature, enviably
composed impression. I, on the other hand, am a bundle of
nerves.

You're trembling, Antje says sympathetically. Why are you trembling? She stares uneasily at each of us in turn. Why look so sad, all of you? He's better off now, she goes on quickly, brightly. Oh yes, he's definitely better off. He found the world a trial. He always found life a trial. Life and me—me especially. A smile flits across her face like a nervous tic. I don't think dying's so bad, is it? It isn't, is it?

She reaches for Pelge's hand. He's sitting there quietly, listening to her without understanding a word because she's talking to us in German.

You're always telling us that everything is in a state of flux, she goes on excitedly. That there's no beginning and no end, I mean.

Pelge just looks at her and strokes her hand.

So this is how I imagine it, says Antje. It's as if a light comes on and everything goes bright, very, very bright, and you enter a wonderful radiance and dissolve into it. Surely that's what they always say, the people who've almost died and had these – she snaps her fingers impatiently – these near-death experiences. He looked contented, too, isn't that what you said, Fred?

I give a cautious nod.

Was he smiling?

I don't reply because of the rule of silence. Franka and Pelge are strictly observing it, and I myself find it genuinely welcome in present circumstances, not knowing what I *could* say. I never know what to say in any case. I'm as dumb, in both senses of the word, as a fish. Maybe I should lie. Maybe I should tell her that Theo looked contented when his face was completely blank. Death had wiped it as clean as an empty blackboard. There was nothing left, nothing at all.

But Tubten Rinpoche says that everything changes, Antje goes on. It's simply different – not the same as before. Theo's dead. That's different, so I must change too because everything else has.

She giggles helplessly. Pelge motions to Norbert and me to leave. We obey with alacrity, perform a cursory bow in the doorway and escape.

It's a clear, starry night. The cicadas are busy sawing, everyone else is asleep by now. The big cauldron is steaming away in solitude on the terrace. We make ourselves some hibiscus tea.

Theo always fetched himself some hot water for his vacuum flask at night, Norbert says under his breath. What does he mean, 'always'? We've only been here three days.

Three days is as long as thirty elsewhere. Time comes free of charge in this place. If you run short, all you have to do is stop and do nothing, and – hey presto!—you've got a superabundance of the stuff.

What should we do now? Norbert whispers.

I'm exhausted and in turmoil at the same time. I nurse my cup with trembling hands. We could meditate a bit, I say.

Norbert stares at me as if I'm a reformed alcoholic trying to sell him a fruit-juice cocktail.

We sit down in the wood just behind the tent. It's pitch dark now. The sky has clouded over, the wind is whistling through the treetops and making the branches creak. I feel my heart pound with agitation and bewilderment. I'd like to run away—away from the ultimate compulsion to relinquish everything: one's hair, one's teeth, one's health, the people one loves, one's life, even my brand-new iMac. It might have been me lying in the road today. Wham, out of the blue. I've no wish to relinquish anything at all, and it won't be long before my reluctance to do so makes me as ludicrous as a seventy-year-old woman in a suspender belt.

My breathing is as tremulous as my whole body, but I breathe on, on and on, the way I did when walking through the wood today. And at some stage, an eternity later, I stop trembling and the wind no longer seems to be blowing around me but straight through me, through my already heavily calcified skeleton: Fred's skeleton. There he is again, that green bag of bones from the shoe shop's X-ray machine. He's all that remains, but for the first time he isn't menacing but really quite peaceable, and at this moment I relinquish all I possess – every last thing, and it isn't so bad after all. I relinquish it willingly because I, Fred, appear to consist of something more than flesh and bone. I realize that the world sees me, not just the other way round – that I exist only because everything else does. All at once, the prison gates swing open.

Hey, says Norbert, everything OK?

Surprised, I open my eyes. All I can see in front of me is his dark silhouette. I smell his grimy jeans and hear myself sob, sob without tears like a man in a dream.

Everything OK? Norbert repeats, laying a hand on my shoulder, and I hurl myself at his bony chest like a three-year-old.

Man, oh man, says Norbert, and again: Man, oh man.

Norbert's feet smell as diabolical as ever. I'm lying inside Antje's little blue tent in exactly the same spot as I occupied some ten hours ago. Leaden fatigue permeates my body like black treacle. Sleep, just sleep and stop thinking. No more emotions, please, and no more tears. Women, who are forever indulging in them, lead a damnably tiring life.

I saw some angels once, Norbert says softly. Oh, please not. Not another New Age angel story – not that too, I couldn't take it, not tonight. I groan.

No, really, says Norbert, even if you don't believe it. The three children who died in that explosion at the school were teenagers, pale, body-pierced, hair dyed black, et cetera. They always looked as if they'd come straight from Hell.

Like Franka, I murmur.

Yes, like your daughter. A girl and two boys. Well, I saw them after their death, at the supermarket. I was wheeling my trolley around the milk and yoghurt island, and there they were, all three of them. They looked exactly the same as before, only friendlier. They smiled at me. Like angels, they smiled. They never smiled when they were alive – never. Just goggled at me sullenly, like fish in an aquarium. But now they were angels their true nature came out. They smiled and looked happy. Well, maybe not happy, but contented. They looked as though they lacked for nothing. Please, I begged them, please show yourselves to your parents like this, it would be such a comfort. They just smiled, though. They didn't speak.

Hm, I grunt.

You don't believe me, huh?

Of course, I say sleepily with my eyes shut.

My feet are rather smelly, says Norbert. They are, aren't they?

No, I tell him, not a bit. Don't worry.

27

THIS MORNING I ALMOST enjoy shuffling to the meditation tent in the first pink glow of dawn, half asleep, there to assume the fakir position and spend an hour and a half watching my thoughts cascade like an endless waterfall. I've no need to say or do anything. It's TV without a TV set, that's all. There are brief periods of calm interspersed with moments when I'm unexpectedly swept along by my thoughts into wild whirlpools from which I emerge bemused and exhausted (it's usually my aching knees that save me from drowning); yet there are also, again and again, moments of peace more profound than I have ever known. I'd like to sit here for all eternity; any other prospect fills me with dread. Claudia still doesn't know of Theo's death – I've turned off my mobile – and even Antje hasn't really taken it in.

Her brain is still travelling along its old orbit, rejecting change. How sluggish our thoughts and emotions are, when they ought to be accustoming themselves to altered circumstances. Just as we rummage a hundred times in the kitchen drawer where the potato peeler used to be, although it has long been kept elsewhere, and just as we still feel the hat on our head, although we removed it minutes ago, so the dead live on for an agonizing length of time. When I open my eyes I see Theo sitting in his usual place in the meditation tent, up front in the sixth row and a little to my right. He's wearing his blue T-shirt, I can see him quite clearly.

After showering I stare at my face in the mirror for a long time. I can clearly discern the skull beneath the increasingly flaccid skin, the deep eye sockets, the prominent cheekbones, the jaws and the teeth with their numerous gold crowns. *This is the end, the very end, my friend*, I sing, and promptly earn myself a look of reproof from a youngster with flaxen stubble and a muscular chest. His skeleton isn't discernible yet, least of all to himself. I flee into the loo to be alone – you can't be alone anywhere else in this place – and stare dejectedly at the notice: *Brothers and sisters, kindly refrain from putting paper in the toilet. It can cause blockages!*

Be happy, you schmuck, I whisper to myself, but it's no use. The prison gates have shut again.

The Grasshopper Family has turned up en masse for the wake in the hospital's tiny chapel: Maya in a shapeless white smock, the ugly twins Renate and Ilse in their perpetual apple green and orange, Nhiem the emaciated monk, the young couple, Giovanni and Ingeborg, and the yoga teacher. Also present are Franka, Pelge, Norbert with his flute, and, naturally, Antje. She's clinging, like a drowning woman, to a bunch of wild flowers. Her eyes are huge, her skin is taut and translucent as a tambourine. Mourning becomes her.

Would some guy think that of Claudia if I were the one lying on the cold steel bier instead of Theo? He's still wearing the red cycling shorts Antje can't abide, and he doesn't look dead, although he hasn't been made up, just unhealthily pale.

We squeeze into the sweltering little room. Antje steps forward and deposits her bunch of flowers on Theo's chest. She says something to him in Dutch. It sounds reproachful and angry. She turns away and rejoins us.

Pelge reads the heart sutra aloud in soft, sing-song Tibetan, and Maya repeats it in German:

185

Form is emptiness, emptiness is form, form is no different from emptiness, emptiness is no different from form. She goes on to say that nothing comes into being and nothing perishes, that nothing increases and nothing diminishes – *What goes up, must come down*, thanks, Tom Petty, put like that I find it a bit more comprehensible – that suffering neither comes into being nor passes away. Meaning that nothing exists at all, or what?

Form is like waves and emptiness like water, says Pelge. Waves are water and water is waves at one and the same time. Waves turn back into water just as water turns back into waves. He says it in his ever cheerful-sounding Indian English – *Wave is water, water is wave* – and it sounds so simple.

I imagine I now understand what he means, and I feel comforted for the first time in my life. I, Fred, am not only Fred the wave but also the Lake of Geneva and the North Sea and the Pacific Ocean. I'm more than my outward form, more than the varicose vein in my left calf, my meagre biceps and my only medium-sized penis. I only make life difficult for myself if I constantly limit, compare and defend my outward form as Fred. It's all nonsense, because it seems that, once I'm dead, my molecules will also be simultaneously present in my sofa, a daisy, and my daughter.

What applies to me must also, I suppose, apply to dead Theo. I only see his outward form because that's the way I've learned to perceive things. I don't see him as a flower, a tree, a giraffe, an ant, a cigarette, or vanilla blancmange – and according to Pelge, I suppose, he's now all of those things. When you're everything, things really aren't that bad.

I sigh with relief, and they all turn to look. But if Theo is everything else as well, is he also Fred? Is Theo now a part of me? Am I Theo? Just a minute, Pelge, fair's fair, but isn't there a limit to this business?

A fly circles Theo's nose and eventually lands on the tip. Although I'm well aware that this fly on the tip of Theo's erstwhile nose is a matter of complete indifference to him, I still wonder why he doesn't brush it off. Why doesn't he shoo it away with a twitch of the hand? Why doesn't he at least wrinkle his nose and persuade it to take off? It's tormenting to see how the fly roams calmly over his nose and nothing happens. I can literally feel the fly's tiny legs on my own nose, and I grow restive.

What was that about form and emptiness? Is Theo the fly on his own lifeless nose as well? No sooner have I captured that realization than it evaporates.

Pelge is singing in Tibetan, and the veterans – Maya, Nhiem, the twins, and Ingeborg – all join in with a will. I'm starting to feel queasy in this heat. I can smell Renate and Ilse's cloying deodorant, Ingeborg's BO, and, along with all the other smells, the strange effluvium of death.

I want to get out of here. Emptiness and form are neither here nor there, I must get out. I elbow Norbert aside, squeeze past Antje to the door, and gain the open air.

I draw in a big lungful of cigarette smoke. Oleanders are blossoming pinkly in the hospital garden, people in bath-robes sitting on benches with surgical stockings on their legs and drip-stands beside them. They look sadder than dead Theo. Their outward form is suffering, it hurts and tor-ments them. What would the Buddhist say? Aren't I their outward form? Am I a daisy? Anyone who remains a prisoner of his silly little vaselike human form suffers twice as much. I find that as clear as daylight, but this eternal transcendence is so tiring.

A buxom young woman in a blue smock passes close to me, pushing an old man in a wheelchair. Closer inspection reveals that the man isn't so old after all, in his mid-fifties at most. I often do that: Good heavens, I say to myself, isn't he or she old? – and they turn out to be only a few years older than me.

Conversely, there are people I've thought of for years as old who are now growing perceptibly younger.

The young woman smiles at me. I return the smile uncertainly. She goes by, haunches swinging like a bell under her smock, and I know they're swinging for me.

A few minutes later she comes back without the wheelchair. She gives me another smile and cocks her head a trifle. Like an obedient puppy I follow her along the neatly raked paths flanked by unhappy patients. I've only one thing in mind, one thing only. I notice to my relief that I'm filled with a single instinct, like an airship with helium: desire, lust – hurrah, nothing else. For a man, there's nothing finer than an unexpected offer of sex – it's like someone handing around sweets at a bus stop. She turns off toward the chapel in which everyone else is still keeping watch over Theo's dead body. I follow her. She smiles at me alluringly over her shoulder, opens a heavy wooden door, disappears into the gloomy room beyond, and shuts the door in my face.

What the devil did I think would happen?

This is what I thought: Through a small window, a shaft of sunlight slants down, spearlike, into a cool, dim room. Please don't think, I entreat my brain, please don't think, and it does me the favour. I can hear Pelge's Tibetan chanting in the distance and adapt my rhythm to it. Yes, yes, yes, this is better than meditation, better than anything else – it's redemption, yes, yes, *yes*! And then it's over. We're scarcely out of breath. She stoops to pull up her panties with a polite little smile, smooths her smock down, and leaves the room without a word.

Yes, that's the way I imagined it.

I return to the chapel as if I'd simply nipped out for a pee. Norbert takes his flute from the leather case and plays an *Ave Maria*. He plays pretty well, though I can't tell if Theo liked it.

Antje starts crying. The message has sunk in, she's starting to cry at last. Franka, my little Franka, goes over and puts her arms round her. She looks at Pelge as she does so, at his utterly serene face, and lets Antje cry. She doesn't shush her or offer her a handkerchief or hug her tight, she simply lets things take their course.

I couldn't do that. That's why I can't fathom how this mature, magnificent young woman could have been lurking, like a butterfly in a grey cocoon, inside the sullen, belligerent teenager of my recollection. I feel ashamed of my blindness. There it is again, the outward form I'm forever being taken in by. Conversely, however, Franka is taken in by my own outward form, by the father she may not think much of, but of whom she would never, ever, dream that his dearest wish just now was to fuck a nurse he didn't know from Eve. Never, it seems to me, have I ever been so mixed up and immature. Even as a teenager I had a better grip on my life than I do now.

We're sitting in the big tent with all the others. Tubten Rinpoche is silent. Antje is sitting in the front row. He may have something to say to me, she told me with a timid smile.

Weeping has transformed her eyes into narrow slits. She looks frail and transparent. I'm to drive her home to Amsterdam – Mother Maya asked me to do so on the family's behalf. Her lower lip was trembling with compassion, and my real reason for agreeing so promptly was to get her off my back.

Since then I've been treated like a hero and wished *bon courage* and *bon voyage* umpteen times. Anyone would think I was Orpheus departing for the underworld. The underworld is the presence of sorrow and suffering. No one enjoys the company of the bereaved – least of all me, perhaps – but I've been landed with the job. I shall drive as fast as I can, buy

Antje some sleeping tablets in the nearest pharmacy and drive to the point of exhaustion. Will it be OK to listen to some music? To laugh from time to time?

Rinpoche surveys our seated figures, then clears his throat and pronounces Theo's name. He utters it three times in succession, then relapses into silence. Hm, he says after a while, although we're forever experiencing change we don't believe in it. We stubbornly insist that everything remains as it is.

Silly, isn't it?

He laughs his hearty, clownish laugh. I wonder if he can simply summon it up like a good actor, to disconcert us, or if he really finds everything so funny.

Shall I be nice to you all, he says, or would you prefer to hear the truth?

The truth, then. So be it. He gives a booming laugh. We all have to die, don't we? But here in the West you don't really believe that. You hold on to everything: your body, your love, even your pain. But these attachments are the source of all suffering. Do you know how to catch a monkey? You put a banana in a cage. The monkey is cunning. Instead of entering the cage it reaches through the bars and grabs the banana, but it can't withdraw it because the bars are too close together. But it doesn't want to let go of it either, not at any price. That's how to catch a monkey. Tubten Rinpoche sighs and surveys us again. Hold out your arms, he says like a kindergarten teacher at playtime.

He extends a fat, bare arm from his red robe, and all four hundred occupants of the tent follow suit. I'm averse to group activities. I never sang *We shall overcome* round the campfire, never held my lighter up at concerts, never went to demos, but I shyly hold out my arm. What the hell, I think. I know what comes next. Antje showed me only yesterday. Only yesterday!

And now clench your fists, says Rinpoche.

We all clench our fists.

Harder, harder!

Grinning, he leaves us sitting there with our arms out and our fists clenched. Hold on tight, he says. Don't let go, hold on tight.

After a few minutes my arm starts trembling.

Nice and painful, isn't it? He chuckles like the lid of a boiling kettle. And now, he says, relax your hands and open them. Aaah ... Much better, no? Freedom. Remember, remember, he repeats softly. And again: Remember.

28

THE WHOLE FAMILY HAS gathered round the car to say goodbye. They all give Antje a lingering embrace with their eyes closed. Then they try to do the same to me, but I don't tolerate this artificial cuddling for long. I simply give Franka a quick, affectionate kiss and get behind the wheel.

Franka darts around the car and leans against the driver's door. I can only see her mouth.

Dad . . . she begins.

Yes?

Dadfred . . .

Mm?

What would you say if I . . . if I . . . I wanted to ask you what you'd think if . . .

So ask away.

You'd only say no, I know you would.

Try me.

I . . . I wanted to ask if . . .

She breaks off and thumps the car roof with her fist.

I draw a deep breath and put her out of her misery. You must have all the necessary jabs and tell Claudia yourself, I say out of the window.

Her mouth shapes a perfect O. But it would be all right with you?

I nod.

She puts her head through the window and opens her blue eyes wide, the eyes she gets from me. Even if I drop out of school? she says.

All I ask is that you have all the jabs anyone going to India can possibly need, and that you—

I'll tell Mama. I'll tell her myself. Oh, Dad!

Her eyes fill with tears and she hugs and kisses me the way she hasn't done since she was around ten years old. You're simply incredible!

I bridle and shake my head, even though I think she's right. Mama will kill you, she says.

Now hop it, I say, and give my regards to Pelge.

She nods. I seize her arm. Is he really a monk? I mean, haven't you ever—

Oh, Dad, she says, rolling her eyes. He isn't a monk, he's a lama, a scholar. He's allowed to do anything.

Well, I say, that's a relief.

She laughs. I'm reluctant to let her go, want to detain her for as long as I can. Five wonderful things, I say.

She looks puzzled. Five wonderful things?

Don't you remember? We played it so often in the old days.

She nods, as faintly embarrassed as any child whose parents talk moist-eyed of the times when he or she was young.

Five wonderful things that happened today? She wrinkles her nose. Today's a bit difficult.

Precisely, I say. That's just it. Come on, help me out.

OK. She draws a deep breath. One, there weren't any mosquitoes last night; two, a mole on Pelge's back I'd never noticed before; three, the fly on Theo's nose, which reminded me I'm actually alive; four, I managed to scrounge some salad at lunch; five . . . She beams at me. You!

Thanks, you artful little monkey.

She gives me a farewell peck on the nose, then walks off very erect, looking like an exclamation mark in her black skirt and T-shirt. Just short of the kitchen building she turns once more and waves. She's already so far away that her features are blurred and she genuinely looks like a grown-up woman. I raise my hand, not that she can see it through the tinted windscreen, and my heart suddenly weighs a ton.

An audiocassette drops into my lap.

Norbert pokes his head through the window. Bob Dylan, he says. It always helps.

Let me know when your trial comes up, I say. Maybe I'll attend.

He nods. Maybe, he says.

Maybe.

I give his arm a squeeze. We both know we'll never see each other again. I start the engine. Antje, who's been dumped on the passenger seat like a piece of luggage, stares straight ahead and doesn't stir. I set off, drive past the injunction ENJOY YOUR BREATH and turn out on to the road.

In the wing mirror I can see our family standing there in echelon like a Chinese group photo, waving in unison. *Objects may be closer than they appear . . .* The warning on my mirror resembles a caption for the image it's reflecting. Very apt. That whole, weird Grasshopper Family came closer to me than I would ever have thought possible.

I stick my arm out of the window and flap it clumsily up and down. We're driving along the asphalt road, and I'm getting ready to turn right, not left, so as to avoid the spot where Theo died, when Antje says, loud and clear, Turn left.

I give her a dubious, sidelong glance. Her face is pale, and she looks much thinner than before. Her plaits stand out as stiffly as a six-year-old's.

Please, she says, so I turn left. My heart judders like a pneumatic drill as we near the place.

A dark little figure is standing precisely where I found Theo.

As we draw nearer I recognize the old Vietnamese nun who walked past our family conclave and pleaded the cause of television. Although the sun is already hot, she's wearing a brown woollen cap on her shorn head.

I brake to a stop. We both get out and bow.

The old nun bows likewise. She goes up to Antje and stands there in front of her, a small, shrivelled figure with an unwavering smile on her face. Then she draws back her hand and gives Antje a vigorous pat on the cheek. Any harder, and it would have been a slap, but this is an affectionate pat that instantly catapults me back into the present.

Antje rubs her cheek, looking startled.

The nun says nothing, not a word. She smiles and bows once more, then glides off in the direction of the meditation centre, one step, one breath, at a time.

29

A T BERGERAC ANTJE SAYS she wants to go to the hairdresser's. I don't ask why. Not wanting to hang around
waiting for her, I have my own hair washed and cut by a sullen
blonde in a pale blue smock.

Our fellow customers in the little salon, a couple of elderly
women and one old man, appear to indicate that going to the
hairdresser is a practice reserved for the more mature. It's a
strange re-entry into normal life, this almost absurd-seeming
cultivation of our outward form. There's stench of bleaching
paste, and tufts of hair litter the floor like duck's down.
Lifeless matter like Theo's body, I tell myself, nothing more.

The assistant in the pale blue smock asks me some unintelligible questions – probably whether I want a conditioner
or something of the kind. I greet all her suggestions with a
nod, and she massages something into my hair. It smells
pleasantly of watermelons but proves to be a colouring agent.
By the time my hair has been blow-dried into a dandelion
clock worthy of a gay fashion designer, it's a glossy chestnut
brown. Not a hint of grey – almost like the old days. Except,
unfortunately, that it *looks* dyed – bogus and affected. I'm
reminded of Aschenbach in *Death in Venice* and wonder why
he, of all people, should occur to me now, when I last heard
his name at film school. The film itself I never saw, but I

distinctly recall the episode in which Aschenbach, infatuated with young Tadzio, has his hair dyed and puts on make-up. I found this fascinatingly obscene, because as a youngster I knew, just like Tadzio, that the old remain old however much they try to be young.

And now I myself am one of their number, and my dyed hair is only the finishing touch. What of my black baggy pants and my efforts to familiarize myself with Ace of Base and the Funky Diamonds? Aren't they just the same?

I stare sadly at the imbecile in the mirror: a peculiar individual – wrinkles everywhere, the poor old guy. That's not me, not in a million years. I'm a boy who's just caught a frog, who's just had his first kiss, a young man reputed to be good in bed, an up-and-coming talent at the film school, a newly-fledged father. To remain young I'd have to smash the mirror – that and every other mirror in existence.

I don't recognize Antje till she's standing right in front of me. She's had her head shaved and now looks like a naked fledgling that's tumbled out of its nest. The pale pink scalp surmounting her heavily tanned face resembles a bathing cap. The assistant gives me an apologetic glance as if to say it isn't her fault.

I'm overcome with envy. Antje has acted in a clear-cut, radical way, whereas I'm just an old fraud, even if the dyed hair wasn't my idea. I run a hand through my rustling, preposterously brown hair, turn to Antje's hairdresser, and say, *Moi aussi, s'il vous plaît. La même chose que madame.* And Antje smiles, and the smile traverses the tender skin of her scalp like a wavelet on the surface of a lake.

A gentle breeze caresses my bald head, soft as the first breath of a newborn baby. I feel alarmingly new. It's forty-five years since I looked this way. Like a monk and a nun, we sit together in a pavement café. Antje mutely indicates the *salade niçoise* on the menu and I order for her. When our food comes she bends over her plate as she did at the meditation centre, eats slowly and deliberately, and concludes with another bow. She's trying to concentrate on the present alone. The nun's pat on the cheek: Be here and now! But it won't work. We're only amateurs, we haven't practised enough.

I shall leave her in peace and ask no questions, I'm only the chauffeur. I order a double espresso because I plan to drive through the night, which should get us to Belgium by dawn and Amsterdam around midday. But, when the sun sinks below the motorway, Antje again says one word only, 'Sleep', presumably meaning that I should call a halt somewhere.

Obediently, I turn off the motorway on to a minor road. We drive through some sleepy little villages without seeing a hotel or a pension anywhere. It's getting dark, and still I've found nothing.

We can either go on looking, I tell Antje, or simply sleep in the car. She looks at me gravely and nods. Her pale scalp gleams in the dusk.

Sleep in the car? She nods again.

I turn down a farm track that leads through fields of sunflowers to a little river, where I park on the bank itself. The moon is nearly full. From the car we can see its light reflected in the water.

OK?

She nods. I put her seat into the reclining position. She wraps herself in her jacket and closes her eyes. I'm tempted to stroke her bald head. She must be feeling rent and raw inside – bewildered by it all. My hand hovers above her head for a moment. Then I resolutely remove it and lie back too.

I can't get off to sleep for ages. I think about luck: how tricky and unreliable it is, how it deserts us just like that, without any warning or explanation. For all that, I think the only reason why I've so seldom been happy is an overdose of luck. No air crash, no tumour, no suicide, no family disaster – nothing tragic has ever happened to me. I've had it too good all my life (My sentiments entirely, says my mother) to be able to tell happiness from unhappiness. Who are the happiest people in the world? According to a newspaper report, the Germans are in fifty-second place and the Bangladeshis come first. Can a person be too stupid to be happy?

I try to list the day's five wonderful things: one, the dawn sky; two, Franka's beaming smile when I said she could go to India; three, the nun's pat on the cheek; four . . . I can't think of any more, and I must have dozed off, because I wake with a start to find Antje shaking me. My eyes snap open, my heart races. What's the matter? I say loudly. What's happened?

Listen to me, will you? she says firmly. Listen to me awhile.

I rub my eyes in bewilderment, stifle a yawn, run a hand over my head, and am surprised to discover that my hair isn't there any more. Antje is talking about Theo. She speaks of him in a rapid, breathless voice, as if it could bring him to life again.

He was quite thin when we met, she says. A thin man with curly fair hair. Shy, too. He didn't go out much. Lived on his own in a bedsit in our commune, studying history and information technology. Sometimes he would come upstairs and complain about the loud music. He pumped up my bicycle tyres for me – that was the first time we had a proper look at each other. He asked me to marry him two weeks later. Nobody got married in those days, but he was insistent. I felt flattered, but I wasn't sure I really wanted to spend my entire life with one man. We eventually got married at Chilpanzingo – that's in Mexico – five years later. An Indian girl played a Schubert song on the piano and the minister likened marriage to a car. At first it goes like a dream, but sooner or later things need repairing, and if you don't put them right then it goes phut, and if you aren't careful you drive into a wall. After the ceremony we had drinks with the minister and his family, and Theo ended up so drunk he passed out with his head on my lap.

She gives a tiny little laugh that bursts like a soap bubble as soon as it escapes her lips.

He slept in my lap like a baby, and that's what he always remained: my baby. I took care of him, though he thought he was really taking care of me.

That's why we didn't have any children, she says quietly. He couldn't have endured it. He had to be the one and only. If I'd had a child I'd have lost him. All our friends have divorced or split up. Not us, though. We were the sole exceptions. Our car also went phut, of course, but it went phut without our really noticing. It still ran quite well, actually.

Antje falls silent. Her eyes are glistening in the semi-darkness, but she isn't crying. I admire her composure. She reminds me of a slender vase, very fragile but still intact as long as it's handled with care.

Theo had fits of depression, she goes on. It was almost romantic at first – poor, suffering Theo – but it soon became boring because he was boring when he had them. All he did was sit there watching television. There was no talking to him, nothing to be done, no sex, his work suffered. He's a TV news editor . . .

We both detect the mistake. He *was*, he *was* . . .

Antje draws a deep breath but doesn't correct herself. I found it harder and harder to maintain the 'loving detachment' recommended by my therapist. I was furious – it seemed such a waste of time! I contemplated a separation. But then a friend introduced him to Tubten Rinpoche's book.

How to be Happy When You Aren't, I say.

She nods. He started meditating, and a miracle happened: he felt better. So I felt better too. I gave up thinking about a separation and fell in love with him all over again. Our car drove on. Then, this Easter, he went off to the meditation centre. Wanted me to join him, but I thought: It's his thing, leave him to do it on his own.

Another silence. I picture Theo and Claudia converging on the same spot like two figures in a video game, then the resulting explosion.

When he came back he was in love, Antje says flatly. We tried to dismiss it as a minor accident, one that had left our car badly damaged but not a total write-off. He was horrified that it had happened to him. He hadn't wanted it. Perhaps our marriage had simply been leaking air over the years like a tyre with a little hole in it – one you can drive on for quite a long time until it suddenly goes flat. And, just as we were staring at our flat in surprise, along came this woman . . .

Is she really ignorant of the woman's identity? Did he never mention her name? Never say what she looked like or where she came from?

There's a bang. I give a jump. Antje has punched the underside of the car roof. All I ever had, she says, was the mild, amiable, melancholy Theo, whereas *she* got the wild and passionate one! *She* got the man I always wanted, and I don't know why!

Face distorted with rage, she slams both fists against the roof of the car, which reverberates like a bass drum. *God verdomme*, she shouts, *God verdomme*!

Wild, passionate Theo . . . Feeling queasy, I open the window, hang my head out, and try to feel ashamed of my hatred for a dead man. I can hear Antje crying.

Oh shit, she sobs, shit! That on top of everything else.

I turn to look, and she points helplessly to a big, dark stain on the inside of her pale slacks. I didn't think, she sobs, I forgot. I completely forgot about it, and I don't have any tampons with me.

I take her in my arms. This minor source of distress is a licence to take her in my arms, but not the major one.

She doesn't want to come to the nearest pharmacy with me, and when I drive off I see her sitting beside the glittering river wrapped in a blanket, like an Indian woman.

There's no pharmacy in any of the next three villages. I find one in the fourth, but it doesn't offer an all-night service. In the fifth an unfriendly, pyjama-clad woman with greasy, face-creamed cheeks hands me a carton through the hatch. I can tell what she's thinking: Playing the hero, huh? Trying to make a good impression, dashing off in the middle of the night, just to get some tampons, when the lady probably has some in her bathroom cabinet. All at once her disapproval makes me feel young, really young, as if this were the first time in my life I'd bought some tampons for a woman – as if it were a token of trust and love, the promise of a future together. I feel almost happy at this singular moment.

Bonne nuit, I say politely.

The pyjama-clad woman doesn't reply. She slams the hatch, returns to her quarters at the rear of the shop, and turns out the light.

I can't locate our bivouac beside the river. And while I'm roaming around and mistaking every farm track for 'ours' and jolting over its potholed surface until compelled to turn back by a wicker fence or an unheralded dead end, I get the feeling, as so often before, that this isn't my real, actual life, and that, although I'm on my way through the night with a package of tampons in my pocket for the widow of the man who was madly in love with my wife, this is only one of my potential lives. A combination of circumstances and coincidences has conduced to this particular one, but occurring in parallel are all the other lives to which I can find no cross connection. At some stage, in infinity, they will meet in accordance with the law of parallels, and it may transpire that my other lives were very much happier and more fulfilled, because I did something right in them that I always do wrong in this one.

I can't find our parking place. It's like an evil spell. Every track looks promising at first but turns out to be the wrong one. Antje will be getting nervous by now – even desperate, perhaps. At this of all times, when she badly needs support, I'm leaving her in the lurch.

Why aren't I capable of acting responsibly and reliably? Why didn't I make a note of where that damned track came out? What made me think I had everything under control? Where does it come from, this confounded mixture of arrogance and inefficiency? For the umpteenth time, I drive along the road between the first and second villages. The turn-off must be somewhere here.

My headlights scour the greenery to right and left of the road, but there isn't an opening or farm track anywhere. It's as if nature has locked up, as if bramble hedges have sprouted the way they did in the fairy tale, so as to bar my path and thwart the return of the Knight of the Tampons.

As ever when I'm in despair, my thoughts turn to Claudia. It isn't fair, I know, but I feel like calling to ask her advice. She'd find the track. She'd have noted the distance in a wholly straightforward, practical way. She's forever trying to save me from going astray, and I reward her with anger and betrayal because I don't *want* to be saved. Dependence is a blot on a knight's escutcheon. No knight wants his beloved to send him on his way complete with Band-Aids, street maps, and muesli bars.

Why don't women understand that? They can bring out the steak, beer and Band-Aids once we're back home. Is that really so hard to understand? No good advice, please. Where am I, Claudia? Where in hell am I?

If marriage resembles a car, ours is a battered old estate, practical but unlovely. I haven't looked after it too well. I've let it go to pot, failed to have it serviced, seldom put it through the car wash, neglected to polish and cosset it. Claudia's in the driving seat. She knows what's what, she keeps us on the go – and that's precisely why our marriage doesn't work any more, because I make her pay for the fact that she's the stronger of us. It was like that from the outset. That's why I wanted to stay with her. That's why I wanted to marry her.

But losers hate winners – invariably. Claudia possesses an inner strength I've never had and will probably never acquire: a hard core that always centres her like a gyroscope, never entirely throws her off course, straightens her up again and again. Being envious of that strength, I like to imagine that she's sucked me dry of the little strength I did possess. I'm weak, like Theo, but pose as the stronger. Male pride, that's the really pathetic thing about me.

Not a sign of a farm track anywhere.

What would *you* do, Claudia? Tell me, what would *you* do now?

I pull up, rest my head on the wheel, shut my eyes, and wish I'd never agreed to drive Antje to Amsterdam, wish I'd never gone to the confounded meditation centre, wish I was back home, watching some first-class subaquatic documentary on TV. Why not sound your horn? says Claudia.

Of course! I get out, reach through the window, and toot. Three long blasts, three short. I listen apprehensively, and the third time I hear a faint 'Here! Here!'

I follow the voice. The mouth of the track really is indistinguishable in the darkness, it's so overgrown. I go jolting along in the direction of the faint cries, and then Antje looms up in my headlights like some lost creature from another planet. Without a word, she takes the tampons I hand her as reverently as if they were the fruit of some arduous treasure hunt.

She sits beside the moonlit river all night long, stoically nursing her grief. I sit in the car, dozing off from time to time, and whenever I open my eyes she's still sitting there like that. In the intervals between my brief dreams I don't know exactly where we are or when. We might be in a Western, at the foot of the Rockies. We'd still have a long way to ride, but then we'd live on a ranch, and I'd buy her a dress and a pair of red shoes, and everything would be all right for evermore.

Except that nothing's all right.

At dawn she stands up and gets into the car, shivering all over with cold. I chafe some warmth into her. We don't speak. She feels small and bony under my hands, sensitive and sore as a patient fresh from surgery. We're surrounded by fields of sunflowers. The sunflowers turn their avid faces toward the sun that's creeping over the skyline like a monstrous orange. Antje leans against the window, looking exhausted.

Theo's favourite flowers, she says slowly. The Italian name for sunflower is *girasole*, something that turns toward the sun. Theo used to say that's how one should try to live. Always turn toward the sun . . .

Sounds just like him, I reflect spitefully. A silly platitude like that . . .

But he never really knew where the sun was at any given moment, Antje goes on quietly, as if to herself. I always had to tell him. He sowed sunflowers in our window boxes every summer, and I watched them carefully. The fact is, they don't turn with the sun at all; they stubbornly face south-east to where the sun goes by every day, and when it sets in the evening they go on facing south-east and wait for the next day to dawn. That's quite different from turning *with* the sun. We

205

argued about it again and again. There's a big difference: either I go looking for happiness and turn its way, or I simply wait till it passes by.

She falls silent, gazing sadly out across the sunflowers, which are now a brilliant yellow in the sunlight, and I drive on because I don't know what else I can do for her.

30

HALF ASLEEP, I PILOT the car along the grey snake of the motorway, heading in the direction of Paris. At Lyon it starts to rain. I don't mind, it's more in keeping with our mood. Antje has lapsed into a kind of stupor, and I don't dare to rouse her.

She doesn't react when I ask if she'd like something to eat or drink, so I leave her sitting in the car while I stop at a motorway service area to take in some sausages and a coffee from the automat.

Sharing my little stand-up table are three French truck drivers with tired eyes. They smell of petrol and black tobacco. Seated in front of the blaring TV set is a party of deaf mutes, middle-aged men and women excitedly conversing with their hands. German tourists homeward bound with their sun-tanned children comb the shelves of the motorway shop in search of a final present, a final totem from the south. Fat, broad-hipped women are debouching from their coach and making for the toilets.

Every human being wants to achieve happiness and avoid suffering . . . A lot of those Buddhistic sayings have stuck to me like burrs. If I apply that tenet to all the people I see, they become alarmingly personal, as if they'd suddenly been turned inside out like peeled-off gloves, disclosing the soft, sensitive inner lining instead of the worn, calloused outer skin.

It's clear that even the most disagreeable, unfriendly, brutal person acts solely in order to be happy and avoid suffering.

Through the café window I see my car standing there in the scorching heat. I can't make out Antje, but I know she's ensconced in that metal prison, in the torture chamber of her emotions. There's nothing, absolutely nothing I can think of that would alleviate her sufferings, and because that makes me suffer too, I'm tempted to run off the way I've always run off and hidden. Except that it hasn't worked – hasn't made me any happier. I'm getting overheated and claustrophobic amid all my fellow happiness-seekers in this stupid motorway café. In the men's room I splash my face with water. Then, at long last, I call Claudia. That way, at least, I won't be hiding from her any longer. Besides, I miss her.

I say my name, which sounds curiously formal and unusual.

Oh, she says, it's you.

Yes.

She sighs.

I'm sorry, I say, but I couldn't call before. Something's happened.

I already heard.

I see.

Franka called me.

Does she really sound reproachful, or is it only my imagination? There's a reproach in almost everything she says. Sometimes open, sometimes disguised, like an object in a picture puzzle: Find the reproach. It's always there. Always.

You said she could go to India.

Yes.

Are you crazy?

Theo's dead.

I know.

I'm driving his wife home to Amsterdam.

I know that too.

Silence. Our phone calls are like minefields. When we've trodden on all the mines, we hang up.

About Theo . . .

Yes?

I wanted to ask you something.

About Theo?

Yes.

Well?

How . . . how well did you really know each other?

Her response is unhesitating. Meaning what?

I'd simply like to know how well you knew each other, that's all.

Quite well.

Quite well.

Yes. Isn't that good enough for you?

No, it isn't, but I don't ask the question that's gnawing at me. I don't ask it for fear of seeming even feebler than I am already.

I don't really care how well you knew each other, I say instead, aware that I've botched the whole thing.

Why ask, then?

Maybe I wanted to know if you're feeling sad.

Oh.

Well, are you?

Yes, I am.

I'm sorry.

Really?

Yes, I am, believe it or not.

Rather than lose her temper, I suspect, she draws a deep breath and expels it loudly.

Thanks, she says curtly.

He had a heart attack, but I expect you know that too.

Franka won't be going to India, she says sternly.

If you say so . . .

You must have been mad to say she could.

I wanted to make her happy?

You wanted to make her happy?

Yes, believe it or not.

Since when have you spared a thought for other people's happiness?

Everyone wants to be happy and avoid suffering.

That's just great! Her voice goes high and thin with anger. You learn that one saying and promptly decide to send your daughter to India to catch dengue fever or cholera and go to the dogs . . .

I'm not 'sending' her to India.

Have you completely forgotten why you went there?

Yes.

What does that mean?

I don't know any more.

Fred, she groans, you're . . . you're just—

An asshole, I put in.

She falls silent. I could weep – I could simply burst into tears and stand here until someone leads me away. I run a hand over my bald head.

I've had my head shaved.

You can't be serious.

I am.

I don't believe a word of it. It's ridiculous!

But I did.

What nonsense! You want to look like a raver? Why tell me such a thing?

No special reason.

Oh Fred, she sighs, can't we ever have a normal conversation these days?

I make my leaden-footed way back to the car. Antje has got out and is lying on a small stretch of grass beside the parking lot. There's a smell of piss and rotting bananas. As soon as she sees me coming she gets up and returns to the car. Just before we get there she takes my hand and squeezes it, just like that. The comforter comforted by the one in need of comfort. Gratefully, I hold her hand. I could stay with her, that's another possibility. Look for a job in Amsterdam, start a new life that would almost feel like the old one – almost. But I'd only drag my old life behind me like a convict's ball and chain. And besides, I don't love Antje.

What do I love about Claudia aside from our memories? I love us and the family we used to be. I love recollections of the three of us in the past, moments I carry around with me like jewels in a casket.

I see us lying in bed together on Sunday mornings watching children's programmes on TV.

I see Franka dressed up as a princess, toddling along in front of us in a fairy hat with a long veil. Claudia and I carry the veil, laughing, as we enter our favourite pizzeria. First Franka, then the veil, then nothing for a long, long time, and then us.

I see the three of us standing on a green hill in the rain, Franka wearing a little red raincoat. I see Claudia breast-feeding her in a skiff on the Starnberger See when she was only a few days old, and me proudly rowing my little family across the lake. I can still sense the happiness of those days like sherbet fizzing on my tongue.

I had the feeling I'd arrived. At the same time, though, I had no wish to reach my final destination or fit completely into Claudia's plans, into the everyday life she handles so much better than I.

I rebel against every day and its attendant problems, whereas she acts in accordance with the Nike motto: *Just do it*. That, as I've since discovered, is a Buddhistic maxim too: Always take life as it comes, nothing more.

My mother was just the same. They're all Zen masters, women. Life's fears are to be overcome just by living each moment without fear.

I found that all far too simple. Why? Because I didn't have a clue. Instead, I manoeuvred myself into a state of constant hostility toward my own life. I thought it was intellectual and artistic to be like that, and now here I am, empty-handed. Empty-handed and pretty damned silly.

At dusk we reach the yellow-lit motorway through Belgium, which is visible even from the moon. The Man in the Moon sees us driving along the Belgian motorway and draws his own conclusions. Antje, who hasn't uttered a word since early this morning, quietly asks me to make a detour via Antwerp.

Of course, I tell her, no problem. She nods and relapses into silence. All at once she seems a stranger, as if I'd never yet exchanged a word with her. She's a widow, I tell myself, trying to associate that bizarre word with the woman beside me, but it simply won't fit.

She steers me unerringly along the wide, deserted boulevards of Antwerp to the station, where we pull up outside a shabby hotel called the *Florida*.

She asks the porter for Room 23, and he hands her the key with a smile that implies prior acquaintance. I'm not sure what she has in mind, but she beckons to me to follow her. I climb a flight of musty-smelling wooden stairs. The stair carpet is rucked up, the varnish peeling off the banisters.

Antje opens the door, and we enter a hotel room straight out of Hollywood. The *Florida*'s bright red neon sign flashes on and off below the window at regular intervals, and looming over the narrow twin beds, with their hole-infested sheets, is a huge, sinister-looking oak wardrobe with a mirror on the door. Only the private eye and his bottle of bourbon are missing.

Antje shuts the door but doesn't turn on the light. Every few seconds she's plunged into darkness, to reappear a moment later bathed in the crimson glow of the neon sign. She sits down on one bed, I on the other. During the next red phase she seems to be smiling.

In the dark she says, We spent a wedding anniversary here. We really wanted to spend it at Bruges, but our hotel room had been given to someone else by mistake. It was much nicer here, actually.

The red light comes on again. So we came here every anniversary from then on, Antje says in red. The last time was three months ago.

We let the intermittent glow play over us for a sequence or two. Then she gets up and sits down beside me, rests her head on my shoulder.

I take her hand and hold it on my lap. I hear myself humming, then start to sing in the dark: *Row, row, row your boat gently down the stream. Merrily, merrily, merrily, merrily, life is but a dream.*

When the red light comes on again, the song is over.

Again, she whispers, so I sing it again, and when I'm through she says 'Again', over and over, and I go on singing till I think I'm dreaming. The wardrobe sways gently in time to the tune, Antje's body consists of warm air, and I myself am a blancmange-like mass that swells and shrinks and changes colour. Red, black, red, black . . .

Thank you, Antje says at length. Thank you. She gets up, takes Theo's blue T-shirt from her bag, hangs it in the gigantic wardrobe, and bows three times *à la* the meditation centre. The next time the light comes on, I'm alone in the room where she spent her wedding anniversaries.

31

WE REACH AMSTERDAM AT dawn. Antje guides me through the city, cool and composed, until we pull up in Prinsengracht. Then she puts her hands over her face.

I can't, she says miserably. I can't go inside. I just can't.

I try to imagine what it would be like to return to our apartment alone and wait for Claudia to be delivered in her coffin in a few days' time. I unlock our front door, and the first thing I see is her yellow Post-it on the wall: Key? Answerphone? Money? To my right, the bathroom. I survey her platoons of cosmetics, her colourful African bead necklaces, her Japanese sponge, the horse-chestnut shampoo in which she believes with almost religious fervour. I see her shoes neatly stacked beneath the wardrobe, her handbag on the chair – all those objects that yearn for her return and are robbed of life by her absence.

Everything will smell of him, Antje says despairingly.

Couldn't we go somewhere else first? I suggest. What about your parents?

She looks at me, her face puffy from weeping.

My mother? she says inquiringly.

Yes, let's go to your mother's place.

We drive across the city, which is gradually waking up, to a suburb near the airport. Antje tells me to park outside a big brick building with an unintelligible sign above the entrance in gold lettering.

Coming?

The brick building turns out to be an old folks' home, and Antje's mother hasn't heard yet. Seated in a green armchair far too big for her little room, she's wearing a nightgown and brushing her long grey hair. She doesn't seem particularly surprised when we appear in the doorway. Antje goes over to her, kneels down beside the chair, and lays her shaven head on her mother's lap, sobbing. The old woman strokes Antje's head, staring at me suspiciously as if I were responsible for her daughter's distress. Antje's body is racked with the kind of sobs a giant might have induced by shaking her. Bereft of her composure, she's weeping as she has never wept in all this time. At last, I think to myself. At least she's letting sorrow gain the upper hand.

I close the door behind me and sit down to wait on an uncomfortable bench near the entrance. I'm back in Amsterdam, and all I can do, yet again, is wait. I rest my head against the cold tiles behind me and go to sleep. Claudia is standing in a coral-red beam of light reminiscent of a disco, telling me what's wrong with our marriage, but the red light goes out every few seconds, and with it the sound track, so I can't hear her any more. She keeps asking me if I've really understood at last, and I nod despairingly and don't have a clue.

That's the last time, the very last time I'll explain it to you, understand? she says during the red phase, and I know that the next time the light comes on she'll be gone for good if I've failed to understand.

Wait, I call desperately, there's something I must tell you! Wait, can't you?

The light goes out, and she's gone. For good. Those two words – for good – pervade my body like a toxin. No! I shout. No!

A woman in a blue smock is shaking me and talking insistently in Dutch. I feel as if I've been beaten. My whole body aches and my neck is so stiff I can hardly move my head. I'm hungry and thirsty. I stare at my watch in amazement: I've been asleep for nearly three hours.

The woman in the blue smock shows me the way to the washroom, where I sluice my face. I look crumpled and squalid, like a relic of bygone pot-smoking days in Amsterdam, a superannuated hippy who has lost his hair.

Gingerly, I knock on the door of Antje's mother's room. It's opened by a young woman who bears a remarkable resemblance to Antje and has her eyes. A fair-haired toddler peers mistrustfully at me from between her legs. The green armchair is now occupied by a competent-looking man in his mid-thirties. He looks up and stares at me curiously. Antje is asleep in bed. Her mother, perched on the edge of the bed, is holding her hand. She's now wearing a grey costume and a white blouse, and her long hair is neatly pinned up. She gives me a nod, carefully deposits Antje's hand on the covers like a fragile object, stands up, thrusts the young woman aside, and fixes me with the same honey-coloured eyes as her daughters'.

Many thanks, she says in German, twice. She holds out her hand, which I fail to see at first, I'm so fascinated by those familiar eyes. I shake her thin but muscular hand, then I'm dismissed.

When the door closes behind me I stand in the corridor and shrug rather helplessly, like a character in a TV movie. An old man shuffles past, mumbling to himself. He doesn't look at me as he goes. I might be invisible, which is just the way I feel. My job is done, I'm no longer needed. Now I must work out – for myself – what to do next.

I drive at random through the city, not knowing which direction to take, and allow myself to be borne along by the traffic like a stray animal in the midst of an alien herd. Seated in the cars around me are resolute-looking people with specific destinations in mind. A little boy with a chocolate-smeared mouth waves to me. The woman at the wheel beside him is back-combing her hair in the rear-view mirror while the lights are at red. A Mercedes driver in a suit and tie is talking irately into his mobile. I feel utterly lost, but the herd firmly leads to a place I'd never have gone to on my own. It steers me along Potterstraat until I see the posters outside the Vincent van Gogh Museum. Sunflowers. Of course. Theo's favourite flowers.

I turn off into the parking lot, get out, lock the car, and resolutely make for the museum. It isn't a Monday and the place isn't shut, as it most certainly would have been if I'd thought of this plan by myself, and the nice cashier miraculously allows me to pay in French francs although it's obvious she'll never be able to change the coins into guilders. Everyone seems intent on getting me to my destination, so I hurry past the gloomy *Potato Eaters*, *The Yellow House* and *Still Life with Bible* until I come to *Sunflowers*.

Yes, Vincent made a really good job of them. He captured their essence. All he didn't do was answer the question of whether they follow the sun or wait till it goes by.

I'm rather disappointed and turn to go, since the other pictures don't interest me particularly. On the way out, however, I pass a glass-topped cabinet containing some letters from Vincent to his brother Theo.

Theo . . . A surprising namesake. Theo and sunflowers.

Dear Theo, I'm writing in great haste. I'm working with the enthusiasm of a Marseillais eating a bouillabaisse, and that won't surprise you when you hear that I'm now painting sunflowers. I work every morning from sunrise onward because the flowers wither so quickly, and I have to do the whole thing in one go . . . I'd so much like to paint them in such a way that everyone – everyone with eyes, at least – would see them. A handshake. I must go back to work. Yours ever, Vincent.

The enthusiasm, the wholly instinctive way in which he knew what he had to do! Envy sticks in my throat and makes me gulp.

How I long to know where my own sun is! I shut my eyes, but if I hoped to see a glow in the dark, a source of light that would show me the way – show me how my life should go on – that foolish hope, of course, remains unfulfilled. Pitch-black darkness, nothing more.

I leave the museum, trudge wearily and dispiritedly back across the parking lot, get into my car, and don't budge for a long time.

I grow heavier and heavier by the minute. Just before I implode like a black hole, I open the door and start running the way I ran through this city a good six months ago.

I run along all the pretty streets that are a bit too pretty and quaint for my taste, past the Grachten and across the bridges. On and on I run, and before long my lungs start to hurt like before. Physically, too, I'm in no better shape than I was then. By chance I come across the little park again. I sit down once more on the bench and wait for the squirrel, which promptly appears, sits up in front of me with its forepaws poised, and watches me patiently. But I'm really waiting for the African fortune-teller, who doesn't appear. I know exactly what I'd ask her today: Where to now?

I wait, staring at the ants between my feet. The squirrel, disappointed, hops off. As a child Franka once had an ant farm. It consisted of a little soil compressed between two sheets of glass with some thin plastic tubes running round them, so the whole arrangement resembled a miniature version of Charles de Gaulle Airport. Franka lost interest in her ants after a few days, but I watched them for weeks, fascinated by the way they dug tunnels and toted breadcrumbs back and forth, or, most fascinating of all, constructed wholly purposeless but aesthetically pleasing towers. They seemed to decide on something and then simply do it. They lugged the soil along the plastic tubes, grain by grain, and built a tower. Just like that. And when it was finished they abandoned it and devoted themselves to their next task. Watching them, I felt not only lazy but completely aimless. I'd gladly have built a purposeless tower myself, if only I'd had the inner compulsion. I've always envied obsessives. Not only Vincent van Gogh with his sunflowers, but every film student who shot some bizarre little movie with burning enthusiasm. The ants, van Gogh, and the film students. Where did they get it from, all that energy, all that self-assurance and staying power?

I take a twig and deflect the ants between my feet from their chosen route, but they're not put off for long. After a brief pause for reflection, they make a detour and steadfastly soldier on. I invoke the African woman – *Row, row, row your boat*, I sing to conjure her up – but she refuses to materialize. She leaves me to stew in my own juice and declines to help me. After four hours I'm feeling almost nauseous, my stomach is rumbling so much. When did I last have something to eat?

Seated around me in an expensive Indonesian restaurant where I can pay with a credit card, not having any guilders, are nothing but chic young people who seem to know precisely how they want to live. The men sport dark designer suits, little goatee beards and glasses with yellow lenses; the women, almost without exception, might have bought their long, flimsy, translucent pastel dresses from the same establishment. Reposing on each table, like the cigarette packets of yore, are several mobile phones of various makes.

A young woman at the next table, her fair hair neatly bobbed, keeps looking over at me. I try to imagine what she sees: an unshaven, unwashed, bald-headed, forty-something man in black jeans and a black T-shirt. He makes a lonely impression but is strenuously trying to look as if he doesn't care, eats too fast, and has almost knocked his glass over twice. A man on his own. Not romantic, just rather pathetic.

The blonde pensively twiddles a wisp of hair and turns back to her girlfriend, a plump creature whose undersized bra compresses her breasts so tightly that her cleavage resembles a baby's bottom. She also gives me the once-over, then shakes her head and giggles. Eventually, the bobbed blonde gets up and comes over to my table.

I'm tempted to run for it but I can't, not having paid the bill.

She asks me something in Dutch, and looks disappointed when I tell her in English that I don't understand.

What did you want to ask me?

We thought you were a television presenter, she says in English. On Dutch television, I mean.

I'm sorry.

She shrugs and turns to go, but before completing the movement she asks where I come from, and I, for some unfathomable reason, say 'Saigon'. Before I know it, I've joined them at their table and am telling them about Saigon as if I'd spent half a lifetime there.

They listen with parted, lipsticked lips, and the longer I go on talking the more I loathe myself. I've always told tall stories as a means of self-protection. I call them fibs, not lies, but they've never protected me, not ultimately, because I'm always better, smarter and more interesting in my stories than I am in reality.

I even lied to Claudia, told her I made my graduation movie at the film school and even won a prize for it, when I really took off without a word one day. No diploma or graduation movie.

The thing I like best about Vietnam, I improvise, is the hot noodle soup for breakfast. It's called *pho*, but I still can't pronounce it properly. The way I say it, it sounds like 'main line station' instead of 'soup'.

They laugh politely.

It's got ginger and nutmeg and aniseed in it. Early in the morning the whole city smells of aniseed . . .

What about the women? asks the plump one. What are they like?

They're the most beautiful women in the world, I reply, quick as a flash. They look like butterflies in their traditional *ao dais* with the baggy trousers and the gauzy tops slit down the sides. They're ethereally beautiful, like angels. The two girls seem saddened by this, so I hastily add that Asian women leave me cold.

That's a racist remark, says the bobbed blonde, and her plump friend nods.

Conversation lapses. They study their fingernails, all of which are painted the same shade of pale blue.

My wife's left me, I tell them apologetically. Could I possibly grab a shower at your place?

32

THE BATHROOM IS STUFFED with cosmetics and redolent of the couple's various perfumes. It's not very clean. There are hairs in the plughole (*Brothers and sisters, kindly remove any hairs from the plughole*), the tiles in the shower are covered with a dirty grey film, and the bathroom carpet is a mass of stains.

I stand motionless under the shower, sluicing away the experiences of the past few days. Everything must be rinsed off. When I'm through, a new, vigorous man must emerge from the shower, gallop home, restore order on the ranch, and put his marriage to rights.

The hot water leaves me pleasantly bemused. I vaguely miss Franka and Antje and Claudia – even the meditation centre. The strange, lulling certainty that everything will be restored to order by the lama's wisdom. No wonder people flock to him in droves. *How to be Happy When You Aren't* . . . I now get the feeling I was happy there. Although I spent most of the time in a state of rebellion, at least I was present in my own life, whereas now it's dribbling away between my fingers like water. I can recall nearly every moment of my time at the meditation centre. Saigon . . . What a load of bull!

I turn off the shower, swathe my hips in the Mickey Mouse towel Connie and Yvonne have laid out for me, and take a few experimental, gliding steps across the repulsive bathroom carpet. Seven paces forward, seven paces back. Breathe in, breathe out. Empty my mind. The bacteria-infested carpet. Claudia, pale and tearful, is mourning Theo. Antje, tucked up in her mother's bed, is mourning Theo likewise. Franka in Pelge's arms. Myself in no one's arms. The beautiful nun. Red neon light. Sunflowers. Where to now? It isn't working. My brain is chattering away in my ears.

Discouraged, I perch on the edge of the bath. Mickey Mouse, that loathsome optimist undeterred by any contretemps, laughs up at me from the bath towel. How does he manage it? Why is he never scared?

Plump Yvonne and Connie, the bobbed blonde, are goggling at me like fish in a tank. Scared? Connie repeats in an uncomprehending voice.

Aren't you ever scared when you watch yourselves living?

Watch ourselves living? Yvonne repeats, eyeing me suspiciously. Either she'll call an ambulance right away, or she'll take refuge from this madman by locking herself up with Connie in the room next door.

No, says Connie. Why should I watch myself living?

Yvonne gives a suggestive laugh. We've got a ceiling mirror for that, she titters. We all look up at the mirror on the ceiling above the couch.

What makes you think you know exactly how to live? I insist.

They sigh like grown-ups pestered by an inquisitive child.

Anyway, I ask their reflections, where are your boyfriends?

We don't have anything to do with men, Yvonne says indignantly, putting her arm round Connie.

I must have been blind. I'd been firmly convinced that their sole motive for taking me home was to try a quick threesome when the hour grew late. I wouldn't necessarily have been averse, either, just for something to do. My boyfriend question had merely been a way of establishing that there wasn't someone lurking in the undergrowth, waiting to hit me on the head with a baseball bat.

I wasn't to know, I say dazedly, and the two of them give me an indulgent smile.

So what do you do with yourselves? I ask in a lame voice, not knowing, now, what I'm supposed to be doing here.

Oh, says Connie, rearranging her cleavage, we go off to work every day and come home in the evening, and so on, and at weekends we drive to the seaside.

They giggle like a pair of hysterical schoolgirls.

And that's enough for you? I ask.

They eye me thoughtfully, as if wondering how to enlighten me on the salient points of their existence.

Why not? Yvonne says defiantly. We've got no money worries and we're both healthy.

I'm an asshole. I simply can't imagine that two girls like these feel a certain gratitude that they haven't yet developed breast cancer, chronic allergies, high blood pressure, rheumatism, or some other ailment – that they wake up every morning, blithely make their coffee, and exchange a kiss before going off to work.

I envy you, I groan.

As if to console me, they give me a beer. They themselves drink tea. They don't just go to the North Sea, they say. Once a year they join a party of women on a walking tour of Nepal. After work Yvonne does T'ai Chi twice a week, and Connie does Feldenkrais exercises because she gets backache from sitting all day long. Both of them are quality controllers at the food-processing factory where they met four years ago. They've been living together for half that time, and next year they plan to adopt a child.

Do you always know exactly what the future holds in store? I ask.

No, they reply cheerfully, but when we don't we ask the stones.

Stones? What stones?

Yvonne jumps up, giggling until her big breasts bounce. She goes over to the bookshelves, which are otherwise devoted to cookery books, and returns with a little black velvet bag and a blue booklet. Then she empties the contents of the velvet bag on to the carpet. They're runes.

I knit my brow. The Nazis used runes, did you know?

They stare at me with wide, mistrustful eyes, as if I were deliberately being a spoilsport.

You mean Hitler used runes? asks Yvonne, shaking her head. It doesn't say anything about that in the book. Are you one?

One what?

A Nazi. Yvonne takes Connie's hand and locks fingers with her.

No, of course not, I retort, a trifle too loudly. Silence. Because of my shaved head, you mean?

You might be, Connie says timidly. After all, a German with a shaved head . . .

Certainly not. What crap! I'm far too old for that. I was in a kind of monastery.

In Vietnam?

Give it here, I say without pursuing her question. Like a school head, I take the book from them and leaf through it. An American edition. No mention of Hitler. It states that runes originated in Scandinavia and are referred to in the *Edda*. All very PC, but I still find it unpleasant to be sitting over a bag of runes in Holland, of all places.

You ask yourself a question, Yvonne explains. Then you put your hand in the bag and bring out a rune.

You always get an answer, says Connie. Always.

They exchange a happy smile and a long, affectionate kiss,

and I watch them like someone standing in front of a brightly lit shop window in winter with his nose glued to the glass.

When they've finally stopped kissing they look at me rather pityingly and challenge me to pick out a rune.

You look like you could use it, says Connie, and I wonder what I could really use right now. Come on, have a go, Yvonne insists. They won't bite you.

I shake my head.

Come on. Connie gets up and sits down beside me. You'll be amazed, honestly. The stones go click as she shakes the bag. The answer's in here, she says coaxingly.

There isn't any answer to my question.

There's always an answer, Yvonne insists. Come on, be a sport.

Be a sport, Connie repeats, nudging me in the ribs.

At this moment I feel as if I've known them for ever. It's a strange moment, like a flash of lightning which discloses that they're no different from me, ordinary people with ordinary lives that go dark and light and are bound to go dark again. Perhaps one of us will commit suicide or drop dead like Theo, but it's more probable that, like the vast majority, we'll be slowly consumed by some disease or, if we're very lucky, by time itself; and all that can console us are these moments that suddenly unfold before us like the petals of a flower – moments at which we believe we'll be utterly and completely happy for evermore. So I shut my eyes and ask 'What now?' and plunge my right hand in the little velvet bag.

I feel a number of cool, oval stones, but one of them thrusts its way to the fore, demands to be taken out into the light. I hesitate briefly, then remove it. Slowly opening my fingers, I find myself staring at a blank white stone. I turn it over, but the other side is just as blank. No rune, nothing. A blank stone. It probably betokens destruction and disaster.

The two girls gasp. Odin, Connie says in an awestruck

whisper, and starts leafing feverishly through the blue booklet.
We've never drawn that one, says Yvonne.

Odin, the Unknown, Connie reads aloud. *The end is as blank as the beginning. This is the rune of total trust, and should be regarded as an exciting indication that you are in direct touch with your true nature, which rises phoenix-like from the ashes again and again. Relinquishing control is the spiritual warrior's supreme task* . . .

Yvonne and Connie exchange a meaningful glance, I stifle a yawn. Stupid mumbo-jumbo. Hitler probably believed he was a spiritual warrior, but he must have missed the bit about relinquishing control . . .

Drawing the blank rune brings your deepest fears to the surface: Will I fail? Connie goes on. *Will I be abandoned? Will I be deprived of everything? The blank rune challenges you to summon up all your courage and leap into the void. Don't be a coward, accept whatever befalls you. And now, jump!*

Connie lowers the book. They both look at me expectantly, so I get up, climb on the futon couch, and jump. The floor-boards shudder.

No, no, Yvonne says sternly, you must leap into the void. You mustn't be a scaredy-cat.

Are you a scaredy-cat? asks Connie.

They both giggle in a silly way.

I don't believe in this stuff, I say firmly.

Connie shrugs. You don't have to, she says soothingly. She puts the stone back in the little velvet bag and replaces the bag and the book on the shelf. We only thought it might help because you've . . .

Because your wife has left you, Yvonne puts in.

Thanks, I say.

She nods. Quite without warning, she unzips her dress and lets it fall to the floor. She stands there in her bra and panties like a bun fresh from the oven, a firm-fleshed figure of a

227

woman of the kind that could appeal to me. She turns once on the spot, beauty queen fashion, then sits down beside me and takes my hand. We like you, she says. Ah, I say to myself, so that's it after all.

Any diseases?

No, I say haltingly. Besides, there are such things as condoms, aren't there?

Hm, says Connie. She sits down on my other side and takes my left hand. Actually, we had something else in mind . . .

Adopting is difficult, says Yvonne, so we wanted to ask you . . .

We wanted to ask you, Connie chimes in, kneading my hand like dough, if you could see your way . . .

We need a bit a sperm, Yvonne says. She might be asking a neighbour for a cup of sugar.

And you appeal to us, Connie purrs.

Yes, Yvonne says shyly.

Because I look like a Dutch TV presenter . . .

Yvonne brushes this aside. That was just a trick. We always say that when we like someone.

Aha. And then you make him draw a rune?

No, that just happened. We only do it ourselves as a rule.

Don't be a coward, accept whatever befalls you, quotes Connie. It fits, doesn't it?

They look at me expectantly like a couple of children waiting for Father Christmas's verdict.

I'm sorry, I say. I . . . I don't have any infectious diseases, but I do have a congenital heart defect. My father had it too – and my grandfather. He died of it, and so did my father. One morning he got on his bicycle and rode off as bright as a button. Three minutes later he was lying in the road, dead. I mustn't exert myself too much.

We only asked, says Yvonne. She rises and picks up the empty beer bottle. Connie collects the teacups, and they take

228

them into the kitchen. When they return they're both wearing long nighties with bears printed on them.

I ought to push off, I suppose, but I'm filled with dread by the thought of the dark, deserted city and my solitary car in the Rijksmuseum's parking lot.

Connie gestures to me. I get up off the couch, and they convert it into a double bed with a few deft movements.

They slip beneath the covers, regarding me amiably, and pat the space between them. I lie on my back with my hands on my flies, so as not to take up too much room, and listen to their regular breathing.

What the devil am I doing here? But what the devil would I be doing anywhere else? Why did I behave like that? Heart defect, death while cycling . . . Forgive me, Theo. A bit of sperm – would that have been so awful? *Don't be a coward, accept whatever befalls you. And now, jump!* But jumping is a proactive procedure. I wouldn't be accepting what befell me, I'd be taking the initiative. I don't want to jump, I've always detested springboards. I even cheated at swimming tests and funked diving in off the three-metre board.

Quietly, I creep out of bed and get dressed.

33

D AYBREAK AT OBERHAUSEN. THE sun is invisible, the sky
gradating from iron grey to mouse grey. Drab, melancholy Northern Europe . . . Streaming out on to the autobahn
are innumerable cars occupied by freshly showered, energetic
people on their way to work. I circulate among them like a
black sheep. I fill the tank and buy myself some cigarettes.
Since leaving the meditation centre I've been smoking like a
chimney again. My throat's all scratchy and my lungs feel sore.

My mouth tastes of ashes, and gas station coffee is burning a
hole in my gut. I'm the loneliest person under the sun – no one
can help me. I'm dissolving with self-pity. I'd leave behind a
big, greasy patch on the forecourt. Nothing would be left in
that greasy patch but my sunglasses, a pair of Oakleys
recommended by Franka, who says they're cool. Movement
is the only thing that helps, so I get back into the car, and soon
the central reservation is flashing past again. A lot of people go
jogging as a means of self-escape; I drive.

Just after Bonn, where the traffic thins out and the autobahn
crosses some hills in a series of dangerous bends, a red Toyota,
the same model as my own, stubbornly hogs the overtaking
lane and refuses to let me pass. I flash my lights and blow my
horn. No reaction. The driver – broad shoulders, thick neck –
is alone in the car. Maybe he's a man who riles other drivers on

principle every morning. Maybe he wants to tempt me to overtake him on the inside, then report me to the police.

I'm soon incandescent with road rage. If I had a gun I'd reduce his tyres to ribbons. Idiot! I thumb my horn for seconds on end, and the sound accompanies me like a flag fluttering from my window. This is too much! He'll have to let me pass in the end! Still no reaction.

I tailgait him closely enough to throw a scare into him, but still he fails to react. We come to a dip, his speed increases. I stay on his heels, willing him to get out of my way at last. Coming up close behind him again, I see his head keel over with a jerk. Perhaps he's got a stiff neck – perhaps he's doing remedial exercises. But his head remains at an odd angle, and it's an age before I grasp the truth: he's unconscious. Or dead.

Not another! Looking back, I believe it was that thought – Not another dead man! – that spurred me into action. Theo was enough. Not another limp, motionless, frightening corpse. Not again!

Watching myself, I'm surprised I seem to know exactly what to do – I, of all people! I overtake, pull in just ahead of the other man, and apply the brakes. Our bumpers connect with a dull thud. The impact shows him down, but it also sends him off course. His car scrapes the crash barrier and threatens to end up in the other lane.

I let him career past me – his foot must be resting on the gas pedal – then pull in behind him again. I must nudge him gently from the left, cue him like a billiard ball and get him to change direction. Another impact, and my bonnet crumples like corrugated iron. Much too hard, now he's veering to the right. The right-hand lane is clear, fortunately, but my rear-view mirror reflects some trucks thundering up behind us like hissing dragons.

Again I nudge him gently from the left. Smoke has started to issue from my bonnet. We're still doing almost 100 k.p.h. At every impact the driver's body flops this way and that like a rag doll. For one brief moment I feel I'm back in a fairground bumper car. The girls used to scream as we youths tried to ram each other, at first in fun, then with mounting animosity, finally with lethal intent. Several of my girl passengers told me later that they hated these displays of adolescent machismo.

I hit him too hard, and my steering wheel digs me painfully in the stomach. Easy, I say aloud, nice and easy. With the precision of a stunt driver I nudge it back in the right direction. We leave the dip and come to a rise, which definitely kills our speed at last. Sixty k.p.h, then fifty . . . I need to force him off the road and into some open country, but here the autobahn drops away sharply to a small wood. We crawl up the incline, overtaken by furious truck drivers who, baulked by our slow progress in the right-hand lane, only just manage to react in time.

Their horns blare angrily as they roar past. We continue to climb, still travelling at thirty. I must force him off the road before he speeds up on the reverse slope. My hands are clutching the wheel so hard I can scarcely feel them, and there's a metallic taste like blood in my mouth. My visibility is obscured by the smoke from the bonnet, which is steadily getting thicker, but my head is clear, completely clear. I pull over to the left as we breast the rise, but fail to catch him at the right spot, and he eludes me yet again. I can already visualize the next truck hitting us, swiping us off the road, crushing us like mice beneath an elephant's foot. He's steadily slowing, but I fail to make it in time. The road falls away, and already he's gaining speed once more.

I ram his left rear wing, engine roaring, and force him over to the right again. Faster and faster he goes. I know I'm risking my life, but the thought seems somehow abstract and utterly unimportant. I keep nudging him at intervals until a rippling field of wheat opens out on my right, then force him into it by drawing level and wrenching my wheel over hard. At this point my engine gives a mighty bang and conks out.

Ears of wheat lash the windows as the two cars cavort across the field like broncos. We leave a long, long trail behind us until the red blob ahead of me comes to rest at last. A final impact hurls me forward. Completely out of breath although I've engaged in no form of physical exertion, I sit there panting until it occurs to me that we'll both be in extreme danger – given that the other man is still alive – if the cars catch fire.

My door won't open any more. I wriggle out of the window and totter over to the red Toyota. Lolling motionless in this seat belt behind the wheel is a fat, bearded man with a blue face. His door does open – luckily, because he would never have gone through the window. I haul him out like a sack of potatoes, unpleasantly reminded of Theo's inert body, through I've no idea if he's still alive.

Grunting with the effort, I seize the bearded man by his arms and his knitted cardigan and haul him clear. The, breathless and exhausted, I collapse on top of him. I lie on his soft, fat stomach, listen for this heartbeat, and hear nothing. I slap his blue cheeks. He tolerates this treatment without demur, his head flopping this way and that.

Come on! I yell. He lets me yell.

I crouch down beside him, pinch his nostrils shut, and clamp my mouth to the cold blue lips in his dark thicket of beard. Having seen this done a hundred times on television, I hope and pray that all those actors got *something* right, at least – that the idiot of a director employed some medic to advise him, and that I'm not making an utter hash of it.

Breathe in, breathe out, in and out, in and out. I'm breathing for myself and this total stranger, who looks a year or two younger than me. In and out, in and out, but nothing happens. He goes on lying there, fat, lazy, and dead. There's a wedding ring on his finger. He probably kissed his wife goodbye this morning. His mouth smells of a last breakfast of cornflakes and coffee, his neck of a final application of cheap aftershave.

Everything is transitory, I hear the lama chuckle, but we refuse to believe it.

Angrily, I continue to inflate the man's lungs. They always massage the rib cage in those hospital soaps, I recall. I picture the scene in every detail: cross hands on chest and exert downward pressure. Breathe in and bear down. Everything I know about life has been gleaned from television. In *Emergency Room* they'd now the hollering for the defibrillator and holding it against the patient's chest. Switch on the juice, and he jumps like a trout in a stream. No, try again. And again. At long last his heart kicks in. All the nurses applaud. Music, credits, The End.

But *my* patient lies there stoically beneath me and doesn't stir. I give myself orders like a swimming pool attendant: breathe and bear down, breathe and bear down. I bear down with all my might on the immaculately ironed shirt with the pale blue stripes, then breathe, bear down, breathe. The ears of wheat around us sway gently in the breeze. I suck in air and blow it into the stranger's body beneath me, breathe in, breathe out, nothing more.

Carry on, keep going, don't give up, Sweat stings my eyes, my heart is pounding.

All at once an insane feeling of happiness surges through me because my own heart is doing its work so conscientiously. I'm alive, I'm actually alive. I'm alive from one moment to the next. That's what occurs to me now, as I crouch over a dead man's chest. Thanks, I whisper breathlessly to my heart as I massage the stranger's silent heart, thanks anyway. You're welcome, says my heart. You may be a schmuck, but I'm happy to beat for you. I'll do better in the future, I whisper back. And suddenly, schmuck that I am, I'm happy – I'm genuinely happy. I grin to myself, and the next time I look down at the bearded man his eyes are open.

While firemen are spraying my car with foam and orange-clad ambulance men busily tramping through the wheat, I lie swathed in a silvery sheet of aluminium foil, blubbering into my mobile.

Ssh, says Claudia, ssh, everything's OK.

Yes, I sob, it is.

34

C LAUDIA TOUCHES WOOD AND whistles three times for luck. See you on-stage, then, she whispers in my ear. The production manager is already leading me away. I just have time to see her turn once more with her hands raised: she's crossing her fingers for me.

Well, Herr Kaufmann, nervous? asks the production manager, a short, balding man with a beer belly and gold rings in both ears.

No, I say, but my stomach is rumbling and my palms are moist with perspiration. He ushers me along a bare green passage, opens a door, and propels me into a brilliantly lit room equipped with a huge mirror.

Right, says the production manager, this is Herr . . . (he's already forgotten my name). He's a 'Hero of the Year', and he's on in seven minutes.

He thrusts me down into a hairdresser's chair with a neck rest. A redhead with bad breath bends over me and drapes a paper bib around my neck. You might have brought him to me sooner, she grumbles.

Don't be like that, Gabi, says the production manager. He doesn't need much done to him in any case.

Are you the guy from the home for stray dogs? the redhead inquires.

I shake my head. Keep still, she says, dabbing some beige cream under my eyes. First let's get rid of those awful rings . . .

Be quick, says the production manager.

Stop hassling me, says Gabi. She bares her smoker's yellow teeth at me in a smile. What would you like on your hair?

Oh, er . . . I stammer.

The production manager plucks at my shoulder.

OK, says Gabi, and removes the bib. You won't look any lovelier than that, not today.

Thanks, I say falteringly, but the production manager is already hauling me out of the chair.

Ciao, he calls. He hurries me out of the room and along some more interminable green passages until we come to a heavy steel door. Opening this, he pushes me into the darkness beyond. Blindly, I take a couple of tentative steps.

Two minutes to go, the production manager whispers in my ear. Then the door'll open and you walk down the steps. Take it nice and easy. Don't trip, they'd only laugh.

My eyes take a while to get used to the dark. I make out some scrawny young women armed with clipboards talking quietly into the little microphones suspended from their necks. The presenter, Arnold Brockmann, is seated on a folding chair. An hour ago, when we were being offered cheese nibbles in the hospitality room, he said a cursory hello and asked me if I'd acquired a new car in the interim.

No, I told him, who from? I deliberately wrote it off myself, after all. He made a note of this.

Now he's hurriedly taking long pulls at a cigarette, which he doesn't stub out until the signature tune strikes up. He rises to his full height, chest out, stomach in, and smiles his toothy, celebrated smile in the semi-darkness. He stands there like that for two or three seconds. Then a door opens and a voice booms, And here is your host, Aaarnooold . . . *Brockmann*! Smiling, he sallies forth into a tempest of frenzied applause like a footballer taking the field. I must have been crazy to get involved in these moronic proceedings.

The production manager nudges me. You're on next, he says.

I ought to make a run for it; instead, I take a leaf out of Brockmann's book. I get into position, draw myself up, and the production manager counts me out like a fight referee in reverse: Three, two, one . . . I hear Brockmann say something unintelligible in a solemn voice. Then he yells, A hero! A Hero of the Year, Fred Kaufmann!

The door opens, and a hailstorm of applause rattles about my ears. Startled, I recoil a step, but the door behind me is already closing. A vast audience is gazing at me expectantly, there's no going back. Below me I see a flight of golden steps. Gingerly, very gingerly, I put one foot before the other and float down them. On the stage is my poor, battered, silver Toyota.

Brockmann welcomes me. He shakes my sweating hand for so long, I wonder if he's forgotten his lines. At length he pushes me into a red armchair and grins. I can see beads of sweat on his hairline, smears of make-up on his shirt collar.

A hero, says Brockmann, levelling his finger at me. A genuine hero, a Hero of the Year.

More applause. I scan the front row for Claudia but fail to see her. I also fail to hear Brockmann's question, so he has to repeat it: How are you feeling?

Fine.

Ah, says Brockmann, so our hero's feeling fine. Well, you'll soon feel even better. We've got a big surprise for you, you see.

He lays a confidential hand on my arm and turns, so I turn likewise. A fanfare rings out, the door opens, and the bearded man emerges.

My patient, Klaus Peter Grünler. The big surprise is no surprise at all, of course, because that was how they lured me here: how happy it would make Grünler to be able to thank me publicly – how I mustn't spoil his pleasure. Grünler is again wearing a shirt with pale blue stripes. He looks fatter than I remember. He peers around uncertainly. Brockmann beckons him down the golden steps, simultaneously motioning me to stand up. He welcomes Grünler, shakes him vigorously by the hand, then spreads his arms wide and proclaims, The rescuer and the rescued! He looks at us encouragingly, looks from one to the other, but we simply stand there without moving, like cattle out to pasture. We gawp at the audience and don't budge an inch until he takes our hands and brings them together. We duly shake hands. More applause, then we're at liberty to sit down.

I've seen Grünler only once since the accident, and that was in intensive care the same day. A few weeks later a nice policeman called me to say that he was doing fine, back at work already. Grünler was a salesman for an engineering company based at Olpe, he told me. He'd been on his way to a customer when he had his heart attack.

Grünler stares at the toes of his shoes and nervously kneads his fleshy hands. I try to picture myself crouching over this man's chest, clamping my lips to his and expelling my breath into his massive body, but I can't. Brockmann regards us proudly, like the father of two sons. Then he jumps down off the stage, walks lithely up the central aisle into the audience, and holds his microphone under the nose of a pudgy blonde with permed hair.

Well, Frau Grünler, happy to have your husband back?

Frau Grünler gives a diffident shrug. Frau Grünler is

ecstatic, Brockmann interprets. How about you? he asks the three equally pudgy Grünler children.

Yeah, says the eldest.

They're all overjoyed, cries Brockmann, and races back on to the stage. Herr Grünler, he goes on, would you care to say something to the man who saved your life?

Silence. I can't see Claudia. She should be sitting in the front row, but she isn't there. I scan the faces again and again. One look from her would reconcile me to this whole inane affair.

Isn't there anything you'd like to say, Herr Grünler?

Silence.

Herr Kaufmann saved your life, Herr Grünler. Haven't you anything you'd like to say to him?

Grünler raises his heavy head and gives Brockmann a bovine stare.

Perhaps, Brockmann suggests, you'd like to thank him . . .

Now it's my turn to stare at my shoes, the expensive English shoes that have carried me so faithfully and dependably through the last few months.

Well, Herr Grünler? Brockmann exhorts.

The studio audience gazes at Grünler in suspense. I conduct another desperate search for Claudia. Has she fled already? What made me lend myself to this idiocy? Vanity, at bottom. Pure vanity, and this is my just reward.

Grünler stares doggedly into space, breathing hard.

Brockmann gives a nervous laugh. Is there absolutely nothing you'd like to say to your saviour, Herr Grünler?

I long to vanish into thin air. The spectators are shuffling their feet impatiently, starting to whisper. It's slowly dawning on me that my patient isn't a very likeable man – if not a creep with whom I wouldn't even care to drink a beer. Just before I get really angry with this uncouth, unfriendly individual, it occurs to me that *he* was really the one who saved *me* – who made me realize that my heart is still beating, and that, on that account alone, every goddamned moment is the best moment of my life. Every moment without exception, the present one included. I laugh aloud. Rivulets of sweat are trickling out of Brockmann's hair, skirting his ears, and disappearing into his collar. He looks at me inquiringly.

This, I say, grinning, is the best moment of my life.

The audience laughs. Brockmann frowns, shakes his head, and turns back to Grünler.

Have a think, Herr Grünler, he insists. There must be something you'd like to say to the man who saved you.

Grünler fixes me with a blank stare, breathing loudly. He gulps like a frog, then blurts out, Well, thanks, I guess.

Brockmann springs to his feet in jubilation, clapping frenetically. After some hesitation, the audience joins in. My old Toyota is trundled off the stage, to be replaced by a red Golf GTI. Some car keys are thrust into my hand.

Grünler looks around disappointedly. Why isn't he getting a car?

Brockmann hastily shakes our hands. The little production manager with the earrings appears and hustles us off-stage.

Obediently, Grünler and I trail after him. At the very last moment, just before we disappear into the black hole behind the stage, I turn to Grünler, grasp his fleshy paw, and fold the keys of the red Golf into his palm.

No, I tell him. Thank *you*.

He stares at me in bewilderment. The gross lips in his thicket of a beard, the lips whose surprising softness I still so vividly remember, open and shut without a sound. Then the production manager tows us away.

We stagger off the brightly lit stage into darkness. I trip and fall into a black void, fall and keep on falling until, at the last moment, I'm caught by a pair of warm arms. Long, soft hair brushes my face, and I fill my lungs with a long familiar fragrance.

I'm home.

Hello, my hero, says my wife. Where do we go from here?

A NOTE ON THE AUTHOR

Doris Dörrie was born in Hanover. She studied drama in the United States and continued her studies at the Academy of Television and Film in Munich, where she still lives and works. She is the author of a number of novels and collections of stories, including *Love, Pain and the Whole Damn Thing* (1989) and *What Do You Want from Me?* (1992), both of which have been published in English. She is also the director of many films including the witty feminist comedy *Men, Am I Beautiful?* and most recently *Enlightenment Guaranteed*.

John Brownjohn, one of Britain's leading translators from the German, has won critical acclaim on both sides of the Atlantic. Among his most recent awards are the Schlegel-Tieck Prize for Thomas Brussig's *Heroes Like Us* and the Helen and Kurt Wolff Prize for Marcel Beyer's *The Karnau Tapes*. He is also a screenwriter whose credits include *Tess, Bitter Moon* and *The Ninth Gate*.

A NOTE ON THE TYPE

The text of this book is set in Linotype Sabon,
named after the type founder, Jacques Sabon. It
was designed by Jan Tschichold and jointly
developed by Linotype, Monotype and Stempel,
in response to a need for a typeface to be
available in identical form for mechanical hot
metal composition and hand composition using
foundry type.

Tschichold based his design for Sabon roman on
a fount engraved by Garamond, and Sabon italic
on a fount by Granjon. It was first used in 1966
and has proved an enduring modern classic.